For Anne Sheldon and Michael Vidor

Acknowledgements

Special thanks to Bill Adamson, John Mahnke, Susan Hoover and Scott 'Fishboy' Odom for lending the details of their professions to this book.

'Any idiot can fall in love. No special talent required for that. The trick is to love somebody who might actually do you some good. That's the part hardly anybody gets right.'

Scott's grandmother

Contents

BOOK THREE: ONE FULCRUM MOMENT

Book One

DIVISION ROAD

Chapter One ⚡

1996
The Headlight Zone

Hayden Reese picked his way on foot in the dark, straight uphill into national forest territory, his Jenny dangling heavy on his right shoulder. Still supple she felt, and almost warm. His only little bit of comfort.

In his left hand, the shovel.

Here and there he'd take hold with his right, grasp the smooth, red, strangely burnished trunk or limb of a manzanita for balance, for pull, gently pressing the fistful of shovel handle to her smooth flank to keep her from tumbling. The sun would be coming all too soon.

He'd kept this trail clear by his own maintenance and concern, hiking by day with a sheathed trail saw hanging on one side of his belt, a strong hinged clipper for smaller branches on the other. He knew this trail the way he'd known his Jenny, could navigate it in the dark, knowing by memory when to grasp, when to duck his head.

What few things Hayden knew, he knew. The rest was a mystery, pure and simple.

As he grasped and ducked he cursed himself, and his burning chest, and promised himself he'd quit smoking again, this time for real, and touched his shirt pocket, wondering if he'd remembered to bring the pack along. It both comforted and disgusted him to feel it there. He'd lean on them now, because he needed to; then, in a day or a week, he'd reclaim his stolen wind.

He reached the saddle of the ridge, the clearing he'd created and maintained, and gently spread her on her side on the cool ground and sat for a moment before going to work. Sat by her side and fired up what he hoped would be one of the last, and set the shovel across his knees, hating the finality of the whole deal. And touched one hand to her cooling side, wishing the sun was up so he could enjoy her smooth blue coat with his eyes and not just his hand. He drew hard on the cigarette tucked deep between his first fingers, watching the red tip glow, hating the way the hot smoke soothed him going down.

Maybe his eyes had adjusted to the dark, or maybe

that odd moment of predawn had found them, because Hayden noticed he could nearly make out the silhouettes of buckbrush, the gnarled shapes and nature-sanded smoothness of the manzanita branches. He felt his thinking change about Jenny. He did not wish to see her, not now. Not like this. And the dawn would bring the heat of the day, the enemy, tormentor of men with shovels. No. It wasn't dawn. Couldn't be. Still long too early for that. But it would be, sometime. He had better get started.

For one brief moment he allowed himself to think about Laurel, let himself feel the need, a touch or a word from her to fill the ache of this moment. Hayden told no one, not even Laurel, when he ached, but he often ached for his ache to be seen, to be known by her. To be cooled and settled.

He put the urge away again but it left an echo, the blank, unfilled shock of a craving deferred.

He set about to dig in the hard ground.

Hayden stared down at his hands, at black dirt still packed underneath the nails, ground deep into the calluses of his palms. He didn't mind dirt, not as such. He minded the lack of sleep, the sandy eyes and dicey stomach from staying up the night, challenging the dry soil inch by inch. He minded that Laurel would come soon to start the cinnamon rolls in the half dark, in the barely-morning light, and what if she reached for him or allowed him to reach for her? What, then, would he do with all this dirt?

More even than this, he minded his Jenny in the ground, lost to him. Minded it so much he could not permit his mind to complete that revolution, to spin its gears around to the new, real, entirely changed day. He needed instead to stay mired a few more moments in that foggy no-man's-land, like the moment between sleep and waking when a vivid dream slides away, one unlikely image at a time.

He sat in the dawn in the cab of his old pickup and waited for her to unlock the diner's back door, thinking, Where will I wash my hands, in case I get to touch her? It was a good moment to cry, or would have been, anyway. Only for one thing, though. Hayden didn't cry. Never had, as long as he could remember. Didn't figure at this late date he ever would.

Even Hayden's mother, whom he hadn't seen since he was nineteen, had told him the story time and time again, along with anyone else who would listen. Maybe when you were in diapers, she would say. But after that, nothing. Not even if you hurt yourself bad. Which was usually. Not even when you broke both your legs that time. And it's a funny thing, she would add, because you were always the most deep-down oddly emotional boy anybody'd ever met. Just no tears.

He sat looking out across the long valley, smoking a cigarette, sighting along the endless line of electrical towers. They always looked like headless lattice giants to him. Long legs slightly spread, short arms extended, strands of wires dangling from their fingers and dipping slightly between towers, traveling off into infinity. Every year some fool kids tried to climb them. A combination of rural boredom and some strange rite of new manhood Hayden wished he didn't understand. This year some poor kid paid the price, which was going to happen sooner or later. Rumor had it his watch was still up there somewhere, half melted and fused forever to that unremorseful steel. Even the crystal melted. Hayden didn't know which tower, and he damn sure wasn't going up to look, but it was possible. He knew such a thing could happen.

He looked in his rearview mirror to see the sun just cresting the mountain ridge, the highway clear in that still air, and an animal worrying over something right on the centerline. An odd sight. And it felt good to be distracted, to wonder over somebody else's problem for a change.

A cat, he decided. Moving a kitten across the highway. Hurry, Hayden thought. It's a mean highway. It's a headlight zone. One of those flat two-lane stretches in the middle of nowhere on which motorists are instructed to run their headlights by day. Only way anybody can think to cut the fatalities. Nobody wants to just do nothing, but how much can you do? People die on highways. It's what happens.

Hayden stepped out of his old pickup and watched the lights of a big rig bear down from the east. Move, cat, he thought, but it wasn't a cat with a kitten, it was a possum. Mother and baby. Which was too bad. A cat he could pick up and move. But possums. Vicious little bastards when threatened. Razor-sharp little teeth.

The rig roared down, and Hayden watched, a bit detached. Somewhat confused. They would move. Of course they would move. Momma possum held her tiny one, eyes barely open, in her teeth, but it squirmed free. Hayden moved closer. Not squirmed, he saw. Convulsed. Something wrong with the baby. Maybe it had been hit already. It seemed to stiffen into little seizures that made it impossible to handle.

Momma possum seemed to know the truck was coming. Death, motherhood – Hayden knew it must be hard to decide. When the headlights fell full across her she abandoned her young and ran. It was late, nearly too late, really, but Hayden stepped into the road and picked it up. It weighed a few ounces at most; it was soft. He jumped back, not even thinking it might bite him. Thinking more about his near miss with the semi. The deep, shocking blare of the truck's air horn pressed into his ears; the wind of the passing monster flapped his big shirt about. The driver flipped Hayden the finger out the window as he blew by.

Hayden only smiled.

The baby possum did not try to bite him. It stiffened into another convulsion in his palm, tiny eyes closed, feeling soft and looking ratlike but innocent. He put it in his shirt pocket, where it seized against his chest. He wanted to return it to the mother but couldn't see where she had gone.

He wondered if it could feel his heart beat.

Old Dr Meecham, the veterinarian, lived over his storefront office. Hayden leaned on his truck horn until Meecham came to the window to ask what the hell gives.

'Oh, you,' he said. The lights came on upstairs and in time he shuffled down.

A hard glare of full morning assaulted Hayden's eyes from the east, over the flat valley landscape; the day's heat already more than threatened. They stood outside, boots in the dirt, two big men hovering over a few ounces of sudden trouble. Meecham wore a shock of pure white hair still tumbled from his pillow.

'Momma abandoned it, huh? That'll happen,' the doc said. 'Born wrong somehow. They know to let it go.'

Hayden didn't bother to say this lady was loath to

let go, like Hayden himself with his Jenny, Meecham being a logical sort of a fellow. Some of us, Hayden considered, aren't fortunate enough to possess that cool luxury.

'Some kind of seizures. Want me to put it out of its misery.' Meecham told this as a fact, didn't ask it.

'No, I want you to fix it.'

'Not everything's fixable, Hayden.'

Don't I know it, he thought. 'You're the veterinarian. You're the one supposed to know how.'

'Well, leave it here. I'll see what can be done. Might cost.'

Everything costs, Hayden told himself, money being the least of it. 'I'm prepared to cover it.'

'Don't get your hopes too high. Sure you want it saved? Just what we need around here, another possum.'

'Do what you can, Doc.'

'Be under somebody's wheels on the highway tomorrow. Born roadkill they are. Just the way of the world, Hayden.'

'You do what you can,' Hayden said, one carefully formed word after another, trying to keep the reasonableness from draining out of his voice.

He walked back to his truck, scuffing his boot toes in the dirt, thinking he must've missed Laurel's arrival at the shop by now, that quiet, untouched moment before life wakes up and shuffles around, disturbing their chances. He said inside himself, That little mass of fur will never grasp the sacrifice.

'How's that good-looking bluetick hound of yours?' Meecham called to his back.

Hayden drove away and did not answer.

When he arrived back at the diner her station wagon was there, along with the car that belonged to the morning waitress.

He stuck his head in the back door and just stood that way a minute, watching Laurel roll the big flat sheet of dough for this morning's cinnamon rolls.

He was that late.

He wondered what might be about to transpire, and whether or not it would hurt. It seemed more or less an even draw, like flipping a coin. Or so the past had taught him.

She addressed him, never once looking up. 'Not like you to sleep in.'

'I haven't slept yet.'

She looked up, as if to confirm or deny that information with her own two eyes; she seemed convinced once she saw his face. He wanted to tell her about Jenny, but it seemed like the morning had already set off in the wrong direction, almost before he'd opened his mouth. So he just stepped inside and watched her work. Watched the place where her apron tied snug at the belt line of her jeans, a pleasingly narrow waist, and the way her hair, kind of brown but red, a dark brown with deep red highlights, had already begun to come apart from the simple way she'd pinned it up this morning. It was better, anyway, apart, mussed looking. It reminded him of other mussed moments, and made his stomach hurt.

He wished she would say something, or that he would.

He moved closer, around her side of the wood table, and slid one arm around her waist, heavy to breaking with his need to do that, but just then the swinging door to the front flew open and the waitress came through. Laurel ducked away from him, he wasn't entirely sure why. He was never entirely sure if they were a secret or not. If they were anything or not.

They waited for the waitress to bustle around and take what she needed and go again. Hayden stood close enough to Laurel to smell her, not perfume exactly but something like it, that blend of soap and shampoo and Laurel that wouldn't come out the same on any other woman, or in his head on a lonely night. It just could not be reproduced.

'This is not a great time,' she said when the girl had gone. 'Jack'll be in any minute. Anyway, we need to talk.'

The words collected in his stomach, gained weight, and settled hard. And then he saw it. Looked down at her hands gone back to slicing cinnamon rolls from the coil of dough, and there it was, half covered with flour, but there all the same. He grabbed her left hand hard and held it close under his face, in case it was only an illusion, and proximity might break it apart, make it go away. But it was still her wedding band. It wouldn't leave him alone all that easy. He felt dizzy, like he might pass out, but in the end was not nearly so fortunate.

'You couldn't have told me about this?'

'I'm trying to tell you about it right now. Could you let go my hand, please? You're hurting me.'

'Oh. Sorry.' He dropped her hand and dropped his own hands to his sides, and looked up to see Jack standing in the doorway, watching them. 'I was just leaving,' Hayden said.

At the doorway Jack did not step out of his way. They stood like that a moment, nearly nose to nose, maintaining eye contact in the manner that any animal will know to do in such a bind. Jack was good looking, which didn't help, with that shiny kind of pretty-boy looks. He had a fifteen-year age advantage on Hayden, but Hayden had a couple of inches and maybe fifty pounds of bulk on Jack. Just for that moment Hayden wouldn't have minded throwing all that into the fray, just to see what would prove more important than what. Wouldn't have minded a bit.

'Guys,' Laurel said, which broke up those thoughts and knocked Hayden onto a different train of action.

'You're in my way, Jack,' he said, and Jack took one step to the side to let him pass. Just as he did, Jack bumped Hayden's shoulder hard with his own, but Hayden just kept walking, at least until it was time to drive.

It was too soon to go back to Meecham's, Hayden knew. Yet he went back there all the same. Where else would he go? Home, to an empty cabin? To no Laurel, no Jenny, no buffer for this roiling disarray spilling around inside him, where it could do harm to himself or others? Better to use himself in some way. If only this had been a working day. If only this had not fallen on his day off from the hardware store, but so it did.

Meecham's assistant was nowhere to be seen. Meecham himself came out from the back examination room, wiping his hands on his lab smock and shaking his head.

'Gone, Hayden. Sorry.' He didn't say it so much like he felt deeply sorry, more like he was sorry to have to tell Hayden something Hayden didn't care to know.

'Seizures killed it?'

'Well, I—'

'What exactly killed it?'

'Can't save everything, Hayden.'

Now it began to rise in him, that hard disdain for being gently tutored in something he knew better than anybody. Meecham stood close up on the other side of the front counter now, and Hayden wanted him to stand farther back. Much farther. To where nobody could get hurt.

'In other words, Doc, you decided not to save it, so you just put it down.'

Meecham seemed to see, or read, or smell the anger in Hayden, packed into and driven in front of those words, and he peered into Hayden's face with a frightened curiosity. He did not stand back. He should've stood back.

'It died, Hayden.'

'You put it down.'

'It died.'

'Fine. Give its body over to me, I'll drive it to the vet in the city, we'll see what it died from.'

'Can't do that. Against county law. Animal dies in this county, remains gotta go in for rabies testing.'

'It wasn't even alive long enough to have late-stage rabies convulsions. You damn well know that. You said yourself it was just born wrong.'

'County law.'

'Okay. Keep what you need to test, give me what's left over.'

Meecham's look had become more frightened, then leveled off, now turned stony with indignation and enough stubbornness, he seemed to feel, to match Hayden's. 'Won't be nothing left over. They got to take a bunch of cross sections of that brain. Look. Hayden. We've known each other for a while now—'

'You killed it.'

'All right, goddamnit. Yes. I put it down. For Christ's sake, Hayden. It was born wrong. It wasn't a hound dog. It wasn't your momma. It was a possum. A goddamn fucking possum. Get a grip, man.'

While Hayden's fist arced, he felt it like a lung full of hot smoke or a private touch from Laurel, soothing deep in his belly, the delivery of something sweet and sorely needed. He threw his upper body half over the counter and caught the doc square on the jaw, fist to face, knucklebones to jawbone, and the jaw gave, and so did the fist.

It was not the first jaw Hayden had ever broken, and he knew the feel of it well, the sickening feel of give, and the sound. Not a clean crack like what one might expect, but an unsettling crunch, the sound of boots on icy crusts of snow on a school day morning in Hayden's long-lost youth.

It was also not Hayden's first boxer's fracture, and he

knew the feel of that as well, the bowing of the outer bone of his hand, then that sudden point of bright pain where it decides to let go.

The vet tumbled to his own linoleum floor.

Hayden came around to the doc's side of the counter, and the old man rolled onto his belly to protect himself, but it was for no purpose. Hayden had finished being angry.

He picked up the doc's phone and called the local ambulance service. Could've called 911 to dispatch them, but it seemed like a lot of histrionics for a simple case of two broken bones.

While he waited on a ringing line he spoke to Meecham. 'Okay down there, Doc? I'm gonna call somebody to come by, take you to the hospital. You just hold steady where you are, okay?'

No intelligible sounds came back to him, just a muffled grumble.

'Morning, Della,' he said into the phone. 'Hayden Reese . . . Good, how're you? I'm over at Doc Meecham's, and I think he'd like it fine if the ambulance came and scooped him up and took him into the city . . .

'Just a broken jaw, I think, but he's in some pain.'

He glanced down at his right hand, noted the early stages of swelling and blackening.

'Me, no, I'm fine, Della. I'm just going to swing by the doctor here in town. You could do me a good favor, though. Once you got that ambulance on its way, could you give Scott a call for me? Tell him to meet me by the doctor's office? . . .

'Yeah, I'll wait for him . . .

'Thanks, Della.'

Hayden sat on the curb and waited. Lit a cigarette with his left hand, held it tightly in his lips, eyes squinted against the smoke, and tapped on the light fiberglass cast. Wiggled the fingers of his right hand around.

He hated the claustrophobic feel of being unable to move most of his right hand. It seemed unreasonable, not enough cause for full-on claustrophobia; still, he knew that in the moments just prior to sleep he would bolt awake, sweaty and panicky, as if his entire body were locked into this forced, armored inertia, mummified.

He took the cigarette in his left hand, where it felt unnatural, and held it between his thumb and index finger, and drew on it, and tried to be calm.

In a minute or two a black-and-white sheriff's unit pulled up, parked a few feet away from Hayden's legs at the curb, and the sheriff stepped out and stood in the empty road in front of him. Hayden looked up into his face, but the sun was full up behind him, and Hayden mostly saw glare.

'Morning, Scott.'

'Hayden, Hayden, Hayden. You were doing so good for a while there. What the hell happened to you?'

'Anybody can have a bad day, Scott.'

The sheriff stood with his arms akimbo, hands at his belt line, face still mostly obscured in the glare, which was okay by Hayden. 'Yeah, I reason that's true,' he said. 'Come on.'

Scott opened the front passenger door of the black-and-white; Hayden thanked him and climbed in. Planted his feet on the familiar corrugated plastic mats, sat staring at the familiar blue dash with the wood-grained strip across it, the Crown Victoria decal.

They pulled away in silence, rode side by side along the flat grid of town, turned left onto the highway at the stop sign. Hayden watched the well-memorized progression of fields. Short brownish cotton fields and almond orchards and tank farms, and wide acres of evenly tilled gray-black dirt. Here and there oil drillers spun their gears around and around, their grasshopper heads pecking slow and regular at the soil. Wide dirt roads named after letters of the alphabet flashed by.

They listened to scratchy transmissions over the radio. Code 6 Mary on a routine traffic stop miles away, which meant he'd have to share the holding cell. An assistance call Hayden translated to mean old Mrs Shuck fell out of her wheelchair again. Every three minutes an alert tone in Morse code, the equipment talking to itself.

'Think he'll press charges?' Hayden asked after a while.

'What do you think?'

'I figure he will. Think I'll get ninety days this time?'

'Depends on the mood the judge is in. Which depends on the mood his wife was in last night. Bottom line, Hayden, our fate'll be determined by the whims of a woman.'

Hayden only grunted.

He sat quiet for a while, noticing the imposing volume at which Laurel's name was not being said. In his peripheral vision he watched Scott's hands tight on the wheel, the short, brushy cut of his thick dark hair. He was young, which Hayden never would be again.

Scott broke the stillness in a voice too serious, a voice reserved for something needing deeply to be said. Something inevitable. 'You knew she would, Hayden. He's her husband. She's got to try at least.'

'How'd you know about that?'

'How'd you *not* know about it? That'd be more to the point.'

'Can we talk about something else?'

'Fine. Whatever. Pick your topic.'

'They won't hold my job for me. Not this time.'

'There's other jobs.'

'Around here?'

'Doesn't have to be around here. There's other places to be.'

'You should be so lucky. You know I can't go from here.'

'Might need to, if you can't get work.'

Breathe, Hayden told himself. Inhale, exhale. Big, full breaths. He did not complicate his breathing by attempting to answer.

'I'll go on by and feed Jenny, you know that.'

Hayden shook his head, slowly, carefully, as though he might dislodge it by not being cautious enough. 'Thanks anyway. No need.'

He felt the sheriff's stare on the left side of his face. Felt it burn there like a brand, like noonday sun.

'When did that happen?'

'Yesterday evening. In her sleep.'

'I'm sorry, Hayden.'

'I know. Thanks.'

'She was old.'

'I know it.'

'Better off this way.'

'Her, maybe.'

'I'm sorry.'

'I know.'

'Tell the judge that.'

'No. No chance.'

'Might go easier on you. Moment of grief. Everybody knows how much you loved that old hound dog. Everybody figured you'd come apart some when you finally lost 'er.'

'I'm not going to make excuses for myself.'

'Whatever. Your funeral. Lord, you're a stubborn man.'

'I know it.'

'Yeah. By now I reason you do.'

Chapter Two

Flame with a Man Inside

'Does it seem kind of funny to you,' Hayden asked Scott a few days further on, 'that they went and put the county jail at the end of Division Road?'

'No, why would that seem funny?'

'I don't know, it just does. You're in check, by the way.'

'Shit. You couldn't have told me that before?'

'I just this minute saw it.'

'Shit.'

Hayden leaned a shoulder against the bars and waited. The sheriff pressed his elbows to his knees, leaned forward on the hard wooden chair, brought his head down into his hands. He raked fingers through his brush cut, as though a proper display of angst might bust him out of check. A staticky transmission came in over his belt radio, and he waited and listened to make sure it didn't require him. Then he returned his attention to the board, frowning and grumbling, transforming his forehead into a plowed field of careful creases. Such a young guy, too, Hayden thought, for the frown lines. But he took his chess game seriously. Too seriously, Hayden figured, especially when you consider he never won a single game. Way Hayden saw it, a person could adopt one of two postures toward a game like chess. Either develop a damn good skill for it or just settle for a cavalier attitude regarding the whole deal. Not being good at cavalier, Hayden practiced a lot, and won.

'Okay, here,' Scott said.

He grasped a knight in the tips of his fingers and marched it around the corner to block Hayden's check. Which Hayden had pretty much expected him to do. And which he answered by reaching through the bars of his cell with his good left hand and sweeping diagonally across the board to take Scott's queen with his bishop. He did not add the insult of any comment.

'How the hell long has that been sitting down there?'

"Bout as long as we've been playing.'

'That's the trouble with you, Hayden. You're all the time lulling people into a false sense of security.'

'Oh, is *that* the trouble?'

Scott sighed.

They sat, almost together, in a room with one cell only, a sort of local version of solitary confinement at the back of the county jail, playing the game from opposite sides of the bars, the board propped on a small filing cabinet between them.

Scott moved a pawn forward, a slow, tedious first step toward getting one of his pieces out of hock. Then he sat back, as if that were an admirable move, one fit to make him proud. 'What's wrong with a county jail on Division Road?'

'I don't know. Just kind of makes you wonder. Makes you ask yourself questions. Like, which side of the law are you on?'

'Yeah. Been meaning to ask you that, Hayden. Just which side of the law you aim to be on?'

'My aim's got nothing to do with it. I'm beginning to doubt my aim these days. You're in check again.'

'Shit.' Scott sat frowning at the board for a moment, then seemed to opt out of the game entirely. His eyes came up and landed over Hayden's shoulder, into the cell behind him. 'What're you reading this time?'

'The *Bhagavad Gita*.'

'More of that weird religious shit.'

'Not religion, exactly, but yeah, okay.'

'What're you lookin' for, anyway?'

'What makes you say I'm looking for something?

Other than the fact that you'll say just about anything at this point not to have to get back to the game.'

'My grandmother had this thing she used to say. "You show me a man who's shopping for a religion and I'll show you a man who's afraid to die."'

'You're still in check.'

'Shit.'

'Got a favor to ask you, Scott.'

'Your timing stinks.'

'When I get out of here, will you go by Doc Meecham's with me? Just so I can apologize?'

'You need me for that?'

'It would help, yeah. I don't want him to get the wrong idea when he sees me coming.'

'That's a point. That's a good point. He might be a trifle gun-shy where you're concerned. Trouble with you, Hayden, you're too big a guy to act this way. Guy your size needs to get some control over his temper. Huge and undisciplined – that could be seen as a piss-poor combination by some.'

'So, you'll go over there with me?'

'Yeah, all right.'

'Good. Now get back to the game.'

Scott levered a hand under one corner of the board and upended the remaining pieces onto the concrete floor. 'What game? I concede this cocksucking game. You want to go see the man? We'll go now. Why wait till you get sprung? He'll be much happier to see you in handcuffs, believe me.'

Scott stuck his head back in a few minutes later, into that solitary area Hayden had been granted more by mercy, not so much as a punishment. Hayden pulled to his feet, thinking it was time to go. But Scott didn't unlock the cell or even move toward it. Just said, 'Got a visitor.'

And Hayden knew, by the way it was said, by his own gut, by sense of smell, by something. He never asked who. His mind flew in a million directions at once. When had he taken a shower last? Had he ever bothered to scrub the black dirt from under his fingernails? Was his hair properly combed? His cell had a piece of shiny metal over the toilet, supposed to work like a mirror, but it was hard for a man to see himself in that. It threw off a distorted image of the man, which might be a lot of what the Department of Corrections had in mind for it. Still, he hated Laurel to see him when he hadn't just had a good look at himself in advance. Too late now, though.

'I'm not supposed to leave a prisoner alone with a visitor, but . . . well . . .'

Scott's face disappeared from the doorway and in she came. Hayden just stood still, both arms leaning on the crosspiece of the bar grid, white-painted bars worn away to reddish orange beneath from other men's leanings. Trying to keep his shoulders straight and square and to stop worrying how he looked to her.

She moved close enough to touch but he didn't dare.

She reached one hand out and ran a finger along the fiberglass of his cast, looking where she was touching. She kept her left hand at her side, to where Hayden wouldn't have to see. Then she brought her eyes up to his, and he wished for someplace to hide. He held her gaze by necessity.

'You okay?' she said, and the sound of her voice changed something inside him that was possibly better left alone.

'More or less.'

'How's the food?'

'Bad. No worse than what I make for myself, though.'

'Happy birthday.'

'That what you came by to say?'

'That 'n' to see if you're okay. Bad deal to have to be in here on your birthday. Specially a big important one like this. Man should get some on his fiftieth, I think. And every one from there on out. Soon as he gets to an age where somebody might doubt his ability, you know? Then it should be part of the celebration, every year.' She shifted her gaze, pushed at a strand of hair fallen away from the barrette where she'd pinned it up in back. Stroked it back behind her ear, a little self-consciously, he thought, then found his eyes again, and looked away. 'Don't you think?' She seemed anxious for him to join the conversation.

'I didn't realize that was still an option with us.'

'Well,' she said. And went no further in that direction. She glanced down at the floor, still littered with the remains of chess. 'Scott lost another game, huh.'

Hayden only leaned his forehead between two of the bars and wished she'd get on with whatever she'd come here to say. There was something there, he could feel it. Waiting. He knew she wanted him to make this easy, smooth into it, but he couldn't oblige her that. He was all too paralyzed in the waiting to make whatever small talk might be needed to guide it home.

'Don't antagonize him, Hayden. Please.' Her voice sounded quiet and strained.

'He can stand to lose a game of chess,' Hayden said. But he knew what she meant.

'Not Scott. You know who I mean. He knows about us. He knows we were keeping time a little bit. While him and me were on the outs.'

'Is that what we were doing, Laurel? Really? Keeping a little bit of time?' With those words he let it out, then, the feelings they both knew to be present in that room, somewhere, just waiting to show their faces and be granted audience to speak.

'Don't twist my words around, Hayden.' She shot it back loud and sudden, leaping right into the thick of the fray herself to meet him, no warming-up period required. 'It's not the point how I say it. Whatever you want to call what it was, he knows about it. Don't set him off, Hayden, please. I got a bad feeling somebody could get hurt.'

She stopped herself then, and reached one hand out to touch his cheek, and Hayden tried not to think about razor stubble and when he'd last shaved. They'd issued him a safety razor coming in, but he'd been feeling unmotivated to use it.

She stepped closer to the bars, and Hayden felt the side of her face on his, her lips on his temple, and he closed his eyes and breathed.

'You know I care for you, Hayden.'

He hated it when she said those words, and she often did. They stank of a condition a few degrees shy of love, seemed to carry a 'but' that followed by nature though never got said out loud. He didn't register objection to any of that, though, because he didn't want her smooth cheek and the scent of her skin to go away.

She ran her fingers along the forearm of his good left, a light touch, and he felt the heat give birth to itself deep in his chest and radiate into his belly and below.

'Promise me you won't start with him,' she said, in that same voice she might use to say, Oh yes, or, Do that to me, yes, that's what I want.

'I promise,' he breathed, nursing that heat and pretending he could make it stay.

'Good,' she said. 'I know you're a man who keeps a promise.'

And she stepped back from him, setting her heel down hard on a pawn and causing it to flip across the room. She smiled once briefly and slipped out.

He blinked and watched her go, and felt the heat follow her away, leaving him colder than he'd been before it came to visit.

Scott stuck his head in the door.

'Ready to go when you are,' he said, and Hayden nodded.

He came and unlocked the cell door and handcuffed Hayden, one cuff left open wider and slipped around Hayden's right arm above the cast. Then he cuffed them both to a chain around Hayden's waist. He led him out the front way, down concrete block halls, past a couple of blinking, half-curious deputies arguing about what sounded like the details of a vampire film. Out to the black-and-white Crown Victoria parked in the dirt out front.

'Happy birthday, by the way.'

'Thanks for the privacy, Scott.'

'You're lucky you got what you did. She's right, you know. You start with that man, somebody'll get hurt.'

He held the passenger door open, and Hayden climbed in up front, waited patiently for Scott to come around.

'I got a theory about love,' Scott said, firing up the engine.

'I can only hope you're not about to share it with me.'

'Fine, you don't want to know, I won't tell you.'

'Good.'

'I'll tell you something completely different. My grandmother had a thing she used to say. She used to say, "That man's got a flame inside." If she met you she'd say, "That Hayden Reese, he's a man with a flame inside." She won't, I mean she couldn't very well, being long departed and all, but if she did, that's what she'd say.'

'It doesn't sound like a compliment.'

'It isn't.'

'Got a cigarette, Scott?'

'Thought you quit.'

'Got one, or no?'

Scott lit two off the dashboard lighter and passed one to Hayden. Hayden held it awkwardly in his left hand and had to dip his head down practically into his own lap to take a draw. Every time he did, his left elbow banged into the wooden stock of Scott's shotgun, stored upright in a rack between the seats.

They waited at a stop sign on Division Road and the highway, and watched a big sedan with a lady at the wheel flash by with no headlights on. Scott hit the gas and made the turn and floored it to catch up. The shiny chrome spotlight on the passenger side nipped back from the force of the wind, the handle turning near Hayden's forehead as he took another drag. Scott pushed a button to flip the radio over to public address and took the receiver in his hand.

'You're in a daytime running light zone, ma'am, please turn your headlights on.'

Hayden heard it echo outside, louder than the actual voice of the man beside him. The bright red back runners of the sedan flashed to life immediately. Scott dropped off a little from her bumper, shaking his head.

He looked at his speedometer and frowned. 'Shit. Now she knows I'm back here, we'll have to do fifty all the way in.'

Hayden said nothing, just looked down the highway, flat and straight, narrowing to a pinpoint at the mountains, with a corrugated strip at the shoulder to let you know by feel if you stray, and a double yellow centerline with two rows of fresh new reflectors. Nothing like fatalities to bring highway money to town.

'Is that asking too much, Hayden? Just to run their damn headlights so I won't have to scrape their sorry ass off the tarmac later on?'

'I'd say not.'

'You know why they don't?'

'No. I don't know why.'

'I reason they're afraid they'll forget to turn 'em off. Run their battery down.'

'But it's posted at the end of the zone to remind you.'

'But they don't know that yet. Because they're not from around here.'

'You don't like people who aren't from around here, do you, Scott?'

'I don't even like half the ones that are.' He buzzed the power window down an inch or two and flipped his half-smoked cigarette out. A blast of hot air rushed in to mix with the AC cool. 'Maybe if everybody used their damn running lights, all over everywhere, always had, maybe you'd still have your wife and daughter.'

'Maybe.'

'That was probably a stupid thing to say, I guess.'

'Probably.'

'Maybe if it's your time, it's just your time.'

'Maybe. Or maybe a simple thing like headlights,

would've saved the whole deal, like just a freak thing that might never have happened otherwise, and then every other part of my whole life would have turned out different from there on in.'

'Which theory do you like better?'

Hayden dipped his head down and stole another hit, already tired of the sorry landscape of his own crotch.

'I think they both mostly suck.'

'Man's got his jaw wired shut, so I expect you'll need to do most of the talking.' Scott held the door open and Hayden stepped out into the day's heat, which blew lightly on his face like a convection oven. He ground the remains of his cigarette under one heel, feeling conspicuous in his orange jumpsuit.

Scott set a hand on his elbow and they walked into the vet's office together.

Doc Meecham's receptionist/assistant was in, a compact woman in her sixties who, according to the local grapevine, assisted the doc with more than just his patients. She brought her eyes up and met Hayden with a wild look.

'Yo, Wanda,' Scott said, giving Hayden's arm a squeeze to say shut up and let me talk. 'Doc Meecham in?'

'With a patient right now, Sheriff. Giving vaccinations to the Burleys' nine cats.'

'We'll wait.'

They sat down together on a blue Naugahyde couch, and Wanda picked up the phone and buzzed the doc and cupped her hand over her mouth and mumbled to him underneath their earshot.

A moment later Meecham appeared behind the counter. Way behind it. Scott and Hayden rose in unison.

'Mr Reese here has something he wants to say to you, Doctor.' He gave Hayden's elbow a squeeze, to say exactly the opposite of what the same squeeze said last time. Talk now.

'Doctor Meecham? I just want to say I know what I did was wrong. I'm awful damn sorry about your jaw. It wasn't ever really about the possum anyway. It was a lot of different things. I was having a bad day. I'm sorry I took it out on you.'

They all stood quiet for a moment, save for Wanda, who sat quiet, and then Doc Meecham said something in return. Hayden wasn't quite sure what, though. He sounded like a man trying to talk around a mouthful of food, more than he ever should've taken at one bite. Or for that matter, like a man with his jaw wired shut.

'Beg pardon, Doc?'

Wanda took over at this juncture. 'He says he probably shouldn't've said that about your momma.'

'Shouldn't matter what he said. I was just wrong.'

'I think he means, you know . . . you being an orphan and all,' Wanda said, independent of anything muttered by Meecham and requiring interpretation.

'I just want you to know, Doc, you won't need to take me to court for your hospital bills. I'll bring the money right to you. Might take me a while, though, being between jobs and all.'

Another muffled short sentence from the doctor. Sounded like something about music and a fence. Hayden wondered if Mrs Burley was still waiting in the back, and how many of the nine cats had been vaccinated so far.

'He says his insurance pays eighty per cent,' Wanda chimed in, seeming comfortable with her role in this game.

'Well, I won't let it be out of your pocket, Doc. That's all I came to say.'

'Good, Hayden,' Scott said quietly. 'Done good.' Then, more broadly, 'I'll just be taking this here heinous prisoner back to his confines now.'

Scott guided him out by the arm like he wasn't capable enough to walk by himself any longer. Nobody seemed noticeably sorry to see them go.

'What the hell did he say about your momma?' Scott whispered before they even hit the dirt of the parking lot, before the oven heat came back to hit them in the face again.

'Nothing, really. He just said it wasn't my momma, it was only a damn possum.'

'True enough.' He held the door for Hayden to climb back in. 'Why didn't you say all that good stuff to the judge at your sentencing?'

'I don't know. Didn't want to seem like I was making excuses, maybe. Maybe I didn't have it all sorted out yet.'

Scott shook his head and slammed the door, came around, fired up the engine, flipped the AC up full-blast, and turned the vents onto his own face. Waited and sighed into the cool before pulling away.

'I never knew you were an orphan.'

'Thought you did.'

'Ever get yourself adopted?'

'Nah, pretty much grew up in the institution.'

'No wonder you spend so much time in mine. Must remind you of home. Didn't you ever even get a foster family or something?'

'Yeah, here and there. At the beginning. Kept getting thrown back, though.'

'Now, why would that be?'

'I don't know. Same reason I keep getting thrown back now, I suppose.'

'Seems like you've had more than your fair share of trouble.'

'Seems like.'

'Some'd say you bring a lot of it on yourself, though. There'd be those who might reason you're practically out there looking for all the trouble you can lay in store.'

'I hope I never have to meet them and hear it for myself, then, Scott.'

'Oh, they're all around you, Hayden. It's just, nobody's quite so sure of you as to say a thing like that to your face.'

'*You* just did.'

'I got you cuffed, though. That's a nice thing about a man in cuffs. You sure you don't want to take this opportunity to hear my theory about love?'

'I got a theory, too. My theory is, never take advice from a man who can't even beat you at chess.'

'Even if he's on the right side of the bars and you're on the wrong?'

'Especially then. Hey. Look. That guy up there doesn't have his lights on.'

And it worked, too. The subject changed and never changed back again.

Just as they streaked by the diner Hayden pressed his face against the glass and watched Jack get out of his brand new one-ton Dodge truck and look right at the black-and-white while it flashed on past, like he'd been expecting Hayden to come along right at that exact moment.

It was an instant that passed almost before it had started, just the count of one, maybe, or two at most, for a couple of men to look at each other and know things in themselves, and between themselves.

Time enough for Hayden to wonder about promises, and if they all had to be kept, and if some maybe just couldn't be, and if this might prove to be one of the latter variety.

Chapter Three

Mister, That's an Ugly Dog

'This is what you might call a shit job,' the man said. 'With no puns intended.'

Mason Nelson was the guy's name. Ran himself a brand-new horse ranch on the far end of Division Road. The far opposite end from the county jail, which seemed like a good deal to Hayden, who'd put in his ninety days and seen the view from the other end of the road quite enough, thank you.

'Thing is,' Nelson said, 'these're good horses, not like you might otherwise find around here. Thorough-breds and Arabs, mostly, stock that might actually go out of here and amount to something on the track or in the show circuit. Wouldn't do to have 'em standing in their own crap. When the investors come by, they don't like to see that. They like to see their little gold mine in a clean corral. How are you on a tractor?'

'Good,' Hayden said. He wanted to ask, If they're such gold mines, what're they doing out here, like as not to die of heat prostration? But he didn't ask. He needed the job. He hadn't ridden a tractor in fifteen years. He didn't mention that. He didn't mention that he was afraid of horses. 'Do you take them out of that corral first?'

'Hell, no. They'll stay out of your way, believe me. They'll get to running around all crazy, but they won't come near the tractor to get hurt. Good exercise for 'em anyway.'

Nelson flipped a key on a plastic feed-company fob into the air, in Hayden's general direction, and Hayden caught it, and looked at it, and took that to mean he'd been hired on the spot.

Nelson walked half into the barn, then stopped and turned around. 'I forgot to say the worst part. All them rocks got to come up outa there. Every damn one. Even the little ones. Got to get in there first and bend down and pick 'em up by hand.'

'Won't the scraper take them up?'

'No, it will not. It'll drag 'em along for a bit, then they'll get caught under the edge of that scraper and lift the whole thing up so it rolls over the rock, and then you'll lose all the manure you been scraping.

Time you're done you'll see all you did is just move it around a little. Nope, they got to be picked up, every one by hand. How's your back?'

'Good.' He'd had two surgeries on his back so far.

'If you still want the job you can go at it starting now.'

'I still want the job.'

'Yeah,' Nelson said. 'I heard you was a little peculiar. Welcome on board.'

It took four hours of bending and stooping to collect the rocks from the first one-acre corral, and since he'd started on the job midmorning, he figured this would be the only one he'd get done today. He moved the tractor to different ends of the enclosure, so he could load the rocks into the front scoop to be hauled away. He thought if he worked fairly close to the tractor the horses might stay back, but with the engine turned off they didn't seem to mind it. The five bay Arabs clustered around behind him, bumping at his back pockets like they might find something good there. If they surprised him, it made him jump, which surprised them and made them jump. They'd scatter and spook and gallop away, throwing clouds of dust into the air, forcing Hayden to breathe through his bandanna until it all settled again.

He didn't break for lunch because he wanted to

show Nelson he could get a lot done and because, not having anticipated getting hired on the spot, he hadn't brought one.

When he fired up the little John Deere and set about to scraping, the horses ran. Hayden worked the fence line first, stopping to pile manure in one corner, then sorted out an even grid, center to side. The heat of the tractor engine mixed with diesel exhaust and the heat of the day and radiated up into his face. When he turned a corner the dust he'd scraped up behind him blew sideways across his face, and he held his breath and tried not to take it into his nose.

The Arabs ran like they'd just been waiting for an excuse. They threw their heads high and raised their tails into flags, and now and then broke gait, down into a long, extended trot that covered a remarkable amount of ground. Hayden watched them as much as he could without taking out part of a fence, and in spite of the heat and dust decided it was a job he could probably do.

At quitting time he had one corral done. Twenty-six left to go. And when he'd finished the last one, the first would be long overdue again. A type of job security, if you cared to look at it the best possible way.

Hayden parked his old Ford pickup in front of his cabin and sat, wanting not to go in. He hadn't been back yet. This would be the first time, if he decided to go in at all.

He sat and looked past his cabin to the dry creek bed and slowly grew into the idea that if Jenny were still here, she'd have come lumbering out to greet him by now. He knew she was gone, but it was a strange, bad situation that he hadn't seen with his own eyes yet, that needed to be absorbed one lousy facet at a time.

He thought about starting the truck engine again and driving back into town. But he needed to ice down his back first and to wash up. Needed it bad, the kind of needing you'd like to ignore but can't. So he'd have to go in.

He found the door of his cabin ajar, the lock destroyed by a crowbar. He picked around here and there and found most of his belongings intact. What came up gone was his food store, a few pans and eating utensils, and a sleeping bag. And of course, the $42 in small bills he'd kept stashed in a cheese crock on the counter.

He opened his little refrigerator and took ice out of the old-fashioned freezer compartment. Ice was the closest thing to food somebody had left him. He put a handful of cubes in a dish towel, broke them up with the handle of a big carving knife, then sat in his favorite chair with the ice positioned against his lower back. He was hungry but couldn't think what to do about that.

He woke up a few hours later. The ice had melted all cold and wet underneath him, and the sun had gone down.

He cruised by the tavern first, just to see who all was there. Scott's off-duty Mustang was parked there, and Jack's new Dodge truck was not, so that seemed like a good deal. He walked a little stiffly across the dirt lot, listening to the weird, ungodly howl of a dog left in a van outside the tavern's back door.

Scott sat at a table alone, nursing a Bud right out of the bottle. He looked up and waved. 'Throw your back out again?' he asked when Hayden sat across the table, and Hayden had to ask him to repeat himself because of the jukebox. Country and Western, which Hayden had never liked.

'Not threw it out exactly, but it's got a few things to say. Hey, Scott, think you could spot me for a beer and a bowl of chili? My place got ripped off.'

'God, Hayden, I'm sorry. I never even thought to go by there. Never had trouble before.'

'We had Jenny looking after the place before.'

'Oh, yeah. I never thought of that. Sure, I could let you have twenty.'

'Pay you back Friday. I got a job today.'

'Good for you. Doing what?'

'Don't even ask.'

The waitress came around, brought Hayden a Corona with lime tucked in the mouth of the bottle without it even having to be ordered, because that's what he drank and she knew it. 'On the house,' she said, a pretty young woman named Rita, whom all the guys in town went after and did not get. 'Welcome back, Hayden.'

And he thanked her, both for the beer and for the welcome.

'Whose dog is that?' Hayden said when she'd left. He squeezed lime down the neck of his beer and poured back three or four good swallows at once.

'I don't see a dog.'

'Out in the parking lot. Making all that racket.'

'All I hear's the jukebox.'

'In that ratty brown van.'

'Oh. Why didn't you say so?' Scott never forgot a vehicle. 'Not from around here.'

'Well, I know that much.'

'So, how am I supposed to know about his dog? Oh, shit. Hayden, do not turn around.'

Hayden closed his eyes and pushed out a lungful of breath. 'Is it just him? Or both of them?'

'Both.'

'Great. Great way to cap off a lovely day. God, of all the places they could be.'

'Of all the beer joints in all the towns in the world, why'd she have to come into yours, is that it? Being there's only one tavern in this town, it's not such a startling coincidence. I mean, I wouldn't phone up the *Unsolved Mysteries* people just yet. Just sit looking at me and finish your beer.'

Hayden watched a spot on the table near Scott's hand, and tipped his Corona back and finished it in one long pull.

'Okay,' Scott said. 'Good. They're over by the bar now. Get up with me and I'll walk you out.'

'I was going to get something to eat.'

'Hayden. I just let you out of jail. You just got your right hand back. You just got a new job. Tell me you're not about to throw all that back.'

'I'm not. I'm just hungry.'

'The burger drive-in is still open. Here's twenty.' Scott passed a folded bill across the table and Hayden wedged it into his jeans pocket. 'Come on. We're leaving.'

Hayden turned to look over his shoulder just as he reached the door, and saw Laurel at the bar, looking back over her shoulder at him. Jack had his back turned and Laurel immediately found a new place to look.

He followed Scott out into the parking lot. The day's heat had barely drained away, leaving a breeze that felt almost cool.

'Why does that man have a gun rack with a twelve-gauge in his back cab window, Scott? He's not a rancher. What does he think he might need to shoot?'

'So he hunts now and then.'

'Is he going hunting now? Or is he taking his wife to the local tavern?'

'Lay off him, Hayden. Just go eat.'

'Listen to that, Scott.'

They stood under the stars for a moment in the parking lot, only that eerie howl breaking the still.

'I'd say that's one pissed-off puppy dog,' Scott said into the evening dark. 'Can't say I blame him, either. He's been parked there since ten o'clock this morning.'

'You're kidding. How's he supposed to pee?'

'Can't say.'

'That's no way to treat a dog.'

'Don't get involved, Hayden. Just go eat, okay?'

But Hayden was already standing beside the old brown van with Scott at his back, talking to the dog through a partly open window. The dog barked and snarled at Hayden, trapped and cornered and more than a little upset with his lot.

'That dog's got no hair on him, Scott.'

'Maybe he's got the mange.'

'There's a cure for the mange. Why doesn't somebody use it? He's skinny, too. And got one eye swollen almost shut. Look at that, Scott. Would you treat a dog like that?'

'You want me to call the ASPCA, I will.'

'And by the time they get out here he'll be gone.'

'Hayden . . .'

'Just don't look, Scott.'

'Hayden. That van is locked. It's against the law.'

'Look the other way, then.'

'That's it. I'm leaving. I do not want to know.'

Hayden could hear his boots stomping through the parking lot and the beefy sound of the Mustang engine firing up and fading away down the highway. He looked once over his shoulder at the tavern and saw no one. He reached his left hand in through the open top of the driver's window and grabbed for the lock button. The dog lunged in and bit him hard, then cowered on the passenger seat while Hayden unlocked the door and opened it wide.

'I'm going to overlook that, this one time only,' Hayden told the dog. 'Owing to your situation. I'm leaving now. You want to come, come. But don't ever bite me again.'

He looked down to see blood from his left hand drop into the dirt. He moved off toward his pickup, then looked back. The dog jumped down, moved stiffly to the front tire of the van, lifted his leg, and relieved himself against it for a prolonged time.

'Come, boy,' Hayden said. The dog followed after him.

They drove over to the burger place together, the dog sitting on the cab seat with Hayden, scratching himself and dropping dandruff onto the seat around him. Hayden pulled into the drive-through and ordered two burgers and a small Coke.

The dog ate his burger pretty much in one bite, then stared and drooled while Hayden ate his.

The light was bad in the drive-in parking lot, but Hayden studied the dog and decided he looked a lot worse than the initial assessment. About fifty pounds when he should be sixty-five, and nearly bald, with two infected eyes and skin all thickened and scaly like an elephant's hide. He was hardly an appetizing sight. Or smell.

Scott's Mustang pulled up next to him before he could finish eating. Scott stepped out of his car, came around to Hayden's driver's side, and peered in.

'I thought as much,' he said. 'Lord, that dog is sorry.'

'Yeah. I'm just beginning to absorb that now.'

'Tell you what. If his owner decides to hang around town to look for him, I'll see if I can't scare up some incentive to get him moving on his way.'

'That's decent of you, Scott.'

'Might want to get that dog to a vet.'

'Maybe when I get paid I could.'

'I'd drive on in to the vet in the city if I were you.'

'Good thinking.'

'Why would you even want a dog that ugly?'

'I never said I did. We're just sitting here having a burger together. Don't make it out a bigger thing than it is.'

Hayden showed up to work at seven, bright and early, hoping the dog knew his way around horses. He brought along a length of rope to tether him up in case he did not.

Mason Nelson came out of the barn to say good morning. 'No offense, Mr Reese, but what the hell is that?'

'It's a dog, Nelson.'

'You sure? How'd he get in a shape like that?'

'I don't know. We only just made each other's acquaintance last night.'

The dog stood close to Hayden's knee, leaning on him, head down, tail between his hind legs. He'd been given a rudimentary bath under the hose, which had knocked off a good deal of the dandruff, but he still smelled like a dog.

One of the trainers, the young one, rode by the barn on a four-wheel motorcycle, craning his neck to see. Hayden had seen him around but they had never spoken. 'Hey, mister,' he called out, 'kinda dog izzat?'

'I don't know. The sorry kind, I guess.'

The trainer spun the bike in a half circle, idled it down, and cut the engine. 'I'll say. Looks like maybe a cross of an Aussie shepherd and some kind of wire-haired something. That just might be the ugliest dog I've ever seen.'

'Nice to find something everyone can agree on,' Hayden said.

He set about working rocks out of the second corral, with the dog bumping up against his heels. The dog didn't go after the horses but growled low in his throat if they came too close, so they did not. Which was fine by Hayden, just fine.

An hour or two into his working day Hayden bent down after a rock, and as he brought himself up straight again felt something go. One of those sudden out-of-alignment things that backs are prone to do, particularly his back, and about which not much can be done in the way of quick fixes.

He couldn't straighten up, so he lowered himself to the ground easy. Not easy enough, though. Got one good wrench out of it, and yelled out loud, and the dog jumped aside, then crowded back in and took to kissing his face. Hayden pushed him away with one hand. But then the horses moved in, a half dozen big rangy chestnuts, maybe not used to seeing a man down. They nuzzled him curiously, looking amazingly tall and dangerous from where he lay, their steel-shod hooves too close to his face.

He thought about rolling out of the corral, manure and all, but as he was unable to straighten himself, it didn't pan out well. So he called the dog back, and he came when called, and sat near Hayden's head, and instructed the horses to stay back, which was better than nothing. Hayden lay curled on his side wondering how long it would take for somebody to miss him. He talked to the dog for something to do.

'I bet you're one of those Lassie-type dogs, who'll go after help if a fellow needs it. Aren't you, boy? Go get Nelson. Remember those guys by the barn? Go on down there, boy. Go fetch somebody back here.' The dog looked into Hayden's face, cocked his head slightly, and set his chin down on Hayden's neck. 'Yeah, I knew I could count on you.'

Nearly an hour later Hayden heard the drone of the four-wheeler and managed to shout loud enough to be heard.

He soaked in a hot tub until it wasn't hot anymore, hoping the heat would loosen things up back there.

Meanwhile the muscle relaxants went to his head and left him still crippled but too high to feel concern. When the tub water grew cold he managed to lever himself out of there and hobble, slow and bent, to his bed.

The dog was sitting right in the middle of his bedspread, scratching his ear with the overgrown claws of one back paw.

'Boo,' Hayden said, and the dog jumped down and ran.

Still wet, he eased in, threw the covers back because it was hot, and lay on his side under the top sheet, drifting in and out of a drugged sleep.

He woke because the dog was barking at the door, defending his new territory. Hayden watched the door – which didn't lock now – drift open slightly, and he hoped this was only a dream.

Then Laurel stuck her head in and he hoped it was not.

'Hayden, what the hell is that?' she said, still wisely holding most of herself outside.

'It would appear he's my new dog.'

'What happened to your old dog?'

'Same thing that'll happen to all of us in time.'

'What's his name?'

'He doesn't have one.'

'Does he bite?'

Hayden glanced down at the bruised swollen tooth marks on his left hand. 'Absolutely.'

'Well, call him, then.'

Call him what? Hayden wondered. He whistled sharply between his teeth. 'Here, boy.' The dog came to him and lay down on the braided rug beside the bed. 'Good boy. Good dog. Laurel, do me a favor, would you? There's some kibble in the broom closet. Feed him some into his bowl, okay? And check and see if he's got water. I'm having a little trouble moving around.'

Laurel stepped rather cautiously inside. 'I heard you threw your back out again at work today. How do you feel?'

'I'm so high on these muscle drugs, I don't feel.'

Hayden watched her pour about seven cups of kibble into Jenny's old food dish, and the dog set about it. 'He looks exactly like my dead uncle George,' she said. 'He wasn't much to look at, either. Had that funny kind of baldness, you know, with about three hairs on every square inch of scalp. Last time I saw him he had both eyes all swollen up from fighting.'

'Maybe he's your uncle George reincarnated.'

'God, let's hope not. He was a nasty man.'

She came and sat on the bed beside him. Ran the fingers of her right hand through the hair on his chest. He'd memorized the words for this moment, if it came, which he hadn't expected it to. 'Not with that ring on your hand. Not if you're on your way home to him.' Now he closed his eyes and said nothing and wished his back were not out, and felt those words melt out of him to where they made no sense and did not feel worth saying.

She threw the sheet back and climbed in beside him, stretched out next to him, and he picked up his head and she held it and set it down on her chest. He threw one arm across her, trying not to get too deeply invested in feelings he was not currently able to see through. Owing to the drugs he drifted out again.

'Peg's gone,' she said, startling him awake. 'Took off.'

'Ran away from home?' he said, thinking the voice didn't sound like his own.

'Ran off with that asshole nineteen-year-old boyfriend from King City. I got a letter from her today. Postmarked Nevada.'

'How long's she been gone?'

'More than a week.'

'What're you going to do?'

'Not sure. It's what I came to talk about.'

And even through the thick foggy glare of the drug, he felt something close down inside him, knowing she'd come here to talk, not just to let him rest with his head on her breasts. 'It's a police matter. I'd call the police. She's underage. He took her across a state line.'

'I was hoping you'd go haul her home.'

'Me? Why me?'

'She likes you. She'll listen to you.'

'Why doesn't Jack go?'

'She's not his daughter.'

'I'd expect he'd think of her as his daughter by now.'

'It's not like he doesn't care, Hayden. Only she's a handful. And he's been on his own from age thirteen, so the way he sees it, she's a big girl. If she wants out, let her.'

'Why don't you go?'

'I don't think this guy she's seeing might be any too keen on giving her back. I was thinking maybe somebody bigger and stronger than him would be good.'

She scooted out from underneath his head, and slid down a little to face him, and kissed him light and soft on the lips, and then on his neck, and kept moving downward. But he stopped her. Put a hand under her chin and guided her up to meet his eyes. He found it hard to focus, but breathing came easy. He wasn't sure if that was the drugs talking, or just the simple cold shower of knowing she'd taken that man back.

'Not if you're going back home to him,' he said.

She flipped the sheet away and jumped to her feet, and he pulled the sheet back over himself quickly, sucking his stomach in at the same time, already missing her closeness.

'Well, he's moved his stuff back in, and I have to go home, don't I? You ask too much from me, Hayden.'

'I don't think I do. Just to state your intentions, is all.'

She came back and sat on the edge of the bed, and brushed his hair back from his forehead. 'I was hoping you'd understand about Peg, since you had a teenage girl of your own once. How old was she?'

'Fifteen when I saw her last.'

'How old would she be now?'

'I try not to think about that.'

'Well, how old were you when—'

'Thirty. She'd be just getting ready to turn thirty.'

'Wow.' They sat in silence for a few seconds. 'She'd be almost as old as me.'

'Thanks, Laurel. That's exactly what I wanted to hear.'

'Sorry.'

'I'll see if I can get Peg home. If she wants to come; I can't drag her. When I'm on my feet again I'll try.'

'Thanks, hon,' she said and kissed him on the ear and slipped away.

When he woke again it was dark, and the dog was up on the bed with him, head up, watching Hayden's face.

'Shoo. Get off the bed.' But he didn't. 'Down, boy. George. Get down off the bed.' But the dog didn't move. He seemed to fully grasp Hayden's inability to enforce his order. 'Okay, fine. Don't get down. But when I'm on my feet again, we're going to have a long talk about this.'

George set his head down hard on Hayden's chest and sighed.

Chapter Four

Ask for Peg Special

Hayden stopped in King City for a pack of cigarettes. First things first. Then he added a street map of the town as an afterthought.

He had a jeans pocket full of money, $400 to be exact, minus the money he'd paid the vet for seeing to George. The wad felt strange and unfamiliar there. Two hundred was from Laurel, expense money for the trip, which he hadn't figured would be enough, but since it was clearly all she could muster, he figured it would have to be enough. She'd left the cash in an envelope on her hall table while she and Jack were working the diner, and she'd said the house wasn't locked, just go and get it, so he had.

Then he'd gone by the horse ranch on Division Road, just to be sure Mason Nelson knew, absolutely and from his own mouth, that he wouldn't be coming back. Duh, Nelson said. Then he'd given Hayden $200 cash, which he called severance pay. When Hayden asked why he'd want to do that for a man in his employ barely one full working day, Nelson stuck a release form under his nose, and Hayden signed away his right to sue the corporation for any injury he might have sustained on their property, inclusive of any workman's compensation action. It was a free $200. Hayden had never intended to sue.

He picked up a pack of book matches from the counter because his dash lighter hadn't worked since 1986.

He sat in the cab of the truck and lit one, and drew from it, and blew a cloud of smoke out into the heat and George sneezed violently and shook his head. His ears looked wet and runny inside from the goop the vet had put in them, and the ointment in his eyes made them look worse, at least temporarily. The mange dip had left him with a strong chemical stink.

'Do not tell me you're allergic to cigarette smoke,' Hayden said. He blew out a few more hits without noticeable reaction from George and drove off, satisfied.

He knew where he was going, and he savored that, knowing it might be the last time on this trip that he would.

* * *

He left George in the truck cab and walked through the gate and up the path. It was a run-down old house, the type that might have been the real old-fashioned original farmhouse before the land was subdivided. The type with lots of character and history but regrettably gone to seed. The roof needed work and a good cleaning, the porch sagged slightly under Hayden's boots. Could have even been a house unfit to live in, but this was the address he'd been given, and besides, there was an old woman sitting right out on the porch. Gray haired and dark olive complected – Hispanic or old-country Italian, maybe – with big jowly cheeks and an old-fashioned air to go with the house. She sat in a dirty webbed lawn chair, fanning herself with a section of the morning paper. She looked at Hayden with expressionless eyes, and Hayden smiled, and the woman did not – just stared out from under heavy lids.

'Morning, ma'am.' The woman only stared. 'You know where I can find Joey Esposito?' No reply. 'Do you speak English?' Nothing. 'Do you speak? I mean, ever? At all?' He waited. *'Yo hablo un poquito español.'* Not a word of Italian, though, so he hoped he'd guessed right. 'Okay. Thanks for all your help.'

He rapped on the door. He didn't expect anyone to answer. Someone did. A woman it was, in her late thirties most likely, but run down, like a car that maybe isn't so old but has seen a lot of mileage and not much care. She had on a dirty apron over her housedress. She didn't seem pleased to find anyone at the door. She didn't seem to want to talk.

'Morning, ma'am.'

'I'm not buying anything.'

'I'm not selling anything. I'm looking for Joey Esposito.'

'He's not here.'

The front door, the kind with window glass in the upper half, began to swing toward his face, but he stopped it hard with his left hand; the woman's look changed. She seemed a little spooked now, maybe less in control, which went down fine with Hayden, who figured the added respect could only work to his benefit. 'I know he's not here. I want you to tell me where he might've gone.'

'Why do you wanta know?'

'Well, it seems he took off with an underage girl, and she's the daughter of a friend of mine, and I'm looking to get her back home. I don't really care about your son one way or the other. I don't want to hurt him or help him. It's got nothing to do with him, really. But I've got to track him down just the same.'

'He's not my son anyway. He's Frank's son. I just live here with Frank. I don't know where Joey went. If you find out, don't tell me. I don't even want to know. I hope he went far away and stays there forever. Can I go now?'

And she swung the door again, and this time he let it swing, because he tentatively believed that she probably didn't know, and he definitely believed that she definitely didn't care. The door slammed hard about a foot from his nose and he took one step back, watching the glass shudder, waiting to see if it would break. It didn't. He looked over to the old woman, whose expression had not changed.

Hayden sighed.

He had lost that one and only perfect moment of his trip, when he actually knew what move comes next, and what direction to travel to get to it. He started his walk back to the truck.

'Pretty little redhead girl?'

The voice turned him. The front door was still shut. He looked at the old woman, who betrayed little. He stepped back onto the porch, walked close to her, squatted down on his haunches next to her chair. 'Yes, ma'am. You know her?'

'I seen her. That a pack of smokes in your shirt pocket?'

'Yes, ma'am. Would you like one?'

'Hell yeah, I would.'

Hayden shook out two and handed her one. He lit

them both with a cardboard match, and when he lit hers, she held his hand in a way that seemed more intimate than absolutely necessary.

'You wouldn't happen to know where they've gone.'

'Nope.'

'Not a clue?'

'He don't talk to me.'

'I had a clue maybe they were in Nevada.'

The woman threw her head back and expressed a long stream of smoke at the porch awning, along with something strangely akin to a laugh. 'I'll bet,' she said. 'I'll just bet they are.'

'But you don't know where in Nevada.'

'Nope.'

'Okay. Thanks anyway, then.'

He rose up off his haunches, bracing both hands on his lower back, stretching out a problem spot. He looked back to his truck to see George scratching hard at one of his ears. He began to move off in that direction.

'Give you two pieces of advice,' the old lady said. She didn't seem anxious to see him go. Neither did he feel any too anxious to stay. 'If you want 'em.'

'Yes, ma'am, I sure do.'

'Check the whorehouses first.'

Hayden leaned back against a rail post, wondering briefly if it would hold him. 'Why would you say that?'

'Because I know my grandson. I know what he thinks girls're good for. I know how he got that fast car and all that pocket cash. I'm not stupid, you know. I got eyes. I see what goes on around me here.'

'I'm sure you do. What's the other advice?'

'Watch out for Joey. He ain't a big guy like you, but watch your back all the same.'

'Well, I thank you for the information, ma'am.'

'Gimme another smoke before you go.'

Hayden gave her two.

Barely into the Mojave proper, Hayden fell under the impression that the truck was running a little hotter than usual. Even a little hotter than desert usual. He stopped by the side of the road, let George out to pee, let the engine cool some. He checked the radiator, which seemed low, but he didn't have water on him. He called George back and started it up and ran it a little, and popped the hood, and saw that he was losing a few drips at a time from the bottom of his water pump.

Great, he thought. That's about right.

There was a rest stop twenty or so miles ahead; he'd seen a sign for it. Maybe he could get some water there. He'd just have to keep filling it and hope the damn thing would hold until he got home. Hope the bearings wouldn't go out.

He sat on the shoulder of the highway with George, in the shade of the truck, sweat rolling down into his collar and sticking his hair to his forehead and the back of his neck. He smoked a cigarette while he let the engine cool some more, hoping to maximize his chances of making it to water. He could probably lay his hands on a reconditioned water pump in the next town. Barstow maybe. Forty bucks or so. But he lacked the tools, not to mention the back, to install it on the road. And to pay a mechanic to do it was clearly out of his price range for now.

He ground out his cigarette and looked off to the horizon. Sand-colored clay hills polka-dotted with scrub, going bald near the top, and mountains in the distance, a rusty gold variegated by light or erosion or both. And hundreds and hundreds of simple three-blade metal windmills, all spinning at once. A whole field of them on the side of that far mountain.

'Look on the bright side, George,' he said. 'At least Scott's not here to tell me I brought this trouble on myself.'

He didn't drive again until night fell.

By the time Hayden pulled into Boulder City, Nevada, the three gallon jugs of water he'd bought in Baker had gone under the hood. He stopped at a service station on the main drag, the Nevada Highway, gassed up, refilled the radiator and the water jugs, and checked the air in his tires. He bought four microwave burritos, ate two, and gave two to George.

Boulder City. That was the postmark on Peg's letter. Which could mean everything or nothing, depending on her smarts, depending on his luck. He hoped it didn't depend on his luck.

He found a dirt-cheap motel room, parked George way around the back, and snuck him in later when no one was looking.

By the time he woke up it was dark again. He rolled over to look for his watch and slammed into George, sleeping on the bed beside him, and George growled. So Hayden picked him up and tossed him partway across the room, and by the time he groveled back, his attitude seemed properly adjusted.

It was eight thirty.

'Let's go get us a beer, George,' he said, knowing full well that a beer was one of the few things he was never going to split with his dog.

'Where's a fellow go to have a good time around here?' he asked the bartender. He leaned on his elbows and tried to appear sincere.

'Depends on what kind of good times you had in mind.'

'This is Nevada, right? I mean, a guy can get stuff

out in the open here he might not in some other state. Anyway, that's what I hear.'

'Right. So why don't you just go over to that pay phone in the corner and look it up in the Yellow Pages?'

Actually, Hayden had never thought of that. Even now it seemed like something that might be true or might be a joke. 'It's just, I'm not too familiar with this area. I don't know what's close to here.'

'You want close, or you want good?'

'Both'd be nice.'

'Well, the close one isn't good and the good one isn't close.'

'I guess I want the good one, then.'

'I was told to ask for Peg special,' he said.

He stood in a sort of ornate old-fashioned parlor, where young women sat and leaned and chatted and smoked and looked bored, like they hoped he'd pick somebody else. He spoke to a black man who wore black sunglasses at ten o'clock at night, who wore his hair shaved close to his scalp, with a line like a part buzzed in at an angle.

'You got told wrong, then. Ain't no Peg here.'

'Anyplace else around here might have a Peg?'

'I ain't in the business of recommending our competition. We got lots of ladies here you'll like.'

'Thanks anyway, then.'

'Nothing Peg can do for you these ladies can't.'

'You could be wrong about that. Where's that place that's closer to town?'

'Look in the Yellow Pages if you need information.'

So Hayden figured whorehouses really were listed in the Yellow Pages in Nevada; either that or the joke about it really got around.

'I was told to ask for Peg special.'

He stood in an entryway of a place that looked like an old flophouse lobby, talking to an equally run-down fifty-year-old woman who sat behind the counter. Her hair was bleached a white-blond color that nature had never handed to anybody. Hayden watched a cockroach disappear between the loose-fitting boards of wainscoting and decided this must have been the place the bartender warned him against.

'She might be busy right now.'

Hayden's heart jumped. This was only the fourth place he'd tried. Without consciously realizing it, he'd fully expected to play this game all night and come up empty handed. 'I can wait.'

'I can set you up with somebody just as good.'

'No. Friend of mine told me all about Peg. Young one. Redhead. Got my heart set on that, you know? No, I'll wait.'

'Suit yourself, hon.'

But there was no place to sit, so he stood. Leaned his back against the wall panels, then thought about cockroaches and stood with his hands in his pockets in the middle of the room.

'You want the hour, or just the half hour?'

'Half hour ought to do.'

'Fifty bucks.' Hayden just stood there. 'In advance.'

He counted it out for her in cash. Fifty bucks. Christ. Last time Hayden had been to a place like this he'd been Peg's age, maybe sixteen. It's amazing really, what inflation will do.

He knocked on the door to room 10.

'Come on in,' the voice said, smoky and smooth, and he couldn't tell for sure if it was Peg or not.

He pushed the door open into a tiny room with a twin-size bed and little sixteen-year-old Peg lying splayed out on it, dressed in some kind of silky black stretch pants and see-through blouse. Hayden didn't want to stare, but he had to see for sure if it was her. The hair was right, a genuine redhead, that bright carroty red, and the face was pretty close, but he'd never seen her all slathered up with makeup like this. Her eyes opened extra wide to see him, and just for that moment she looked like a kid again, not seductive or womanly, just surprised, and it was absolutely Peg.

It made his stomach roil a little, thinking of her here in the filthy dark with cockroaches and potbellied old men.

'Hayden?'

'Yeah, it's me.' He stepped in, shut the door behind him.

'Hayden, what're you doing here?'

'I came to see you.'

'Well, you're seeing me,' she said, and grabbed that silky black see-through blouse in both hands and pulled it right off over her head. Hayden got a flash of a glimpse of hard little teenage breasts before he turned his face away, turned his back to her. He rested his forehead on the bedroom door.

'Peg? Would you kindly dress yourself?'

'You want me to put my shirt on?'

'Yes, I want you to put your shirt on.'

'You just paid fifty bucks for me to take it off.'

'Is that what you think I came here for? I can't believe that. Why in God's name would you think I want to lay down with you?'

'Well, every other older guy in town always wanted to.'

'Are you dressed yet?'

'Wait a minute. Yeah. Okay.'

Hayden turned back and saw Peg sitting up on the side of the bed, her blouse on again. But it wasn't much of a blouse, didn't hide much, so he sat beside her and pulled the shiny red sheet off the bed, all but the part of it she was sitting on, and draped it over her. She wrapped it around herself and disappeared inside it like she'd only just now thought to be ashamed.

'What'd you come, for then? What'd you pay fifty bucks for?'

'Just to talk to you.'

'Never knew a guy who'd pay fifty bucks to talk.'

'What're you doing in this place?'

'Making a damn good living.'

'Joey's idea?'

'We gotta eat.'

'Both his arms broken? Why can't he work a job?'

'You don't understand how it is, Hayden. My mom told you to come here, didn't she?'

She looked at him then, straight into him for the first time. He didn't answer for a minute, just sat quietly with her, realizing he'd found her, and that was a good thing. He took a cigarette out of his shirt pocket and fished for the pack of matches to light it up, to help him think.

'Give me one,' Peg said.

'You're too young to smoke.'

She rolled her eyes and pulled open the drawer in the little bedside stand, and in it Hayden could see three loose cigarettes and six foil-wrapped condoms.

She took out a cigarette and Hayden lit it for her, not to approve, just to be polite. He felt at a loss for words, kind of awkward and slow.

'Joey loves me,' Peg said.

'Did he make you go away with him?'

'No.'

'Is he making you stay?'

'He'd be mad if I left.'

'Are you here of your own free will?'

She took a draw and blew three clean smoke rings one right after the other. 'I wish you wouldn't come here acting like my daddy, Hayden. You're not, you know. Joey loves me.'

'Do you love him?'

'Everybody needs somebody that loves them.'

'Do you love Joey? You haven't said yet.'

'Why I gotta tell you all this?'

'Because I paid my fifty bucks, so you have to do what I want. That's the trouble with your new line of work, little girl. Guy pays his fifty bucks, he can take you all kinds of places you don't want to go.'

'It's an honest line of work. It's legal.'

'Not when you're sixteen, it's not.'

'Will you keep your voice down, please? I got a fake ID. I got some kind of life here. I can't go home.'

'Why not?'

'Things're no good at home.'

'Jack give you trouble?'

Peg laughed, a kind of snotty, disrespectful laugh. 'You wish, Hayden. No, Jack gives *you* trouble. Jack and me, we get along good enough. He treats me like a grown-up, which is more than I can say for some people I know. It's my mom gives me trouble. I know she sent you here. Just go on, Hayden. Just go away. I don't want to go home.'

'You like it here?'

She stamped her cigarette out in a glass ashtray on the floor, then sat huddled forward over her own knees. She looked so little. She brushed her long, straight hair back along her head with one hand. She never did answer the question.

'Because if you don't like it here, but you don't want to go home? I mean, there are other places to be.'

'Joey wouldn't want that.'

'I don't give a fuck what Joey wants. What do you want?'

'He keeps a pretty good eye on me.'

'You let me worry about that.'

'Where would I go?'

'Anywhere you like. You could go to one or another of your grandparents. You could come to my house and we'd get you a place to live on your own in town.'

'And when Joey comes looking?'

'You let me worry about Joey.'

She lay back down on the bed and sighed, still wrapped in the sheet, and looked at her watch in the dim.

'How much time do I have?' Hayden asked.

'Twenty-five minutes.'

'Good,' he said. He propped himself up on the pillows beside her, as respectfully apart as possible on a twin, and folded his arms across his chest, and wondered if George was okay waiting out in the truck by himself. 'Good. You got a while, then, to think what you want to do.'

They sat together, side by side and quiet for a bit.

'Joey loves me,' she said.

'Nice to know you're making so much progress over there. Let me tell you something, little girl. When you love somebody you want them all to yourself. When you turn them out to shop their body around, well, I can't say exactly what that is because it's foreign to me. But it's sure as hell not love.'

'Oh, right. And you're the big expert on what love is.'

'Meaning what?'

'She walks all over you, Hayden.'

'Wrong. You are so wrong. Don't be turning this around onto me. This is not my life we came here to talk about.'

'Oh, no? Then why're you even here, then? You're

here because she snapped her fingers and said, "Go fetch my girl home, Hayden." Like she's telling you to go and pick up a quart of milk or something. And you do it, because you do everything she says. You are so whipped and you don't even see it.'

'She turns to me when she needs help.'

'And then she turns away from you when she doesn't.'

'Okay. Fine. Whatever you say. I don't need any more of this.' He was on his feet now, on his way to the door. 'I did what I said I'd do. I came here to give you a chance. You don't want that chance, fine. I'll tell her I tried.'

He felt his hand on the doorknob.

'Hayden.'

He heard her voice, sudden and a little shaky, like it was important to her to stop him. That's when he realized it didn't matter all that much if she came along or if she didn't. He'd done what he swore he would do. He'd been smart enough or lucky enough to find her, he'd offered to get her home – now he was done. Blessedly done. Now he could go back to his old familiar truck, where George was waiting for him. He could nurse his leaky water pump home, and then sleep in his own bed and be done with all of it.

And the next time Laurel asked him for too big a favor, maybe he'd tell her it wasn't his job anymore. It wasn't his role anymore, so it wasn't his problem. Next time maybe he'd tell her to go get the same from Jack.

'Hayden, hold on a minute. Don't go just yet.' But he wanted to go. He wanted to get out of this place. He really did. But he waited a minute, because maybe Peg did, too. 'How long could I stay at your place?' she asked.

Chapter Five ⚡

Searchlight

'That's not Jenny,' Peg said. She stood on the passenger side of his truck on a street corner, with the door held wide open, looking at George while George looked back at her.

'Would you get in, please?'

'What happened to Jenny?'

'She passed on. Now would you please get in before your boyfriend comes by to pick you up?'

'Is he going to bite me?'

'Get in. Now.' Hayden grabbed George around his neck and held his head away from Peg, and Peg climbed in.

'God. I didn't know Jenny died.' Hayden hit the gas before the door on her side was even closed. 'Christ, Hayden, what're you trying to do, throw me out again?'

He made a sharp left, and the door swung closed, but he could tell by the sound it hadn't quite latched shut. He slowed slightly and pulled over toward the curb. 'Slam that proper,' he said, and she did. He pulled away again.

The plan had been that she would cut her last client five minutes short, appearing on the street corner at 3:55 A.M. instead of the usual 4:00. That would give them a five-minute margin for Hayden to pick her up instead of Joey. But she'd been late, more than four minutes late, cutting their safety margin down under a minute.

'Put your seat belt on.'

'God, Hayden.'

'Do what I say, please.'

She frowned and grumbled, but she put it on. Hayden let go of George and he sniffed at her side, then lay down on the seat between them, his front paws hanging over near the gear shift.

'No, don't go this way,' she said when she looked up. 'This is the street Joey takes to come get me.'

'Great. Now you tell me. You might want to get down.' She tried to duck down across the seat, but George growled at her and Hayden had to cuff him lightly on the side of his head. 'Duck down on the passenger floor,' he said, but there wasn't that much time.

Before she could even try, a black BMW pulled by, going the opposite direction, and Peg said, 'Uh-oh.'

Hayden didn't even bother to ask if that was Joey. 'Think he saw you?' Hayden watched the car in his side-view mirror, watched it swing a U in the deserted street, the lights coming right up behind him. 'Never mind answering that.'

'What're we gonna do now, Hayden?'

'I guess we're going to drive.'

'Jack's a nicer guy than you make him out,' she said after fifteen or twenty minutes of stony quiet.

They were out in the open desert now on 95 south toward Searchlight, a flat, unpopulated highway with mountains on either side. Hayden glanced obsessively in his rearview mirror. The lights of the BMW were still back there. No closer, no farther behind. Neither of them was speeding much. It was just back there. Keeping up. Following along.

'I'm sort of trying to think, Peg.'

'Better than my other stepdad.'

'Maybe this is not the right moment.'

'Better than my real dad. Now, *he* messed with me. Why do you think my mom took me and left? I was four years old and she couldn't keep him off me. I know you want to think Jack's like that so you got some good reason to hate him. I bet you'd be awful happy if I said he messed with me. Then you could put something behind how you feel about him. Sorry I have to disappoint you. He's pigheaded. No more so than you, though. But he's not like that.'

Hayden scratched his head behind his ear for a minute. It *was* a little disappointing, really. 'I'm sorry you had to go through that with your dad.'

'Wasn't your fault.'

'I'm just sorry you had to grow up thinking that's all you're good for. I'm sorry you had to end up in a place like where I just found you. With a guy like we got behind us. Now maybe I better think what I'm doing here.'

They rode in silence for a handful of miles. Hayden checked the shoulder of the highway, and it was always the same. Wide tarmac giving way to good, hard, wide dirt. Plenty of space to pull off all along, if he needed to. He shifted his eyes from the rearview mirror to the temperature gauge and back again.

The sky took on that pre-predawn look, something short of full-on black. Above the mountain on his left it glowed slightly with a preface of morning, white at the edge going to metallic blue, the stars still alive above, the edge of the range sharp and black in relief. One bright star hovered over the mountain, standing out from the rest.

He saw a sign in his headlights. *Searchlight 22.* He

looked at the gauge again. It wasn't in the red, but high. He knew they couldn't do this much longer.

Her voice startled him, and he jumped. 'You got a gun?'

'No.'

'Why not?'

'Why not? That's a funny question. A lot of people don't have guns. Why would I? Who do you think I want to shoot?'

'Might be a good thing to have from time to time. You know, just for protection.'

'Joey has a gun? Is that what you're trying to tell me here in your own indirect way?'

'Yeah, Joey has one. For protection.'

'What kind of gun?'

'I don't know.'

'Handgun?'

'Yeah.'

'Automatic type of a thing?'

'I don't know. I don't know nothing about guns.'

'You know how he goes about putting bullets in it?'

'Yeah. They go in that round kind of cylinder thing. Six at a time.'

'Okay, good.'

'I think it might be a Smith & Wesson. 'Cause, like, before he bought this new car, his old one had a bumper sticker in the back window that said, 'Protected by Smith & Wesson.' But maybe that's just a figure of speech. I don't know.'

'Okay, Peg. You can stop talking now.'

She appeared hurt. Slumped down in the seat and put her arm around George for comfort, like a kid reaching for a doll or a teddy bear, and George picked up his head and set his chin down on her thigh.

He looked at his temperature gauge again. Wondered if it paid to let it get any higher. Just postponing the inevitable. What would be gained by driving farther? Light, he thought, and that was a good answer. He would prefer to face Joey in the light of dawn, see what all he was up against. He thought about what, if anything, he had to use in the way of weapons.

'Peg, feel around behind your seat there, see if you can feel a tire iron.'

His own was up under the bed of the truck with the spare, but he'd borrowed a much longer one from Scott. He'd been overhauling his brakes and couldn't get enough leverage on his short little bar. Not with his back being what it was. So he'd borrowed a longer bar and a can of brake cleaner from Scott. Couldn't remember if he'd taken them back, though. That was the only possible problem.

'Yeah, I feel something back here,' she said. 'A bar and a big can of something.'

'Hand them both to me, okay?'

He took the iron from her, snugged it under his right thigh, where it showed from Peg's side but not from his driver's door. He popped the cap off the can of brake cleaner and set it on the driver's floor behind his left heel.

'You're not going to stop, are you, Hayden?'

'I think in a while I'll need to.'

'Couldn't we just drive to a police station or something?'

'I don't think Searchlight at four thirty in the morning will be much help to us.' Maybe this had been a bad idea. Maybe he should've gone north to Vegas, even if it was out of their way.

'Are we getting low on gas?'

'No, water. The engine's leaking water. It'll get too hot in a little bit.' And we're only a half hour out, so this will be a long, slow trip home, he thought. If we get that far.

'So? Drive it hot.'

'That won't help anything. Just blow the engine.'

She exhibited the first signs of obvious outward stress then, blowing air out of her mouth in a raspberry noise, raking her hair back with both hands, exasperated. 'So, you can get a new engine, Hayden. We can't get another one of us.'

'You don't get it, little girl. What does a blown engine do?'

'Ruins the engine,'

'Then what?'

'I don't know.'

'It stops. It seizes up, and then it doesn't go anymore. Get it now?'

'Yeah. I get it now.'

They drove in silence a few more miles. The sky above the mountain added one layer of color, a flat gold. All the stars except the bright one faded. He stared again at the mirror, at the temperature gauge. Flirting with the red zone. Maybe better to stop now, while he still had the option to go again, depending on how things panned out. It wasn't all the light he would've wanted. Then again, if it got full-on light, maybe Joey could aim a shot without anybody even pulling over.

He drove a mile or two more. He could feel it moving around in his stomach, but he didn't turn his attention on it full. Still it worked at him, crept through his muscles, radiated out along his arms and legs. He chewed on the inside of his lip and wished Laurel were here so he could yell at her for getting him into this.

His headlights hit another sign. *Truck Lane Ahead.* And Hayden knew immediately what that meant. Long, unrelenting uphill stretch. Overheating territory.

'Okay, let's get this over with,' he said.

He looked over at her face and it looked pure white, like china. She didn't say anything at all. He pulled over onto the shoulder, well off the highway in the dirt, and cut the engine. A light mist of steam came up from his radiator grille. In the mirror he watched the BMW pull up and park behind them. Hayden could see the outline of it now, when Joey cut his headlights, like a shadow. Like the edges of the dark of a new moon. That's how much light he had to work with.

He felt his hand on the tire iron and George growled at nothing, feeling a threat he couldn't locate.

He watched in his side-view mirror, and spoke to Peg without turning his head to look at her. "You do exactly what I tell you, whatever it is. Don't question anything I say. Just listen to me and act fast.'

Joey got out and came up alongside his truck, on the driver's side, both hands out straight in a shooting stance, cautious, the gun at the level of Hayden's head. Hayden opened his truck door.

'Close it!' Joey shouted. 'You just stay right inside.'

Hayden eased the door back but did not latch it closed.

Joey stood at the open window, gun aimed at Hayden's face, a big 357, and peered past him to Peg. He was a little guy, like his grandmother said, small and wiry. He wore his dark hair slicked back, wet looking.

Hayden knew by his stance and his body language and his voice that he was scared, probably as scared as they were. That didn't make him feel any better, though. A scared man is a dangerous man. Hayden had learned that years ago.

'You come on out of there, Peg,' Joey said. His voice betrayed his age and lack of confidence. 'You just stay put, old man. This was a stupid move, Peg. Don't try nothing like this ever again.'

Hayden shifted his head right and looked at Peg. Terrified. And although it wasn't the moment for it, he thought, Isn't it crazy, what we'll mistake for love? George snarled at the driver's window and Hayden clamped a hand over his muzzle. 'You better go to him, Peg.'

Her eyes flew wide. 'You're just giving me over to him?'

Hayden breathed deep. He knew this would happen. He'd told her clearly to do what he said, fast and without question, yet was not the least bit surprised that she did not. With his head turned fully to her, fully away from Joey, he gave her a look he hoped would drive the point home. 'Will you do what I say for once?'

She just stared at him, frozen. Then she opened her door slowly and got out of the truck. She looked at him again from there, standing on the shoulder in the dirt, and he gave her a little flip of his head to say, The front.

Go around the front. Hoping she could see in this bad light.

She went around the front.

He shifted his head back and the gun was just an inch or two from his left temple, and he held his breath and watched her, walking slow. She crossed in front of the truck and turned and came around the driver's side, slowly, toward Joey. And Joey, who was only nineteen after all, and a rank amateur at being so bad, did what Hayden wanted him to do. He lowered the gun slightly and turned to face her.

With the tire iron tight in his right fist he swung his body around to face the driver's door, fast, all in one move, pulling his legs up onto the seat to brace them against the door. Then he kicked it hard, and it flew open and hit Joey and sent him sprawling out on the paved shoulder of the highway.

Hayden picked up the can of brake cleaner on his way out of the truck, in case Joey hadn't lost his grip on the gun. He jumped out over Joey's downed body. Joey rolled over onto his back and tried to rise and Hayden sprayed the brake cleaner in his face, right in his eyes. Toxic stuff, brake cleaner. Says right on the label make sure you don't get it in your eyes. Joey yelled out and both his hands flew to his face and neither one held a gun. Hayden couldn't see where the gun had gone, but he knew the worst was over.

Joey sat on the tarmac, face in his hands, knees drawn up in front of him, and Hayden raised the tire iron high and swung it hard and smacked it across Joey's left knee, and Joey screamed, and doubled into a fetal position, and Hayden found the scream to be a satisfying sound. He hadn't really needed to break Joey's knee, not with that stuff in his eyes. He could've just poked around and found the gun and put water, in his radiator and packed up Peg and left. He did it more to satisfy himself, because his fear had made him mean. Another example of the danger in a frightened man. And he didn't even feel done yet. Just felt it all flow into him, the rage to replace all that scared he'd been trying to suppress. Bigger than everybody there, that's how it felt, so he picked Joey up by the shirt and threw him against the side of his truck bed, and held him up that way, and stuck the tapered prying end of the tire iron up against his throat.

'Think you're bad, don't you, boy? You are such a rank amateur. What were you gonna do, boy, beat her up? Beat her real bad so she'd know not to leave again? About a hundred pounds of sixteen-year-old girl? That makes you a real man, huh, Joey. How does it feel to you? You like having somebody bigger and stronger take control of you? Decide if you get to live or die? If you get to keep all your parts?'

Joey's head bowed back with the pressure of the steel

wedged under the Adam's apple of his throat, and he gurgled and tried to breathe, and tears ran out of his eyes, and his jaw set tight against his pain, and sweat and tears dripped off his jaw and onto his collar. And Hayden leaned in even closer to see all of that in the half-light. He was beyond any control now, could feel that clearly, and he hoped in a disconnected way that he wouldn't kill the kid, but knew he'd have to watch and see.

'Now listen, you little redneck asshole.' He hissed the words out through a hard-set jaw, right into Joey's face. 'Let me talk to you in words you can understand. You think you own that girl. Wrong. I do. You fought me to get her back but you lost, didn't you? So she's mine. Think of us like two stallions fighting over one mare. You can relate to that, right? We fight to the death, now I get to kill you.'

Joey gurgled something, and Hayden eased up a little with the tire iron and felt himself back off a step inside, and know that maybe nobody would have to die out here. 'What did you say? Talk so I can hear you, boy.'

'Please don't kill me.'

'Why not? What'll you do for me if I don't?'

He let go of Joey's shirt and Joey folded like a sock doll, crumpled to the dirt at Hayden's feet, his back up against the rear tire. He cried like a baby, rocking slightly over his knee, gray with the pain, trying to hold it without quite touching it. Hayden stood over him and waited.

'Um. Go away and not bother you no more?'

'What about her?'

'She's yours, like you said.'

'Well, that's a hell of a good offer, boy.' And with that Hayden felt himself turn back to himself again, and he hauled a gallon of water out of the truck bed, and walked it around front and popped the hood. 'Find that gun, Peg, then go sit inside.'

He touched the radiator cap and decided it was too hot to put water in with the engine turned off, so he went around and hit the key, and idled it, and eased the cap off with his bandanna and replaced a gallon of lost water. When he'd slammed the hood again, Joey had dragged himself halfway back to his shiny black car, and Peg was sitting up straight in the passenger seat, her arm around the dog, the gun in her lap.

Hayden got in and slammed the door and set Scott's tire iron on the passenger floor. He popped the truck into first and pulled away without looking back.

'I'm sorry you had to see that, Peg.'

He wanted a cigarette, but his hands had taken to shaking, along with a place deep in his gut. Even the muscles in his thighs had set up shaking, so he just kept his hands tight on the wheel. He drove a mile or so, then pulled off to the side of the road and set his head down on the wheel and tried to breathe through the dregs of adrenaline and cold plain fear.

'You okay, Hayden?'

'Light me a cigarette, would you?'

She lit one for each of them, and he steadied his arm on the steering wheel and took a long, shaky pull.

'Well, now you have a gun,' Peg said. 'See what I told you? It's a good thing to have sometimes.'

Hayden picked it up off her lap, and stepped out of the truck and into the middle of the empty highway in the half dark, and wound up and threw it as hard and as far as he possibly could. He stood looking off in that direction a few seconds, then got back in and drove, feeling a little closer to settled.

'What'd you do that for?'

'I don't want a gun.'

'I could've kept it.'

'There's a lot about life you don't understand, little girl.'

'Like what?'

'Like he might've committed a crime with that gun. And it's not a good idea then to have it in your possession. Like when guns are around, people die. Like if you're trying to defend yourself with a gun, and your hands are shaking and you're not such a great shot and you miss? All a guy has to do is take it out of your hands and use it on you. You want to live a long life, Peg? Then live fairly clean and stay out of trouble. Don't make trouble and then try to shoot your way out of it.'

She sulked for a while without answering. Stroked George's back and set the side of her forehead up against the window.

'Like if I'd known where that gun had gone, I probably would've killed that boy, just out of being wound up and scared.'

'You weren't scared.'

'Hell I wasn't.'

'I saw it, Hayden. The whole thing. You were fierce, you're not scared of anything.'

'There's a lot about life you don't get yet.'

'Stop saying that to me.'

'Okay. Fine. We won't talk.'

They crested the hill and there was Searchlight, below them, predictably asleep.

They stopped at a café in Baker for breakfast.

Peg sat across the table and brushed her hair back with her fingers and kept looking at him shy and funny out of the corner of her eyes, and smiling in a way that felt unsettling.

The waitress brought coffee and took their orders

and left them alone again. And Peg looked at him straight-on this time, with that funny shy smile.

'You were really good back there.'

'Wrong again, little girl.'

'You're my hero, Hayden.'

'Then you got lousy taste in heroes.'

'I know one when I see one.'

That's when Hayden realized what was unsettling about that smile. It was flirtatious, that's what. 'Peg, I shattered that little boy's knee back there just because I was in a mean mood.'

'So what? He deserved it. He put you in that mood.'

'That boy will probably walk with a limp his whole life. I could've just driven away.'

'But this way you scared him bad enough he probably won't come around again.'

'I hope you're right about that.'

'You'll take care of me, won't you, Hayden?' She set her hand down on his, but he jerked it away.

'Don't do that.'

'Why not?'

'You don't get it, do you? My feelings for you are more like you were my daughter.'

She frowned for a few minutes, and played with her hair.

Hayden wet his big paper napkin in his water glass

and handed it to her, badly aware in this light how she looked.

'Wipe all that goop off your face, okay? Try to look sixteen.'

She sighed and took a pocket mirror out of her purse, and set about cleaning the makeup away.

'How old would your own daughter be now, Hayden?'

'God, you're just like your mother.'

'I'm not your daughter, though.'

'I know it.'

'You'd always take care of me, though, anyway. Right?'

'Nobody can make you a promise like that.'

When the food came, Peg announced she hadn't wanted toast, but Hayden told the waitress it was okay, he'd eat it. Then he wrapped it up in a napkin with two pieces of his bacon, to take back out to George.

Seventy miles closer to home they passed a sign that said, *Horses for Rent by the Hour*, and Peg, who had grown several years younger in the past couple of hours, decided they should stop and go riding.

'Let's, Hayden. Please?'

'No.'

'Why not? I love horses.'

'I don't.'

'Just do it for me, then.'

'I don't ride.'

'It doesn't matter. They have beginner horses.'

'Don't make me say this.'

'Say what?'

'I'm scared of horses.'

'You are not.'

'I am.'

'You're not, Hayden. You're not afraid of anything.'

'I'm afraid of everything. I've been trying to tell you.'

'You're making it up so we don't have to stop. You can't be scared of horses. You're my hero.'

'I told you before. You got lousy taste in heroes. I'm just a bad tempered, middle-aged guy with no self-control where it's needed most.'

'You're still my hero. I saw what you did back there. You shoulda killed Joey. Make sure he never comes back again.'

'You don't know what you're asking, little girl, when you ask a man to kill for you.'

'You wouldn't kill for me?'

'No.'

'Would you kill for my mom?'

'I hope I never have to find out.'

'Do you love my mom?'

'That I do. Yes.'

'Do you love me?'

'Different, though.'

'Would you kill to save my life?'

'Will you stop asking me all these questions?'

Peg sulked and refused to speak to him the rest of the way home, which was a marked improvement.

Chapter Six

It's Like This, Scott

By the time he pulled up to Laurel's house it was that sweet dusk, about eight o'clock. He turned off the engine and sat a minute and looked over at Peg, who'd fallen asleep with her head back over the top of the seat, her mouth wide open. He wanted to beep the horn so he wouldn't have to knock on the door. So he wouldn't have to see Jack, or at least wouldn't have to see him at such close range. But he didn't want to jar Peg awake.

He stroked the back of George's neck, the only place he had a little bit of hair. He wanted to tell Laurel he could have been killed on that little errand she'd sent him on. He wanted to ask if she knew how dangerous this was going to be, and if not, why not, and if so, why did she ask him to do it? Was he really that expendable?

And he *would* ask, too, he decided. Wouldn't just sit here and want to. He would. He would have to.

He tapped the horn two light little beeps and Peg did not wake up. A few seconds later the curtain in the front window moved aside. Then Laurel came out and stood at his open driver's window and looked inside and smiled.

He had his hand stretched out along the door, his fingers on the side-view mirror, and she put her hand on his arm and said, 'You're amazing.' The combination of the touch and those words, it warmed him.

'She's not quite ready to live home again.'

'Where's she gonna live?'

'I told her she could stay with me awhile.'

Something crossed her face then, something hard to read, and she took her touch away. 'This's not a romantic thing, is it?'

'You know me better than that.'

'I mean, I can see you might want to lash out at me, under the circumstances, and it's not like we owe each other anything at this point, but still—'

'Laurel. She's sixteen years old. I'm not looking to spend any more of my life on Division Road. This guy she was with is dangerous. Even if she did want to live home, what's the first place he'd look for her?'

'Think he will?'

'Frankly, no I don't. I think I scared the piss out of

him. But let's not take any chances, okay? She'll be with me a few weeks at most, and if he stays away, well . . . I told her we could look into getting her a place of her own. But really I'm going to try to talk her home.'

'Where does she sleep in that tiny little place?'

'She can have my bed.'

'And where do you sleep?'

'In a cot. Right in front of the door. Where any little assholes from King City would have to go right through me on their way. She'll come home. Give her time. Did you know this kid was packing a gun?'

'No, how would I know that?'

'There were some touch-and-go moments.'

'I'm sorry, Hayden. I didn't think it would get that bad.'

They both stopped talking for a few seconds, and then her touch came back, stroking along his arm, and he closed his eyes to the dusk and her face and just dipped inside his own self for a moment. 'Remember when you came by last? When my back was out? You didn't know Jenny had died. You said, "What happened to her?" And I told you.'

'Yeah? What about it?'

'You never said anything. You never said, "God, I'm sorry, Hayden, I know how much you loved that dog. I know you raised her from a pup and had her fifteen years, that good-looking legendary hound everybody loved so much, and I just can't imagine how bad you must feel."'

The front door of the house swung open and Jack stood in the doorway and looked out. Laurel's hand disappeared from his arm. Then the door swung shut again and he was gone.

'God, I don't know, Hayden, I was busy trying to get used to your *new* dog, I don't know. I'm not a dog person, much, I mean . . . what's your point?'

'I don't know. I guess I don't have one.'

He leaned forward to the ignition and fired up the engine again, and shifted the truck into gear.

'Thanks for what you did with Peg,' she said, and leaned in and kissed his cheek.

'You're welcome,' he said, and drove toward home, feeling for the first time how beaten down and tired he really was.

Late the next afternoon Scott came by the cabin to see him. Peg was inside, amazingly still asleep. Or maybe it wasn't so funny, really, since she had her days and nights turned around.

Hayden was out front with his head under the hood of the Ford. He had the fan belt and the fan and the pulley off, sitting on an old sheet on the dirt, and he'd just pulled off the bad water pump, spilling greenish coolant all over the hard ground, when Scott pulled up. Scott was driving his official car, his black-and-white. Hayden sat down on the ground with the water intake housing and a paint chisel, to begin the task of scraping off the old welded-on gasket so he could replace the thermostat while he was at it.

Scott came and stood over him, and said, 'Where do I sit?' because he had his uniform on, and Hayden indicated with a flip of his head where a lawn chair stood folded up against the side of the toolshed. Scott came back with it and sat by Hayden's side.

Neither said anything for a minute or two. Scott just watched him scrape the gasket, and Hayden could hear the radio on Scott's belt crackle with static.

Then Hayden said, 'Tell me it's not bad news.'

'Well, I guess it's not, exactly. Just funny. Something funny happened while you were gone.'

'I can only hope you mean funny as in amusing.'

'No, I mean funny as in weird.'

'I figured you did.'

'How many kids have you had in your lifetime, Hayden?'

'Just the one daughter.'

'That you know of.'

'I'd say it's a safe bet.'

'Well, then, my next question would be, just how many girlfriends you got?'

'Oh, now, let's see,' Hayden said. He set the housing

down and wiped sweat off his forehead with a shop rag. 'At last count I believe the number was . . . none. Yeah, that's it. Unless my math is off. I've got no girl-friends. Why? What's this about?' He picked up a wire brush and started to clean the gasket mating surface with it.

'Young woman came around here looking for you while you were away. Not real young. Maybe Laurel's age. Younger maybe. A few years younger. Thirty or so.'

'And she said she was my girlfriend?'

'No. She said she was your daughter.'

Hayden stopped brushing. Just sat there, he wasn't sure how long, with the clean housing in his hand, then got up and went back to the truck to clean the mating surface on the engine side.

'I just thought that was kind of funny,' Scott said, 'being as you only had one daughter and she's been dead a long time now. If this was your daughter and she's fifteen years in the grave, she sure didn't look any the worse for wear. What was your girl's given name?'

Hayden pulled his head out from under the hood, leaned on the grille, and scratched his head for a minute. 'Allegra,' he said, not having figured a way out of saying. 'Her mother named her Allegra.'

'Well, that's what this woman said, Hayden. Said her name was Allegra Reese. Said she was getting married in a couple of months and she wanted to find you to see if you'd give her away. Can you think what an explanation for that might be?'

'Did she leave a number or an address?'

'No. I just told her I knew you, and she said she'd check back in a week or two. See if you'd got back. What gives, Hayden?'

'An explanation, huh, Scott?'

'That's what I was thinking, yeah.'

'Tell you what. Why don't you just go back out on patrol, and I'll go back to putting my truck together, and then by and by I'll see if I can't think of one you'll like.'

He stuck his head back under the hood.

It took Scott a long time to go away. But he did, eventually, without saying more or asking further questions.

When the new water pump and thermostat had been snugged in and he'd run the engine for a while to check for leaks, Hayden went back inside to shower and maybe have a beer. Peg was up, sitting on the floor with George, rubbing hand lotion on the worst scaly patches of his elephant skin.

She looked up with a hopeful expression, which changed quickly. 'What the hell happened to you?'

'Nothing happened. Why?'

'You look upset.'

'I'm fine. Thanks for looking after George.'

'I thought it might help the hair grow back faster.'

'Put some of that goop in his eyes while you're at it, will you? He holds still for you. I have to practically sit on him to do it. I'm going to go take a shower.'

'What did Scott want?'

'Nothing. You need to think about school.'

'What about it?'

'You should go back. You need to think about maybe going home, too. Give your mom another chance.'

'I'm never going home, Hayden. I'm going to live here with you forever.'

'Beg to differ, little girl.'

'But I love you, Hayden. Can I make you something to eat? I can cook some. And I'll keep the place nice. I know you're in love with my mom, but you'll get over her after a while and here I'll be. You'll see.'

'Jesus Christ, Peg.' Hayden sank down into a kitchen chair and set his head down on his folded arms. It all just sort of conspired to collapse him. 'Do us both a favor. Get it out of your head that it's going to be that way. Okay?'

She never said if that was okay or not.

He got up after a while and took a shower, and came back out dripping wet with a towel around his waist, and stood in the middle of his little cabin, feeling

Peg stare at him. He felt noticeably self-conscious. He also felt like it wasn't really his own little place anymore.

He took all those details into consideration when he gave himself permission to spend the evening in town and get drunk.

After his fourth Corona, his conviction that he didn't owe Scott an explanation began to evolve. After all, Scott was asking not in any official capacity, more like a friend, and he had gone to bat for Hayden on any number of occasions. It wasn't Scott's fault that the question put Hayden in a bad mood.

So he started to memorize how he would say it, barely able to hear his own thoughts over the din of the jukebox.

It's like this, Scott. Guy comes to a rural spot, not really expecting to stay. Just that he has to start somewhere. And there's a job available. He figures he'll just work it until he's set to move on, but then somebody has a piece of cheap land for sale and he gets given a pretty little bluetick hound pup and builds on the land, and next thing you know it's fifteen years later, and he's still just kind of stalled there . . .

'Rita,' he said as she passed his table. 'Bring me another round, would you please?'

He still had a small wad of money in his pocket,

though mostly tens and ones now, and he owed twenty of it to Scott. When it was gone he had no special plan, other than maybe to go into the city and file an unemployment claim, because he didn't leave his job voluntarily, it was a bona fide health problem. Unless the fact that he'd previously been unemployed for ninety days would screw him out of the claim. He'd have to see.

Rita brought the beer, and he took it, and put a ten on the edge of her tray. While she made change he tipped the beer back, drained it in a long series of deep swallows, and set the bottle on her tray again. 'Let's do that one more time,' he said.

'Slow down, Hayden. It's early yet, you got all night.'

'Easy for you to say.'

And she shook her head and went off to get him another.

It's like this, Scott. There's this narrow zone that people let you live in, just for a little while. You get to drag around and feel sorry, and spin your life around in circles, and people just sort of pat you on the back and say, Buck up, guy. We're with you. But only just for a certain time. Depending on what happened to you. Then you cross over some imaginary dividing line, and they don't pat anymore, and your life is still spinning in a circle, but now they say things like, Life goes on, buddy. Get over yourself. But you're still just spinning . . .

Rita came back with the beer, and he thanked her, and set it in front of him and stared at it with his brow furrowed down, and rubbed at the sweat on the bottle with his thumbs.

'You okay, Hayden?'

'No, I'm not. Thanks for asking, though.'

'Poor Hayden.' She gave his shoulder a little pat, then disappeared between couples dancing on the floor.

See, Scott? Now do you see how it is?

But it was ten thirty and Scott still hadn't come in. So he sat in the corner and had another round and practiced some more.

Okay, Scott, we've known each other a long time, and you've been more than fair with me, but before I tell you this, I need to know you're not judging me, I just need to . . . pee. Yeah, that's what I'm trying to say. First I just really need to pee.

He swung up out of his chair and stood, swaying, the bar floor the deck of a ship, tilting and rolling with the uncertainty of the sea, trying hard to rise up to meet him. He didn't get full-on drunk often, and he didn't realize he already had tonight. He tried to compensate, to get his sea legs. He grabbed at the back of a chair to steady himself.

Then he picked his way toward the men's room.

And it was going fine, just fine. At first. Then he looked over to the door and saw Scott come in, and just when he turned his head some idiot pushed his chair back, smooth and sudden, without ever thinking what or who might be behind him, and Hayden's boot caught on one leg of the chair, and he flew forward and landed hard on his chin. It knocked the wind out of him, and made him embarrassed, which made him mad.

He found his way to his feet, and the man was right there to brush him off, to see that he wasn't hurt. Only the man was Jack. And Hayden looked past Jack, across the table, and saw Laurel sitting there with her eyes half averted, trying not to watch him make an idiot of himself in front of everybody.

'Feel better now, Jack?'

'I didn't do it on purpose, Reese. I didn't see you.'

'Just a coincidence,' Hayden said. 'Make a fool out of me in front of her.'

And he reached both hands out and pushed Jack. Not real hard, but hard enough. Enough to make him take a step back.

Then Jack took the step back in again, only he came in swinging, and aimed a hard right at Hayden's face. Hayden hated that, when someone hit him in the face. That or a loaded gun aimed at his face. Just set him off somehow. The whole world just kind of went black. Only Jack never really managed to hit Hayden in the face, because the punch was high and he ducked his head in time, but it must have been the principle of the thing, because the world went black just the same.

With his head ducked down he just hit Jack straight on, just rammed his head into the middle part of Jack and kept ramming, and Hayden flew forward and Jack flew backward, and it seemed to Hayden, whose senses were all a little off anyway, that they flew that way for ages. Way too long. A city block maybe. And then Jack hit his back up against the wall and stopped dead and Hayden's head kept driving, until it had to stop, too, and all the air came out of Jack in this big whoosh that Hayden could hear and feel, both.

Then Jack was down on the floor, somehow, and Hayden was straddling his chest and hitting him in the face, hard but natural. It just felt natural to Hayden, like something he might never need to stop.

But he did stop, though not of his own accord.

He felt himself pulled away with an arm straight and hard at his throat, and felt himself jerked backward a long way and let go. He felt his back hit the opposite wall of the tavern. And then Scott was there, in his face, his long side-handle baton out and used to pin Hayden's neck to the wall. Hayden could mostly breathe, but not swallow at all, so he just held still.

'What do I have to do, Hayden?' Scott was yelling at him but it sounded far away, and over his shoulder he saw Jack make his way to his feet. And he saw that everybody had stopped drinking and dancing and talking, and just stood or sat staring at him. And just then the song on the jukebox ended, a ringing silence just as Scott yelled again. 'What do I have to do, keep you on a leash? I'm just about at the end of my rope with you.'

Hayden closed his eyes and tried again to swallow, and pointed at his throat. Scott eased up a little on the baton.

'Face the wall. Put your hands behind you.'

Hayden did as he was told and felt the familiar cool steel, heard the sound it makes clicking shut.

Then he got turned, and pushed, and the cool outdoors hit him and made his head spin, made him feel a little sick. When they got to the car it wasn't Scott's off-duty Mustang, it was the black-and-white. Scott put a hand on Hayden's head and ducked it down to clear the car roof and put him in the back.

Then he left for a while and went back inside the tavern.

Hayden sat and felt at his tender knuckles and looked around. He'd never been in the back of Scott's black-and-white before. It had a steel guard all across the back of the seat in front of him, and almost no leg room, forcing him to sit sideways. A three-piece Plexiglas window separated him from the front, with the spring-loaded center section left open. He closed his eyes and tried to focus on not throwing up.

After a few minutes the front car door opened and closed, and Hayden heard the engine start, and they were moving. He tried to remember what it was he'd been practicing to say.

'I was hoping you'd understand how it is, Scott.'

'I don't, though.'

With his eyes still closed Hayden felt the car stop at the corner. Then the left turn out onto the highway. The engine whined and pulled reaching highway speed.

'Scott. Do you believe in love?'

'I suppose I do. Why?'

'I do. I believe in love.'

'Listen, Hayden. Listen to me. Let me tell you something. I know you're stinking drunk, but if you only remember one thing in the morning, I hope this is it. Any idiot can fall in love. No special talent required for that. The trick is to love somebody who'll actually do you some good. That's the part hardly anybody gets right.'

'Your grandmother tell you that?'

'As a matter of fact, yes.'

'So it's really her theory. More than yours.'

'It's mine now. You ought to try it on sometime.'

*   *   *

Hayden woke with a start because Scott slammed something hard against the bars. He came to in the daylight, in the private cell in the back of the county jail, with too much light in his eyes. He sat up gingerly, trying to postpone throwing up, and bent over his own ailing midsection, and blinked his eyes and saw that it was a breakfast tray.

'Welcome back to Division Road, Hayden. Decide yet which side you want to be on?'

'Morning, Scott. Could you take that food away, please? The smell is making me sick.'

'Nope, sorry. It's the law, I got to feed prisoners three times a day. Whether you like it or not.' He slid the tray through the specially provided slot in the side door. 'Now I'll just leave you alone awhile to eat your breakfast, or lose your breakfast, or whatever you're prone to do here, and then we'll have our little talk.'

'Do I have an arraignment this morning?'

'That's what we're going to talk about. *Bon appétit.*'

Hayden heaved over the squat, seatless toilet long after the heaves were dry and useless and painful, threatening to turn him inside out. Then he lay back down and tried to close his eyes. Tried not to smell cereal and orange juice.

When Scott came back, God only knows how much

later, he banged his baton on the bars. Hayden sat up and said, 'Ow.'

Scott pulled up his wooden chess chair and sat.

'How long do you think this time, Scott?'

'Well, there's bad news regarding that, Hayden. For me, anyway. Seems I'm obliged to let you out.'

'Excuse me?'

'I tried to talk Jack into pressing charges, but he declined.'

'That doesn't make any sense.'

'That's what *I* said. I've wasted my whole morning trying to find something to charge you with, but I'm sick of trying. Seems public drunkenness is not a terribly serious crime in this county. I can hold you overnight, which I did. So, you're out. I got to say, though, this is not a good sign on Jack's part. This is not his way of being magnanimous, let me tell you.'

'What exactly did he say?'

'Oh, we had a long talk about you. You steal money from that man's house?'

'No. You know I don't steal.'

'I thought you didn't lie, either. Now I don't know. He thinks it's an awful coincidence how two hundred dollars came up missing the same day his neighbor saw you go in his house while nobody was home.'

'Laurel left me that money. To go get Peg.'

'She must've forgot to tell him that. Here's how he

sees this thing. You sleep with his wife, but what can he do? They were separated at the time. You sleep with his stepdaughter, but it's not like you tied her up first. He figures that's her own bad judgment.'

'I did not sleep with Peg.'

'Well, she called her folks and said it's true love. Then you steal from him, but it was just before you did that expensive favor with Peg, so he reserved judgment, thinking maybe Laurel didn't tell him the whole story. Are you getting a picture here? That he's more of a reasonable guy than you credit him for? Only now you've gone and beat him silly in front of said woman and most of the rest of the locals. He's not a happy man.'

'So why not press charges?'

'He just said, "It's between me and Reese." That's all he would say. I'd guess he wants to hang you with his own hands. Why let the county have all the fun? So I'm letting you out. Though, truthfully, you'd be safer in here. But that's your own problem.' Scott unlocked the cell and stood back, the door wide. 'If he kills your sorry ass dead, don't come running to me.'

They stood in the dressing-out area together, on opposite sides of the counter. Scott brought Hayden's blue mesh property bag to the counter, stuck a form under his nose to sign, then gave his personal belongings back, a jacket, his wallet, his belt, some folded money, and a copy of the form he'd signed coming in.

'I owe you this,' Hayden said, and peeled off two tens for Scott, cutting his total life assets down under $30.

'You do indeed,' Scott said, and put it in his pocket.

'Something missing here,' Hayden said quietly.

'Oh, right. Sorry. I was reading it.' Hayden followed him to the front desk, the control area of the holding cell complex, where Scott picked up Hayden's paperback copy of the *Tao Te Ching* and slapped it down on the counter. 'If you don't mind my saying so, you're not getting the most bang for your reading buck here, Hayden. That book is all about peacefulness and non-action. Either you didn't read it or it's not working on you.'

Hayden stuck the book in the pocket of his jeans jacket. 'We still friends, Scott?'

'You tell me, Hayden. You tell me.' They stood quiet for a moment too long, then walked to the door together. 'You wouldn't happen to remember what I told you last night?'

'Actually, yes I do. And it's funny, because I don't remember much else.'

'Power of suggestion,' Scott said, and held the front door open wide. 'Have a nice day.'

Chapter Seven

Red

It took Hayden almost two hours to get home, in part because it was a long walk back to the tavern, where he'd left his truck. And also because he stopped at the hardware store where he used to work, to spend half his life savings on a new lock for his cabin door. Should have replaced it long ago, he knew. Now leaving his door unsecured no longer seemed a viable option.

Then he forgot and left the lock in the truck, and went inside without it. His head throbbed, his stomach felt rocky. He was dirt tired, sore, and down. Really in no mood to be assaulted by a hysterical teenager.

'Where the hell were you, Hayden? You were gone all night.' Peg came at him, yelling, and he wanted to turn the volume down. She beat on his chest with both fists, but it didn't hurt much. 'You were with another woman, weren't you? Don't lie to me, Hayden.'

He grasped both of her shoulders, held her out at arm's length. She just kept swinging, slicing the air between them with both fists, and Hayden saw she was crying.

'I was in jail.'

She stopped swinging, so he let go of her shoulders. 'Really?' She raked the hair off her face, wiped her eyes and nose on one sleeve. 'What'd you do, get in a fight?'

'Yeah.'

'Beat some guy up?'

'Unfortunately, yes.'

'Cool. Want breakfast?'

'God, no.' He eased himself down into a kitchen chair.

'Who'd you beat up?' She sat across from him, surprisingly composed now, eager almost, though her eyes were still red.

'Your stepfather.'

'Oh.'

'Go to school, Peg.'

'I hate school.'

'Do it for me, then.'

'Would you like me better if I did?'

Hayden leaned his forehead into one hand. The

world felt too bright, too loud and complicated, and his palm granted less asylum than needed. 'I would gain respect for you, yes.'

'Then I'll go.'

'Thank you.'

'Anything I can do to make you like me better. You just tell me, Hayden. I want to be exactly what you want.'

'Oh, God, that is so wrong, Peg. That is getting love so completely backwards.'

'All right. Then I just want you to respect me.'

'Then there's one other thing you can do.'

'Anything. Name it.'

'Stop by the diner on your way. And tell your folks we're not sleeping together.'

'I never told 'em we were.'

'Well, whatever you told them made them think we were.'

'So? Let people think what they want.'

'Peg, listen to me. I need you to do this. This is important. It could even save somebody's life here. Maybe even mine. This is one of the misunderstandings we have just got to get cleared up.' He looked up from his own palm to see her sulking, slumped back in her chair playing with her hair and frowning. 'Please, Peg.'

'If it'll make you like me more.'

'It will.'

'Okay. I'm going.'

He rose with some difficulty and walked her to the door.

'Come here,' he said, and held his arms out, and she came in for a hug. But it was wrong, right off the bat wrong, not at all the sort of hug he'd intended, so he backed her up again. 'Whoa, little girl. I didn't mean it like that.'

'I'll do what you want on one condition.'

'Let's hear it.'

'That you never call me "little girl" again.'

'Deal. Now let me give you a hug like the kind your daddy would give.'

'*My* daddy?'

'Well, no, not your daddy. A good daddy.' And he pulled her back close again, and put his arms around her and held her tight, because he knew suddenly how badly she needed him to. He kissed the top of her head. 'I'm sorry I hurt your feelings, Peg. I do care about you. I do. Even if it's not the way you want me to. Hell, I watched you grow up. Of course I care for you, but it's like you were my own girl. Let me love you like a daddy, would you please? Now go to school.'

*   *   *

Hours later, in the middle of a sweaty nap, Laurel came in and sat on the bed with him, and Hayden mistook it for a dream, but spoke his mind just the same.

'This war has got to be over, Laurel.'

'What war is that?'

'Jack Hatfield and Hayden McCoy. I can't keep doing this. It's like those dominoes you set up when you're a kid, and then you just touch one and everything falls down. Everything just knocks over everything else. It's all predetermined. It's too late to get out of it by then. You know exactly what's going to happen because you set it up that way.'

'This is coming from the same guy beat him black-and-blue last night.'

'Apparently it is.' Hayden sat up, naked under the sheet, and reached out to touch her shoulder. He always woke up slowly, and in a fog, now even more so than usual, and it was only just dawning that she was not a dream. 'What are you doing here?'

'I wanted to see you. Is that okay?'

'Shouldn't you be at the diner?'

'They can do on their own for a while.'

'Jack's not there?'

'No, he went into the city to that restaurant supply. Peg came by. She said there's nothing between you two.'

'Good.'

'Is it true?'

'Of course it is. I told you I wouldn't do that.'

'Oh, Hayden.' And she smiled and fell into his arms. And he just held her like that, feeling somewhat electrified, in some good ways and some bad ones, all at the same time. He also felt pretty well awake by now.

'I was so jealous.'

'Jealous? Of me and Peg?'

'Yeah.'

'You were jealous?'

'Yeah. Why? Does that seem so strange?'

'Well, yes. It does.'

'Why?' He felt her face, her lips tuck into his neck just above the collarbone.

'I didn't think you cared that much.'

'I never had to think of you with somebody else before. Thing like that, it puts you in touch with how much you care.'

She slid down onto the bed on her back and pulled Hayden down on top of her, and they just lay together for a few minutes. His brain told him not to keep moving forward but his body and heart wouldn't let him back up, and it formed a kind of holding pattern that he could've happily spent the day nursing along.

'I missed you, Hayden.'

'I missed you, too.'

'I'm so relieved you're not sleeping with her.'

'So Jack knows I'm not, right?'

'No, Jack was in the city like I said.'

'Oh, right.' The holding pattern fractured, and he rolled away from her and lay at her side, no part of them touching.

'Now what's wrong?'

'You didn't tell him you gave me that money.'

'I didn't think he'd give it voluntarily.'

'He thinks I stole it.'

'Oh.'

'He still thinks I'm sleeping with Peg. And he doesn't know I didn't steal from his house. And I beat him up last night. And I'm in bed with his wife, right this minute. Scott thinks he'll come after me. That he might try to kill me.'

'What do you think?'

'You know him better than I do.'

'He's pissed all right. But he's not a killer.'

'Never know what a man might do until he's right up against that moment. Until somebody just pushes him one step too far.'

'He's in the city anyway. He can't kill you from there.'

'But it already is, though, Laurel. It's killing me now, right now on the inside. I have to get off this ride.'

'Are you saying you don't want to see me anymore?'

'I'm saying I think I better not.'

'I can't believe you really mean that.'

'You made your choice. You took him back. You can't have it both ways.'

'Maybe I want to change my mind now.'

'Maybe I don't want you to.'

'How can you say that, Hayden?' He had his eyes closed when she said it, and her voice sounded strange, on the verge of a tightly reined-in hysterical tone, and he opened his eyes to see she was crying. 'I thought you loved me.'

'I do love you, God knows I do, but it never seems to get me anywhere. It just keeps taking me all these places I never wanted to go.'

'So that's it, then? You're just telling me good-bye?'

'I'm telling you go make a life with your husband, I mean, you decided to be with him, so be with him. Don't be sneaking around into another man's bed while he's away. Give your whole self to at least try, you know? You threw us away for that, so at least make it work. Otherwise it just went for nothing.'

'I can't believe you don't even care enough anymore to fight for me.'

'It's not about how much I care. I couldn't care for you any more if I tried. I just don't want to fight anymore, period. I'm just tired of fighting, Laurel. I'm just so tired. Can't you see that? I'm old and I'm tired and I just can't keep doing this.'

'Make love to me one more time.'

'I might change my mind if I do.'

'Just to say good-bye. I mean it. Just the once more. I miss the way we used to. It was gentle with you. I could never figure out how an angry man could be so gentle.'

'And what if Peg comes home from school?'

Laurel held her left wrist in front of his face, her watch under Hayden's nose. 'Two hours.'

He'd been walking in the heat earlier that morning, though, and hadn't showered, so he felt unclean, which made him feel unworthy, which, he remembered, he always did when Laurel came this close.

But her closeness overcame all those reservations, and one more time after all they'd meant to each other didn't sound like such a wrong thing, so they made love for what he knew in his gut and in his heart would be the last time. And it was more gentle even than usual, so much so that it hurt. If Hayden had ever been a man to cry, he would have left a few of his tears on Laurel before they dropped off to sleep.

When Peg threw the door open, Hayden woke up and Laurel did not. Peg didn't even scream. She didn't come at him, yell at him, accuse him, beat on him. Her jaw just set hard, and the color drained out of her face, and she just stood looking. She had George with her, and Hayden had forgotten to notice that he hadn't been around for a while. Then she picked up her mother's keys off the table by the door and disappeared.

Hayden heard Laurel's station wagon roar to life out front, and the crunch of wheels spinning and skidding on gravel as the car flew away.

'Laurel,' he said, and shook her hard.

'What?'

'Get up, get dressed. Now. Right now.' He climbed over her and went after his shirt and jeans, hanging over the back of his favorite chair.

'Shit, Hayden, we got time.' Her eyes fluttered open and she peered at her watch close-range. 'Oh, shit. No we don't.'

'Peg just took off in your car. I'll have to drive you out of here.'

'She's not allowed to drive my car.'

'Good. You go catch her and tell her that. What time is Jack supposed to get back?'

'I don't know exactly.'

'Could he be back at the diner by now?'

'Shit, it's almost four. I guess he could be.' She jumped out of bed then, and started getting dressed.

'What if she runs straight to him and tells him what she just saw?'

'Why would she do that?'

'Because she's mad, and she's hurt.'

'Okay, we better move then, huh?'

But it was only a three-minute drive to the diner, a six-minute round trip if one obeyed the speed limit and stopped at the two stop signs. It could be done an awful lot faster than that. Had been before, maybe would be again. And a couple of minutes had gone by already. There just wasn't any way to move fast enough.

Before they could even make it down the gravel drive to Hayden's truck, Jack's one-ton Dodge blocked their path like a cloud blotting out the sun. Hayden's eyes jumped to the gun rack in the back window, and it was empty. A relief. Short-lived. Jack stepped out and stood in front of Hayden, and he had the 12-gauge in his hands.

Hayden looked at Jack's face, amazed by the damage he'd done the night before. Fear twisted his thoughts, making what he saw feel strange and distant and out of proportion. Jack's left eye was swollen near shut, purple and black, and one whole side of his face was too big, all unbalanced and unmatched. It seemed hard to believe he'd done all that with his own fists.

And then the shotgun blocked his view of that face.

Just for a split second Hayden wanted Laurel to do what he would have done. Or at least, what he thought he would have done. Hoped he would. Stand right between them and say, No, Jack. No. Don't. But she ducked away to save her own life.

'You pushed me to this,' Jack said. He sounded desperate, more scared and sad than angry.

Shuck shuck. The ugly sound of Jack cocking the weapon, of a shell slamming into the chamber, ready to go. The little plastic gun protector – the mock shell that sits in that chamber, keeping it oiled, waiting for a real one – flipped out of the way. Hayden saw it bounce on the gravel, heard the light click of it. His nerves jangled with too many orders to his legs and feet at once, and they jammed, and canceled each other out, and besides, it just happened too fast. There just wasn't time.

The report of the shot hit his ears first, just a fraction of a second ahead, the kind of fraction he might not have identified at any time other than this. Then the shot itself tore into his chest, knocking him up off his feet and backward, picking him up and throwing him, like a big wind that hit hard but didn't exactly hurt, at least not the way he expected it to. His back hit the gravel, and he lay there still and found it strangely hard to draw normal breath.

But he could still see.

His eyes were open and he could see the leaves of the big oak that stretched over his home, shifting back and forth across the sun, causing a blinking effect, like twinkling stars. And the power lines. The all-seeing, all-knowing electric.

And he could still hear.

He heard Jack's truck pulling away, tires squealing and crunching on the slight turn of his gravel pathway, and Laurel's voice saying something about a phone, going for a phone.

She'd always told him he should have a phone, and he always said there was no one he cared much to talk to, except maybe her, and she knew where to find him, and now she had to pry his truck keys out of his hand and drive to the nearest neighbor to call for help, so he should have listened to her and gotten a phone. Because what were the chances, really, that he would survive between now and the time she called 911? He never listened to good advice.

And he could still feel.

Warm wetness at his back that he knew in a distant way to be his own blood, and a faraway, light, high feeling in his head, which probably meant he'd lost too much blood already. And another warm wetness in his crotch and down the inside of his right leg, but he didn't know if that was more blood or if he'd urinated on himself, which was probably a reasonable thing to do when you've just been shot.

But not pain.

And not his left leg, not the whole lower left quadrant

of his physical self, really. It had come unplugged somehow, cut off from signals. And it was hard to breathe. So he took shallow little breaths and waited either to pass out or die, whichever came first.

He closed his eyes for a second or an hour.

When he opened them Scott's face was there. He knew maybe it wasn't, really, but he was glad to see it all the same.

'Heard the call come over the radio, buddy. Ambulance is right behind me. Listen, you can hear it.'

Hayden listened but didn't hear anything. He wondered if Scott was really here, and whether it really mattered, but he wanted it to be real.

'It doesn't hurt, Scott.' He could barely hear himself. His voice came out cracked, breathy, a scratchy whisper cutting in and out like a bad radio connection.

'Can't hear you, buddy. Listen, don't try to talk, okay?'

Hayden reached up with his right hand and touched Scott's uniform shirt, felt his chest hard and solid behind it. It made him happy, that Scott was real. He grabbed a handful of the shirt and pulled Scott down close to his face. 'Doesn't hurt.'

'Did you want it to? Listen, don't try to talk, Hayden. Just lie still. Listen, can you hear that? That's the ambulance coming up the path. You're just in shock, is all. You just don't feel pain because you're in shock.'

'I might be dead.'

'You're not.'

'If it doesn't hurt, I might be.'

'I can hear you talking to me, buddy. You're not dead.'

'I can't feel my leg.'

'Hayden, goddamnit, don't talk. Save your strength.'

But Hayden felt surprisingly strong for a dead man, and he held Scott's shirt even tighter, so he couldn't go away. 'I'm afraid to die, Scott.'

'Then don't.'

'Your grandmother was right about that.'

'She was a smart lady.'

'Want me to tell her hello for you?'

'Shut up, Hayden, just shut up. Stop talking like that. I'm not letting you die.'

'I can't breathe right.' And his voice was slipping, moving further away, his words coming in more divided segments, between gasps for air.

'I know CPR, though, so if you stop breathing, I'll just start breathing for you, okay? One way or another, buddy.'

And Hayden tried hard to breathe, thinking it would be much easier to have Scott do it for him, and his breath caught somehow, caught on something, and he felt a kind of gurgle inside, and coughed hard, and a splash of bright red blood splattered against Scott's uniform shirt.

And then Hayden could hear it. The siren.

And he closed his eyes and let go of Scott's shirt and wished again that he would pass out. He got his wish, just for a brief moment. But he got jogged aware again when the gurney was moved, picked up with him on it, and he could feel himself immobilized, strapped down with his neck held stiff, and he could hear voices, see a strobing of red, but the words made no sense, the colors didn't seem real.

He saw Scott's face one more time, suspended over him, disembodied. 'I'm right here with you,' Scott said.

Then the inside roof of the ambulance, more like a dream than anything so far, and an oxygen mask clamped over his face.

He tried to say something to Scott. Tried, to say, You lied to me, Scott. You said you didn't care if he killed me. Liar. You are my friend, you know you are now. Admit it.

But the mask cut off his words, which were probably only in his head anyway.

He was sure he only closed his eyes for a minute.

Then the pain came, dragging him up through that heavy sludge of unconsciousness. He opened his eyes.

He saw an off-white room in early morning light, saw a monitor on his left side, the jumpy line of his heart beating, and a television set dark and silent suspended in an upper corner.

A nurse came in and did something with his IV, something he could only half see, and relief flowed into his veins, that heavy, unmistakable morphine kick, and he thanked her for that, though not out loud. The pain was still there, somewhere, but he stood apart from it now, relaxed.

He closed his eyes, opened them again. Saw a pleasant older woman's face.

'I know you,' he said. He couldn't believe how it sounded. A tiny whisper, like a child, barely audible. Not even enough breath to blow out a candle.

'I don't think so,' she said. 'You've been in a coma since they brought you in.'

'I know you. You operated on me.'

'I operated on you. But you couldn't have seen me.'

But he had seen. Not from the table but from some other part of the room. Watched her remove half his left lung and pull out pieces of shattered rib and locate a piece of shot lodged in his spine that this doctor, the woman who stood over him now, did not dare try to remove. It could easily have been a dream, except that he knew her now, both her face and her voice.

He could have told her all that, told her he

remembered what she'd said, that a man who'd lost this much blood should be dead. 'How is this man alive?' Those were her words exactly. But he didn't know where all that breath or energy would come from. And he didn't need to convince her. And he didn't want to remember that last thing she'd said, just as they wheeled him out of the operating room, how she'd snapped off her gloves and shook her head and said he probably wouldn't last forty-eight hours.

He mostly needed more sleep. He didn't feel like talking anymore just now.

Book Two

JONAH WAS AN ANGRY MAN

Chapter One

1967

Steam

Hayden sat up, then woke up, more or less in that order. Naked, half under the covers, he sat for a moment or two, trying to identify the sound. Not that he didn't know that sound, what it was, what it meant. He did. Just that he woke up slow, foggy, and it took a minute to clear his head. It was one of those sounds requiring something, an action he knew well. Like the phone, only not the phone.

He felt Judith roll over next to him. 'I'll get her, honey,' she said.

'No, let me.'

'No, you have to be up at three.'

Hayden peered at the alarm dock, which did not glow in the dark. It was almost two already. 'Then it hardly pays to go back to sleep.'

'You sure?'

'Positive. Let me.'

He climbed out of bed and found his pajama bottoms draped over the end of the bed, and stumbled into them in the dark. Ordinarily he would wear them to sleep, but Judith had wanted to make love last night, even though it was late.

Now, fully awake, fully aware of the sound and its meaning, his chest filled with a swell of appreciation for that noise. That wonderful noise. Even though she was crying. Even though she was unhappy. He knew he could fix it.

'Leggy, Leggy, Leggy,' he said, letting himself into her tiny room. She heard and knew the sound of his voice, so her crying thinned to a little burble. 'You need a diaper, Leggy. You need a bottle and a fresh diaper, Leggy. Daddy knows. Daddy knows what Leggy needs.'

He picked her up and held her snug against his bare chest and felt her warmth and heard her light fussing. He bounced her a tiny bit and she fell silent. Even with the old wet diaper she fell silent and reached for his chin with her perfect little fingers. And he set her back down in the crib and she fussed just the tiniest bit while he unsnapped her jammies and peeled off the soggy wet diaper. He dropped it in the pail, and wiped and powdered her, and snugged her into a fresh one, snapping her up and feeling better himself, as though he could feel the dry comfort on his own skin.

Then he held her again, held her up against him, her head on his bare shoulder, her fine blond hair soft on his skin, and wrapped the blanket around her for warmth. 'Leggy, Leggy, Leggy. Daddy's going to make you a bottle of formula. How's that sound, little girl?'

He carried her into the kitchen with him, and turned on a thin glow of light from the fluorescent fixture above the stove, and rocked her slightly while he made a bottle with one hand. A little bit of an awkward process, and not fast, but he was getting pretty good at it, and it pleased him to acquire the skill. He set the bottle in a saucepan of water on the stove, blew lightly on the burner as he turned on the gas.

Out the kitchen window he saw the lights of the city at night. He'd be out there, all too soon, in the dark. In the cutting cold and fog, riding, running, and throwing. Shivering and blinking. But from here, from this vantage point, in this fellowship, it was a beautiful city. Lights glowing hazy and indistinct through the mist.

'Daddy loves his Leggy,' Hayden said. 'Just wait a few months, kid. You'll get big and start to talk, and then you'll be saying, "Leggy loves her daddy." You wait and see. Never too soon to start practicing. Just listen, to see how it sounds. Leggy loves Daddy. Leggy loves

Daddy. I know you do. You don't even have to say it and I know.'

He picked up the bottle, dribbled formula on the thin skin inside his wrist. Turned off the burner. The little girl reached for the bottle, reached out with both hands, fingers spread wide, lips sucking before she even pulled it in.

Hayden cradled her in the crook of his left arm, steadied the bottle with his right hand, though she was old enough, really, to hold it by herself, and looked out the window again, into that strange hour of San Francisco night he called morning.

Joel would be by in an hour, beeping his car horn lightly downstairs. Then Hayden would be off. First to the part-time, then a quick breakfast and on to the day job, then to school. Cradling in his mind, in his gut, that moment so much later this evening when he would get to come home to them. Joel would be here in an hour to get him for work. But he wasn't here yet.

He wasn't here yet.

Hayden felt Judith's hands on his bare back, felt them stroke down to his waist, drift around to his stomach. He felt the front of her press up against the back of him and he closed his eyes, freezing one of the moments that proved he was lucky.

'I don't know how you do it,' she said.

'Same way you do, I guess.'

'I get twice as much sleep as you.'

'I needed the love more than I needed the sleep.'

'Want coffee?'

'Not yet.'

'Want me to take her while you go back to sleep?'

'I'm awake now. She's almost done. She'll go down right away. You'll see.'

'Want me to put her down?'

'If you want to.'

'I do. I want you to go back to bed.'

'I'm going.'

And he handed her over to Judith, the bottle resting on her pajamaed belly, her fingers draped across it, still sucking with her eyes partly closed.

Hayden went back to bed and waited. Climbed back out of his pajama bottoms, sat up on one elbow under the warm covers, and waited for Judith to come back.

When she did, just a few minutes later, she said, 'You're not asleep.'

'True.'

'You're not wearing your pajamas.'

'Also true.'

'You're not serious.'

'I am if you are.'

'You'll never make it through the day.'

She climbed in with him, and he pulled her close

and kissed her ear, and the side of her neck, and that nice place between her breasts, that bony hollow that her nightgown dipped down to expose. The little gold necklace he'd given her, with the opal inset, slipped aside to make room for his lips. Then he pulled back and looked at her face. Sometimes her face was so pretty it hurt to look at it. This proved to be one of those times.

'I'll make it through the day because I have to. I won't have any choice.'

'You need sleep.'

'I need the love more than I need the sleep.'

And she took him at his word on that.

Joel's eleven-year-old Plymouth roared along deserted city streets, slowed going up hills, bounced and creaked ominously coming out of dips. Joel ran red lights and stop signs, and made illegal lefts, because there was nobody to hit and probably nobody to notice. If they were lucky.

Then he'd pull onto a residential street, slow to a crawl, and both their hands, Hayden's and Joel's, would reach into the back seat. Reach into the mountain of tied, folded papers, take one each, Joel throwing left, across the street, Hayden throwing right out the passenger window. The air that screamed in felt indecently cold, wet and cold, a cold like a scalpel, making short work of coats and scarves and hoods. A thermos of coffee rested on the floor at his feet, but unless they caught up to schedule, there would be no time to drink it now. Not until seven. Not until the sun broke the fog and every last paper had found a stoop, a mat, an apartment door, a grumpy morning reader incapable of appreciating how long he'd been allowed to sleep. How warm he was in his home.

Short work of this street, fine, but the next was an apartment zone. Joel stopped the car and banked the wheels and pulled muscles tearing at the hand brake and complained about it. They left the motor running, and collected eleven and fourteen papers, respectively, and split apart. And Hayden ran up and down stairs, down long carpeted halls, knowing by heart, by rote, that 2A does and 2C does not, knowing not to give the torn one to 3B unless he cared to hear about it later.

Then he hit the cold air again, with Joel gunning the motor and shooting him this rolling hand signal. Come on, come on, come on, come on. They'd gotten a late start again today.

They cruised down a long stretch of boulevard, a dead spot, just motoring fast to the next sector. Hayden picked up the thermos and unscrewed the top, and poured into the cap/cup with his arms extended, to spill scalding coffee on anything that was not his lap.

'Try to keep the screaming down when I turn this corner.'

'You don't turn here and you know it.' Hayden took a long gulp, still leaned forward, and the coffee scorched him going down, sloshed onto his chin and dripped off onto the bare metal of Joel's passenger floor.

'Gimme some of that,' Joel said, and cheated by slowing almost to a stop to drink. 'Okay, enough luxury.' He shot away again, handing the empty cup back, wiping his mouth on his jacket sleeve. 'Take me with you tomorrow.'

'With me where?'

'When you go out and get drunk. I live to debauch.'

'Who said I was going to go out and get drunk?'

'It's an immutable fact. It's legal, so you do it. All twenty-one-year-olds do exactly the same thing on their birthdays. It's actually an obscure law that exists on the books to this day. If you don't go out drinking, the sobriety police will come and drag you out of your apartment. Right in front of your wife and kid. Very embarrassing.'

'If I'm going to skip class, I'm going to spend that time with Judith.'

'So? Bring her along.'

'I'm sure a twenty-year-old will have a great time watching the of-age boys debauch.'

'Hayden, my boy, you can spend every night of the

rest of your entire goddamn, overlong, boring life with your wife and daughter. This is one exception. Bring her or don't, but we are hitting the bars, my boy. Mañana, on the dot. You need to let off some steam.'

'I need to catch up on my sleep.'

'Don't you worry. We'll be out like a light at a reasonable hour. Okay. Here we go.'

Joel made the turn, back onto a residential street, and threw left. Hayden threw right.

Hayden sat on a stiff typist's chair in the photo lab, blinking from the fluorescent lights. He could feel breakfast sitting heavy in his stomach. He could feel his foot on the pedal. Shift, click. Shift, click. Cutting the three-by-five prints off the printing paper roll. Lining them up in a three-by-five metal window. Trying to center each one first, no white borders showing, but that would require no break in concentration, ever, at all; an impossibility. Then stepping on the pedal.

This morning the prints came fifty at a time. Fifty prints of the same photo, with a slight overage for error, one right after the other. His favorite way, because then the subject of the photo didn't distract him so much. Even though it was porno. Of course it was porno. What else gets printed fifty prints at a time? Photos for sale, period. Nobody gets fifty prints of Aunt Pauline in front of the Washington Monument. Porno.

Boring stuff today. A big black man wearing a cowboy hat and chaps, nothing else, with a big black erection. Which Hayden stopped focusing on after the first four or five. Shift, click, shift, click. The cut prints fell into a basket under the machine. A trace of white border on each upper edge.

Maybe he should go out and get drunk tomorrow with Joel. Let off steam. That's what Joel said. That's the part that sounded good. Something that would earn no money, no credits or degrees. Wouldn't make him a doctor, or make Judith a doctor. Just done for its own sake. One evening, one life decision, one quick motion that didn't direct itself toward their future, their purpose. One night off without a goal.

The photo changed. A woman, in shadowy lighting, masturbating with a lighted candle. Not the lighted end, of course. And the light of the candle, he realized, was the only light used. So, sketchy and dark. And not pornographic, because pornography requires light and detail. Hayden shifted it across his machine. Shift, click, shift, click. Five, six, seven times. Liking it better each time. Feeling himself respond to its subtlety. Physically, but in other ways, too. Fifty-three of these, there would be, a margin of three on each shot. A margin for his error.

He pulled another through, framed it badly, cut it at an angle. It fell into the basket on the black cowboy, showing an unacceptable border of white at the upper left. Hayden picked it up and slipped it into his jacket pocket.

He'd give Joel a call right after work. Mañana, buddy, on the dot. We go let off some steam.

'Tell me something, Hayden, my good man.'

'Will if I can.' Three empty Heineken bottles sat on the table in front of him, four in front of Joel, and Hayden still had $7 in his pocket, exactly what he'd had leaving the house. He wondered how it must feel to be Joel, to take your paycheck to a bar and spend it without undue consideration.

'You're going to be a doctor.'

'Indeed.'

His head had begun to spin lightly, not so much the beer itself as the beer tapping into the exhaustion like a fuse, lighting it and letting it go. The jukebox throbbed in his head in a pleasant way, replacing mental activity. He watched couples dancing close on the floor and wished Judith had agreed to come along. It felt so strange, not being at school or at home or at work. Just being.

'So you get married at nineteen, and have a baby at twenty. Is this smart?'

'Yes.'

'Figuring how?'

'You think I'd get in more units per semester in Da Nang?'

'Oh, shit. Yeah. I always forget. I get a few beers in me and I forget other guys got to worry about that.'

'And you don't.'

'Four F, man.'

'Because . . .'

'I'm a homosexual.'

'You are not.'

'I am if you want me to be,' Joel said, and leaned in close to Hayden, batting his eyes and forming little kisses in the air. Hayden hit him on the arm. 'Ow. Okay, I'm not. It's a combination-plate deal. One from column A, one from column B. Extra-high blood pressure and flat feet.'

'Flat feet? That's it? And you get to stay stateside until the war ends? If it ever does?'

'And extra-high blood pressure.'

'You're so lucky.'

'Yoo-hoo, pretty barmaid. Another round for the birthday boy.'

So Hayden drank another Heineken straight out of the bottle and realized Joel wasn't lucky, not at all. Hayden was lucky. And it felt important that he never forget it again.

'Look at this, Joel.' Hayden took the photo out of his pocket and set it down on the table between them.

'Whoa. That's kind of freaky. What about it?'

'Doesn't do anything for you?'

'Should it? You can't see anything. There's a naked woman in that picture. Turn the lights on.'

'You have no soul, Joel.'

'No, that's true. I don't. But I'm buying tonight. So watch what you say.'

Hayden sat on the slope of cold damp concrete, his back up against a building unfortunately not his own. He had lost Joel, he had lost home. Everything was lost except him. And it was after midnight, so Joel would come to pick him up in less than three hours, but how would he find him? Hayden knew he should get some sleep, but the cold damp held him just at the edge of a sludgy consciousness.

A minute or so later three faces appeared above him, floating. Probably they had bodies, but it was dark, and Hayden's focus was off. Just floating faces. A tattoo of a teardrop at the corner of one eye. A gold tooth in the mouth of another. Oddly pleasing floating faces.

'Hello,' Hayden said.

'What's your problem, man?' The gold tooth flashed in the light of the corner streetlamp. A cloud of frozen breath formed around the words, heavy white steam in the city dark, a cumulonimbus hovering over damp urban pavement.

'Just kind of got drunk and lost where I live.'

'Got some money?' The teardrop spoke into a similar cloud, backlighted, and Hayden shivered slightly against the cold.

'Seven bucks.'

'You're joking, man.'

'No, that's really it.' Hayden pulled the wad of folded one-dollar bills out of his jeans pocket, turned the pockets inside out to show them. He held the money out for the gold tooth to take away. After all, he'd fully expected to spend it tonight, anyway. But it remained there, in his extended hand.

'You got seven bucks to the world.'

'That's it for now. At least until payday. Then I pay bills and that's it again.'

The faces retreated, leaving dull foggy streetlamp light, traces and curls of frozen breath floating alone, independent of their creators. The seven ones still rested lightly in his right hand.

'Nah, forget it, man. You need it worse.'

'You sure?' He wasn't certain in which direction to speak. Then he heard boot heels on the steep concrete to his right, and turned to look uphill, and saw there were at least five of them, walking away. 'Have a good night, then,' Hayden said, to no reply. Watched them walk toward the corner, which looked oddly familiar. 'Nice meeting you.' But they turned the corner and disappeared.

Hayden closed his eyes, opened his eyes. And there she was, standing over him like a dream. Like a beautiful dream that you try to get back to if something rattles you out of sleep, but it never works. That beauty only ever comes one dream at a time.

'Judith.'

'Hayden, why aren't you coming home?'

'I couldn't find it.'

'You are really drunk.'

'Probably so, yeah. I guess so. How did you find me?'

'Hayden. That's our building. Right there.'

'Where?'

'There. Right there on the corner. Across the street. I could see you out the window.'

'Oh. Yeah. Wow. It was lost, I swear. Where's Leggy? Who's looking after Leggy?'

'Oh, Hayden. Why did you get so drunk? How did you get so drunk on seven dollars?'

'My good buddy . . . Joel . . . whom I have misplaced . . . was buying.'

'Come home, Hayden.'

'You look so beautiful.' He took her hand and pulled

her down closer to him. To better see her face. She had this small, wonderfully shaped nose, like Allegra's baby nose, the skin soft and almost translucent. Delicate and innocent. And lots of straight blond hair, which he now held aside. To better see her face. Then he closed his eyes to that beauty, because, sweet pain though it was, it was pain. 'You know I love you, don't you, Judith?'

'Come home now, Hayden. I'm worried Allegra might wake up while we're gone.'

'You really shouldn't be out this late, Judith. It's not safe, really.'

'Please come home.'

'Do you love me, Judith?'

'You're scaring me, Hayden.'

'But you do. Right?'

'I love you so much it scares me.'

'I don't want you to be scared. I'll be scared for both of us. And for Leggy too. You guys just be happy, I'll be scared for everybody. That's my job. I get so scared, Judith.'

'Why? Of what?'

'I just get so scared.'

'Of what, Hayden?'

'I love you and the baby.' He squeezed his eyes tighter; he knew he was holding her hand too hard, but he didn't loosen up and she didn't complain.

'Why is that scary?'

'I'll always take care of you. You know that, right?'

'Hayden, please come home.'

'I'll never let anything bad happen to you or the baby. You guys mean everything to me. What would I do without you and the baby? I wouldn't even be anybody anymore.'

'You're scaring me, Hayden. Please come home.'

He opened his eyes and looked at her face, watched her breath come out in foggy curls of steam from her perfect little nose. The concrete felt damp and hard and cold. Home sounded good. A warm bed. And Joel would know how to find him there.

'Okay. Help me up, okay?'

And she held his arm and pulled, and he swayed to his feet and nearly sent them both tumbling again. But his hand shot out and found the building to hold him up, and the wad of dollars dropped to the concrete, and he steadied himself there, upright on the problematically tilted street, while Judith retrieved it again. Then he put his arm around her shoulder and they walked home together.

'I'll always take care of you,' Hayden said.

Two forty-five the alarm clock blasted him up again, and he showered and dressed and looked out the kitchen window waiting for Joel, who never showed.

He sat at the window wondering when he would feel sick, fully expecting to feel sick, but instead he felt drunk. Still drunk. Which was probably better than sick.

At four he called Alex, their supervisor, and said Joel's car must've broken down again, because he hadn't come by to pick him up. And Alex grumbled and agreed to run the route himself, which meant papers would all be late this morning, grumble grumble grumble. But when Hayden hung up the phone he realized he had the morning off, and wasn't due anywhere until nine. An amazing freedom.

He undressed and climbed back into bed with Judith, tucked up against her, curled up to her back, and breathed gently against her ear.

'You okay?' she said.

'I'm sorry I got so drunk.'

'It's okay. You needed to.'

'I let you down.'

'It almost never happens.'

'Now my check'll be one day short from the paper.'

'We'll get by.'

'I have no idea why I got so drunk.'

'I do.'

'Did I say why last night?'

'Sort of.'

'What did I say?'

She rolled over to face him and they wrapped their arms around each other, and she kissed his cheek. 'I think you just needed to let off some steam.'

Just then the baby started to fuss in the next room.

Chapter Two

1971

No More Baby

'Eat your cereal, Leggy. We're going to be late.'

'Where's Mommy?'

'She had to go.'

'Who's gonna walk me?'

'I am. Your loving daddy. Me. Now eat your cereal.'

Hayden sipped at his scalding coffee and watched her push the soggy cereal around with her spoon. Fine blond hair, and that tiny nose, and eyes the color of the sky in some mythical Indian summer you could waste your life dreaming about. If he weren't due at graduate school, Leggy at nursery school, he could easily stare at her until bedtime tonight.

'Where'd Mommy go?'

'She had an appointment.'

'What's a 'pointment?'

'It's being a certain place at a certain time.'

'What kinda 'pointment did Mommy have?'

'The kind you have to be on time for.'

'Oh.'

'I'm taking you to nursery school, and Grandma Thea will come pick you up like always, and you'll spend the afternoon at her house, and when you get home, Mommy will be here. How's that sound, Leggy?'

'Daddy . . .'

'What?'

'Don't call me Leggy.'

'But I always call you Leggy?'

'But don't. It's a baby name.'

'What should I call you?'

'Al-le-gra.'

'What do they call you at school?'

'Al-le-gra.'

Hayden sighed. 'Okay. No more baby Leggy.'

And he packed her off to nursery school, and himself off to grad school, nursing that sweet pain of loss.

Hayden got home before anybody, and sat chewing his thumbnail down past the quick, waiting for Judith to get home from work. Thea and Leggy – no, Allegra – showed up first.

'Daddy!'

'Allegra. Hey, kiddo. Give Daddy a big hug.' He squatted on his haunches to meet her flying body, and she nearly knocked him down. 'No more baby Leggy,' Hayden told Thea over Allegra's little shoulder.

'Yes, I know. I got the lecture, too.'

'Have a good time at school, kiddo?'

'Pretty good.'

'If you go pick out a game I'll play it with you.'

'Okay.'

'Pick carefully, though. Don't hurry.'

'Okay.'

And she let go of him and ran into her bedroom.

Hayden stood up and met Thea's anxious gaze with his own. A tall, handsome woman with a reassuring smile. Hayden hoped it was true what they say, that you can preview your wife in twenty-five years by looking at her mother. Sometimes he wished he'd been born to Thea instead. He just knew she would have handled things better.

Thea watched Allegra skid into her bedroom. 'Any word yet?'

'No, there's no good way to reach me at school. But she should be home any minute.'

'Have you talked about what you'll do?'

'Well, sure. I mean, how could we not talk about it?'

'Poor Hayden. You two have worked so hard. I hate to see anything get in the way.'

'We'll still get there, though. Maybe I'll lose half a year of school. Judith'll miss a year, I guess. But still. Leggy got in the way, but God knows we wouldn't trade her in. How do *you* feel about it, Thea?'

'Me? It's not my decision.'

'I don't know what we would have done without your help with Leggy, though. I mean, maybe it wouldn't be fair to you. Maybe it's pushing a favor too far.'

'Don't worry about me, Hayden. You two just talk it out and let me know. Maybe we're worrying about nothing, anyway.'

'Right. Maybe.'

'Call me when you know.'

'Judith'll be home any minute now. Hang around.'

'No. You two need to be alone at a time like this.' And she kissed his cheek before leaving. 'She did a smart thing picking you.'

And Hayden felt his cheeks redden, and Allegra hit his legs like a steamroller, the Candyland box under her right arm.

'I'll call you,' he said.

When Judith walked in the door Hayden asked the question with his eyes, and she answered with a barely perceptible nod.

He felt the news tingle around in his stomach, and

behind his eyes, and it was terrifying but good. It felt good.

'Hi, Mommy. How was your 'pointment?'

'Fine. Who's winning?'

'She's mopping up the landscape with me. I concede, kiddo.'

'What's that mean?'

'It means you win. Run put the game away, okay? Dinner's almost ready.'

'You cooked,' Judith said when Allegra had left the room.

'I thawed. I'm glad, Judith!'

'Are you really?'

'Yes. Really.'

She sat on the couch beside him and touched his cheek. He wanted to reach out for her, pull her close, hold her, but the tingle of the news had disconnected all the stations, and the nerve signals just crackled and died in his limbs.

'It'll make everything harder.'

'Leggy made everything harder. But she was a good idea, right? Oh. I forgot. No more baby Leggy.'

'Yeah,' Judith said. 'She explained that to me, too. So I guess we tell her over dinner.'

'We should, yes.'

'So we're happy, right, Hayden?'

'Yes. We're happy.' A signal got through and

he reached for her and they held each other for a moment.

'Are we scared, too, Hayden?'

'Oh, hell yes. That's us, all right. Happy and scared.'

Hayden couldn't sleep, much as he needed to. He sat up on one elbow and watched Judith sleep, in the faint light from the bedroom window. She was far enough along now that she slept only on her back, which made her snore lightly, but he didn't mind. He liked that reminder of her presence. Their presence. He wanted to reach one hand out and place it on that sweet hill of her belly, but was afraid to wake her.

A few minutes later she shifted around, tried to roll onto her side, corrected herself, opened her eyes, reached her hand out to take his when she saw him watching. He placed the other on her belly, hoping to feel movement, a kick maybe, but apparently everybody could sleep except him.

'You're worried,' Judith said.

'Just thinking.'

'About what?'

'Do we have the same deal as last time? If it's a boy, we name him Daniel?'

Judith opened her eyes again, pulled herself up a little, and propped up with the pillows behind her head. He suddenly wished she'd go back to sleep, so he could watch her in silence. Not have to deal with any questions.

'I thought that was just a name you liked.'

'It is.'

'It must be important to you if you remembered it all this time and it's keeping you awake.'

'It's not keeping me awake. I was just thinking.'

'I can always tell when something's important to you. Do you know somebody named Daniel?'

Say it, or don't say it? Time to decide. 'I had a brother named Daniel.'

'I didn't know you had a brother. I thought you were an only child.'

'No, I had a brother.'

'You never mention him. You never tell me anything about your family.'

'Nothing to tell. I just grew up, like everybody.'

'You never go see him. Where does he live?'

'I'm thinking I should have a vasectomy.'

'Really?'

'We want to stop at two, right?'

'Well, yeah. But no point rushing into it.'

'Why not? We know that's what we want. Why, wait? I mean, accidents can happen. You know. I'm not sorry this one did. But I feel bad, you missing two semesters of school. You have as much right to get through med school as I do. I'll call around in the morning. See what it costs.'

'At least wait till I have the baby.'

'Why?'

'Why not? We can't have an accident while I'm already pregnant. Just wait and see that everything works out okay.'

'What do you mean, "works out okay"?' Hayden sat up, pulled his hand back from her belly.

'Well. You know.'

'No. I don't know.'

'I'm just saying.'

'What would go wrong?'

'Well there are things that can go wrong.'

'Why would you think they would?'

'I don't think that.'

'Then why would you even say it?'

'Hayden.' She sat up and put an arm around his shoulder. 'I'm just sayings yes, in a little while, maybe you'll get a vasectomy. Now please stop worrying and go to sleep.'

'Okay.' They lay back down together, Hayden tucking up as close as he could to her side. He placed a hand on her belly again, something that often helped quiet him to sleep, and listened to a distant siren. 'I just wish you hadn't said that.'

'Poor Hayden. I forgot how much you worry. Don't

forget we have a Lamaze class tomorrow at seven.'

'Try to keep me away.'

'Where the hell is the labor nurse?' Hayden said, and sat down and breathed into the brown paper bag. It was part of their Lamaze kit, for hyperventilation, but of course it was supposed to be for Judith. Hayden had felt teased and belittled at first, when Judith suggested he use it, but the labor nurse, now irritatingly missing, had said hyperventilation was extremely common in a labor partner. And said it in a nice way. But where the hell was she now?

'More of those ice chips,' Judith said, and Hayden dropped the bag and spooned a few more out of the paper cup for her. She had to grab his wrist because his hand was shaking.

A sheen of sweat had broken out on her brow to replace the one he'd just blotted away. So he did it again, lovingly, and winced when another contraction hit her, visible, and painful even to him.

'Hayden.'

'What?'

'I feel something funny.'

'Like what?'

'Like my water breaking.'

'It broke a long time ago.'

'That's why it seems funny.'

Her forehead looked wet again, her expression a cross between curiosity and panic. She threw the cover back and they both saw it. On the sheet between her legs, and on her gown, a pool of blood the size of a saucer and spreading.

Hayden looked up to see the labor nurse walk into the room, with a younger nurse a step behind. He tried to scream, wave his arms, signal her, but nothing moved, nothing happened with him except on the inside. But the nurse noticed the situation immediately. So fortunately there was nothing Hayden needed to do. He could just stand there, paralyzed and mute, hating himself for his sudden overwhelming uselessness.

The labor nurse shot instructions over her shoulder to the nurse behind her. 'Page Dr Seagrave, tell him she's hemorrhaging. And get a gurney in here, I want her in a delivery room now. Okay, now relax, honey. We're getting the doctor.'

Hayden looked down at the pool of blood, about the size of a dinner plate, but it wasn't getting any larger now.

The nurse held a strange-looking stethoscope to Judith's huge belly, a stethoscope with a metal band that fit lengthwise over the top of the nurse's head. Hayden wanted her to say something. What she heard, what she was thinking. Something. But she just furrowed her brow. She looked down at the site of the bleeding. 'It stopped,' she said in an official way, seemingly to no one in particular.

'That's good, right?' Hayden said, thrilled and amazed that he'd spoken. But she didn't answer. 'Right?'

'The doctor will be down momentarily.' She pressed the call button, and another nurse appeared. 'Start an IV of D5W right away. We may need a transfusion. Type and cross two units.'

Two orderlies ran in with a gurney and transferred Judith onto it. Hayden ran after them down the thinly carpeted hall, listening to the cries of babies in every third or fourth room.

The 'in' half of the delivery room door swung open when an orderly hit it with his back. At the corner of his eye Hayden saw Dr Seagrave pull level and pass him. At the door the doctor turned and stopped Hayden with one hand on his chest.

'This is an emergency, Mr Reese. I know you're her labor partner but I'm sorry. I'll have to ask you to wait outside.'

'What's going on with my wife? I have a right to know.'

'That's what I need to find out, Mr Reese, so I really have no time to talk right now.'

Hayden just stared at him a moment. Both their

jaws were set. Seagrave had a schoolteacherly manner, and Hayden resented that authority. He was a small enough guy, and Hayden could flatten him easily, but it didn't seem prudent to do so.

The doctor spun around and proceeded through the swinging door, and Hayden followed. Seagrave seemed to notice immediately, to see his shadow or hear his footsteps, and he swung back and pointed at Hayden's chest, the door resting against his back. 'You're not scrubbed,' the doctor said, curt and simple. 'Your shoes are not covered. You're not wearing a cap or mask or cover gown. You're putting your wife and baby at risk coming in like that, Mr Reese. I can't believe you'd want to do that.'

Hayden blinked three or four times, took a few steps back. The door swung shut near his face.

Hayden found the mask, the gown, the paper shoe covers, and cap right where the labor nurse said they would be. She'd told him this earlier, much earlier in the labor, when no one had predicted he would not be welcome.

He scrubbed and suited up in a shaky flurry, making a mess of everything, but getting there eventually. Then he marched back down the hall and through the door into the delivery room.

Dr Seagrave stood at the foot of the table between

Judith's legs, a nurse on either side. She had an IV in place, and one nurse still listened with the strange stethoscope. Green paper drapes lay over her legs and belly, and her arms were strapped at her sides in wide leather restraints. An oxygen mask covered much of her face.

Seagrave turned his head slightly as Hayden entered the room. 'Get him out of here. Where's the anesthesiologist?'

'He's on his way, Doctor.'

'Why are her arms strapped down?' Hayden said. It felt wrong to talk, but he did anyway.

'I'm not getting a heartbeat,' a nurse said.

'There's no heartbeat?' Hayden said.

'She didn't say that. She said she can't hear one. Which would you like me to do first, Mr Reese? Save your wife and baby, or answer your concerns?' He waited only a split second for an answer. 'What was her station when you called me, Nurse?'

'She had a dilation of ten, Doctor, fully effaced with a plus two station.'

'Plus two. We might need to section. Get an OR crew in here. Would you please get him out of here?'

The anesthesiologist burst in, set up, replaced the oxygen mask with a heavy black anesthesia mask. As Judith's eyes fluttered and closed he placed a tube down her throat. Hayden knew he was lost without her. Meanwhile the two nurses just looked at each other, and at Hayden. Hayden saw Seagrave's gloved hands working between Judith's widespread legs. Saw the leftover blood. Knew he wasn't leaving.

'Call an orderly if you can't get him out yourself. She's plus three now. Forget the section. Get her legs up, get the forceps. I want this kid out. Now.'

'Should I still call an orderly, Doctor?' The young nurse.

Hayden stepped back into a corner, out of everyone's way.

'No, forget that. We don't have time.'

Hayden could see the crown of his new baby's head appear, Seagrave's forceps grasping that delicate little structure. Then the whole head came clear, facedown, and Seagrave wiped the face, suctioned out the tiny nose and mouth, Hayden wished he could see the baby's face. To know something with his own eyes.

Then the doctor was holding the head in his hands, freeing the tiny shoulders, and Hayden could see the whole head, and the face, and it was white, so white. Too white. And too still. Then he was out, all of him; in a great rush he just came, slipped free, the whole baby, streaked with blood and yellowish fluids. A boy. Hayden could see from here. But so white and still. Seagrave clamped the cord, cut it, and handed the baby to one of the nurses.

'Resuscitate him,' he said. 'Where's the pediatrician?'

'On her way, Doctor.'

Seagrave returned his attention to Judith, working over her as though there were something more to deliver.

'I need an ambu bag,' the nurse said, and one was placed in her hand, a mask with a bag attached, and she slipped the mask on Daniel's silent white face and pumped air in and out of him.

And that moment just went on. Just kept going. Judith asleep. Daniel silent and still, his chest rising and falling on command. Hayden leaning in the corner, brilliant white tiles and stainless steel blinding in his periphery, not knowing what anyone was doing or why. Not sure if he was breathing himself.

'We've got a velamentous insertion on our hands.' One of the nurses drew a fast, audible breath. Seagrave broke the instantaneous pause. 'See how fast you can get the transfusion,' he said to the young nurse. 'What's the heartbeat?'

'Less than thirty, Doctor.'

'We don't have much time. Nurse!' The young nurse seemed frozen, and she jumped when the doctor raised his voice. 'Now.'

She ran out of the room.

The pediatrician arrived at a dead run, and they

worked over his son. And he lay still and white and the nurse tried to breathe for him, but the pediatrician said, Poor little guy, he just had nothing to circulate. Damn it, where is that transfusion? What's the heartbeat now, Nurse? Damn it. Damn it. And then she monitored the heartbeat with her own stethoscope.

The young nurse who'd gone after the blood came back and said it would be just another minute on that crossmatch.

And the pediatrician shook her head.

The bag was removed, and Hayden's little boy, Daniel, was placed on a thin white blanket. Nobody was rushing now, nobody was yelling. The moment slowed to a long crawl and Hayden stayed several steps back from what he knew that meant.

Hayden came in close and looked at Judith to see if she was okay. But there was no gauging, nothing to help him know. 'Is she okay?' he asked the young nurse, whose eyes seemed marred with sadness on his behalf.

'She'll be fine.'

'But the baby . . .'

'I'm sorry, Mr Reese.' Seagrave, behind him. 'This is an extremely unusual event. It's only the second one I've seen in my career. I want to sit down with you, explain what happened.'

Hayden turned around. The doctor stood holding

Daniel, still and white, in both widely spread hands, the blanket bunched underneath him, mostly hanging down, Hayden wanted to cover him, because he looked so cold. Smears of blood provided his only color. Hayden could see the clamped cord at his belly, the shape of his perfect genitals, every tiny finger and toe. He was perfect. Absolutely perfect. Except he wasn't alive.

'Give him to me,' Hayden said.

'The nurse has to take him down the hall and—'

The nurse stepped in to take the baby.

Hayden reached out with his right hand and took a firm grip on Dr Seagrave's throat. The nurse stopped dead. Seagrave's eyes opened wide.

'Give him to me.' Every word measured, metered, precise. The doctor placed Daniel in the crook of Hayden's left arm. Hayden pushed with his right, not hard. It didn't seem to him that he pushed hard. But Seagrave stumbled backward and hit a rolling table of instruments and knocked it over, landing on top of it.

Hayden took Daniel down the hall, to the hospital chapel.

Hayden sat in a pew, the frontmost of three, staring through the leaded glass window, which sat over a simple altar. Just a few candles, some of them burning. So much to pray for in here.

Too cheap for stained glass, he figured, for crosses or statues, but after a few hours he conceded that it was probably not to save money. It was probably to help one tiny chapel serve for every possible religion, to offend no one.

Doctor Seagrave came in, accompanied by a uniformed policeman. The policeman stood in the corner, Seagrave sat by Hayden's side. In his peripheral vision Hayden could see the angry finger marks he'd left on the doctor's neck.

'When you're ready,' he said, 'I'd like to explain.'

'Am I under arrest?'

'No.'

'What's *he* here for?'

Hayden looked up at the cop, who leaned against the wall, thumbs hooked in his belt, returning Hayden's gaze with a steady, unflinching stare. I'm not afraid of you, the stare said. But Hayden could tell it was a carefully rehearsed lie.

'Just to make sure there's no further trouble.'

'You're not having me arrested for assaulting you?'

'No. I didn't see what purpose would be served. I told the officer there was no real harm done.'

'Thank you.'

'We need to talk.'

'I'd like to be alone with my son, please.'

'It's been several hours, Mr Reese. I understand your

grief. And I'll give you more time if you really need it. But sooner or later you have to give him up.'

'Later,' Hayden said.

Seagrave exchanged a look and a barely perceptible shrug with the officer, and Hayden was left alone with his son.

The light through the leaded glass told him night was falling, which seemed odd, since it had been seven in the morning when Judith's labor went so suddenly and completely wrong.

Now and then a door had opened behind him, but no one seemed to actually come in, and Hayden never once looked around.

After a while the labor nurse came and sat with him, the officer taking his position in the corner. 'Your wife is awake and asking for you. She needs you now.'

'Tell her I'll be in when I can.'

'She's going through this alone.'

'We all are.'

'Don't you even want to see her? To comfort her? To let her comfort you?'

'I know Judith. She'd tell me to let him go.'

'Maybe you should now.'

'Go away.' He turned to face her for the first time, and the look in his eyes made her jump to her feet and stumble back a step. 'Before I do something I can't take back.'

The cop moved in between them, his baton drawn, though no one had done more than look and speak. 'I'll take care of this, ma'am.'

'No, you won't. You can't beat him into it. He has to be ready to give it back.'

And she led the policeman out.

'He's not an it,' Hayden said over his shoulder as they left. He heard their footsteps pause.

'What did you say, Mr Reese?'

'He's not an it. He's a he. His name is Daniel.'

'You're right,' the nurse said. 'I'm sorry.'

Hayden spent the night in the chapel, by the light of someone else's candles, sitting up, talking to Daniel and to God, intermittently. Nobody answered.

Chapter Three

The Book of Reese

Morning rose early behind the leaded glass.

Hayden sat with Daniel on his lap, completely wrapped and covered in the blanket, because it had been nearly twenty-four hours now, and it felt somehow less natural and more unwholesome to still be here with him. And if the time had brought changes, Hayden didn't care to see.

A policeman came in and stood in the corner of the chapel, but the shift must have changed by now, because it was not the same man. And Hayden accepted that this was ready to end, come to a head one way or the other, and was glad to see someone he wouldn't mind tearing apart.

A minute later a young nurse came and sat beside him, and Hayden turned his head to look at her, and recognized her from the delivery room. The one who froze for just a split second. She couldn't have been any older than Judith or himself, and looked to weigh about ninety pounds. And it made a weird degree of sense, somehow, that they would send someone tiny and fragile and powerless to overpower him.

'Good morning, Mr Reese.'

'I really wish you wouldn't call me that. I wish you'd call me Hayden. Whenever someone says "Mr Reese" it makes me think of my father. Which I don't care to do.'

'Hayden. I'm Angela. I was there during the delivery.'

'I know. I remember. Good morning.'

'Mind if I sit and talk a minute?'

'I guess not.'

'If you don't mind my asking, Hayden, are you a religious man?'

'No. Not at all. Why do you ask?'

'Well, you came here to the chapel, first thing.'

Hayden looked up at the cop in the corner, whose face he didn't like, and felt constrained by his presence. And Angela must have seen that, because she got up and stood close to the officer and exchanged a few quiet words with him, and the cop reluctantly moved to the door.

'You just yell if you need me, ma'am,' he said at the door. Too loud. An insult to a place of worship.

'I won't need you,' Angela said.

Hayden heard the door swing shut and liked Angela for sending the cop away. And decided that maybe, just maybe, in a few minutes, he'd give Daniel to her. But what would he do then? Where would he go if not here? That was the problem.

'I'm not going to hurt you,' he said.

'I know you're not. Now. What were we saying, Hayden?'

'I guess it was force of habit. I came from a religious upbringing.'

'I read on your admission form that you're an Episcopalian.'

'I *was*.'

'You're completely separated from the church?'

'Completely.' They sat in silence for a minute or two, and it didn't seem to make her uncomfortable to spend a moment not talking. Then he decided he missed the warmth of the words. 'Why do you ask?'

'I'm an Episcopalian, too. That's why I asked if I could come in here and talk to you.'

'You needed someone's permission to come in here?'

'It's cordoned off, yes.'

'Great. I'm a menace to society.'

'I know you're not, though. I don't have any children, Hayden. And I'm not married yet. But I hope when I do get married I find a man who cares as much as you do.'

'You better hope he cares a little less. There's such a thing as too much caring.'

'No, there's not.'

'Yes, there is.'

'Poor Hayden,' she said, and put one warm hand on his arm. And he felt that warmth radiate and wondered why he wasn't going to Judith, why he wasn't letting her warm him. 'When I have a real crisis in my life, I have a priest I can talk to.'

'I don't want to talk to a priest.'

'Is there anybody you would like to talk to?'

'Right now, just you.'

'Okay.'

'Would you hold Daniel for me? Just for a minute?'

'Of course.'

Hayden handed her the little bundle, and waited to see if she would run out the door and send in the cop, or if she'd just hold Daniel and talk. She just held him. Gently.

'Would you please explain it to me?'

'Dr Seagrave—'

'I know. I know he tried. But I just can't talk to him. It's not his fault. I just want to hear it from you, in plain language. What a velamentous insertion is.'

'Okay. I'll tell you as best I can, because it's the first one I've ever seen. It's rare.'

'How rare?'

'I don't remember exactly. It's only the second one Dr Seagrave has seen and he's been an OB/GYN more than twenty years. I think it's something like one in every four or five hundred thousand births. I could look it up if you want.'

'Maybe later. Why does it happen?'

'No reason we know of. It just does. It's just a rare defect in the attachment of the umbilical cord to the placenta. There's no way for the doctor to know about it until the delivery. Then blood vessels tear away and the baby loses all his blood. It happens before anybody can really do anything.'

'So that was Daniel's blood on my wife's bed.'

'Yes.'

'All of it.'

'Yes.'

'That little tiny pool.' Hayden held his hand out to form the size of the circle. 'Is all the blood from a human baby.'

'Yes. I'm sorry. The only good thing I can say is that it's random, not congenital. When you and your wife get pregnant again, it's no more likely to happen to you than anyone else.'

'We won't.'

'Don't say that. You don't know. Let some time go by.'

'I'm getting a vasectomy.'

'Wait to decide. Are you sure you don't want to see a priest?'

'Whose fault is it?'

'No one's.'

'We didn't take good care of Judith's pregnancy?'

'No. You did. It's not your fault. It was there all along. Nothing you did could have changed it.'

'Seagrave didn't make any mistakes?' But he knew before she answered, because that was Daniel's blood, all of it, he'd seen it with his own eyes, and Seagrave hadn't even arrived on that floor yet.

'It's an act of God, Hayden. That's all anybody can call it. That's why I thought you might want to see the priest. The church is not that far. You could even walk there. It's a long walk, but it might do you good.'

'I know where the Episcopal church is. Will you take good care of Daniel?'

'Of course I will.'

'Get him all cleaned up so he can have a proper burial?'

'I'll treat him just the way you would.'

'Thank you. Will you give Dr Seagrave a message for me? Tell him I'm sorry I laid hands on him?'

'I think he knows. But, yes, I'll tell him. You really

might want to stop and see your wife before you go. She's been asking for you. She can't understand why you haven't come to see her. She's getting kind of desperate. She really loves you.'

'Please take care of Daniel,' he said, and walked out of the chapel. Walked past the cop without incident. Past the gift shop, with its bright flowers and balloons. Out the front hospital doors into a cold city morning, alone.

'May I speak with you, Father?'

The priest approached Hayden when he spoke out. A stocky older man, maybe in his seventies, with a full head of gray hair, wearing a clerical collar and a plain black jacket. His eyes a frosty color of blue, but not the least unfriendly.

Hayden didn't rise to meet him, just sat in the front-most pew watching him approach, the riotous primary colors of the stained glass overwhelming his senses even in his periphery.

'How may I help you?'

'You can tell me why God decided to kill my son.'

'I see. A difficult question. Would you want to go into my office in the rectory for privacy? Or are you more comfortable here?'

Hayden looked up, looked around. Cast his eyes up into the clerestory, the great arches of rich wood.

Looked forward, to the stained glass depiction of Jesus behind the ornate altar, the light of midday behind and through. No one else around. No one to disturb his privacy here. 'I've been here for a couple of hours,' he said, 'so I'm used to it here.'

The priest sat on the pew beside Hayden, lowering himself carefully, as if his bones hurt. 'How old was your son?'

'He never drew breath, Father.'

'Stillborn?'

'Yes.'

'I'm so sorry for your loss. A difficult loss to understand. No one of us can really claim to know God's ways. To understand His full purpose. He oversees a much wider scope of human events than we can even imagine.'

'So, you're saying there is no answer.'

'I'm saying there is an answer, but we may never know. Are you familiar with the scriptures?'

'Probably as well as you are. I can still spew out chapter and verse.'

'You might do well to review the book of Job.'

Hayden felt his jaw set. He swung himself up off the pew, his hips stiff from sitting so many hours on hard wood. He began to pace. 'I have no Bible anymore, Father, and I was forced to learn the book of Job almost by heart. I didn't come here for a reading assignment.'

The priest rose, ambled out of the church, down a long narrow corridor, the reverse of the way he had entered after Hayden's hours of waiting. Well, that's it, Hayden thought. Say one thing they don't like, they just wash their hands of you.

He paced back and forth, deciding whether or not to leave. Where would he go? Back to the hospital? He couldn't. Home? An empty apartment? He could go to Thea's and pick up Allegra, but it wouldn't be healthy for the girl to be around him now. He wasn't the right sort of company.

He paced in front of the bank of candles, thinking of lighting one, thinking of breaking them all. He paced down the aisle toward the door, kicking each pew, one harder than the next, wondering how hard he'd have to kick before he felt even the slightest bit better.

The priest's voice echoed out through the cavernous room, wavered off the high ceiling down to Hayden's ears. 'Take this.'

Hayden turned to see him holding a Bible in his hands. Walk out the door, he said to himself. He walked back to the priest.

'I don't want a Bible, Father. I want answers.'

'This is a book of answers.'

'No, Father. Real answers.'

'You don't believe the Bible contains the word of God?'

'I don't even believe in the word of God.'

'Then why have you come here?'

Hayden accepted the Bible into his hands. Small and black covered, a King James with gold imprinted letters.

'I have always hated the book of Job,' Hayden said quietly.

'Many people have trouble with it. Careful study leads to understanding.'

'I will never understand—' Hayden realized he was shouting. Couldn't bring himself, even after all these years, to defile a church with his shouting. 'God punishes this poor Job,' he continued, more collected, 'not for anything he did. Just to prove His point to the devil. Just to win an argument. Not with a man or another God. With *the devil*. Like God doesn't even know when He's being manipulated. He destroys this man's life. Seven sons and three daughters. He kills them to make a point. And then smites Job with sore boils, just for good measure.'

'You're saying God misbehaved.'

'I am.'

'Men misbehave. God behaves in ways men sometimes don't understand.'

'So killing ten children is a good thing. If you just get His point.'

'If God performed this, then it was good.'

'So killing my son was good.'

'In ways we may never understand. It is God's way, my son. Remember that God restored all of Job's children and property.'

'So, is God going to do that for me, Father? If I read this book yet again, and try to understand His ways, is He going to restore my son back to life?'

He gripped hard at the spine of the Bible, waiting to throw it. Waiting to stomp on it, or slap it against the priest's face. Waiting for his answer. He watched the creases around the priest's eyes, tried to read the thoughts behind them.

'How would He feel?' Hayden said, shouting in church now and liking it. 'What if it was His son?'

And he marched up onto the altar, straight to the stained glass window, infuriated by the face of Jesus, His eyes cast heavenward, hands folded in a weak, gesture of supplication, surrounded by lambs who gazed at Him adoringly.

And he struck the glass with his fist.

It cracked slightly but did not break, so he struck it again, and a thick piece splintered away. Now, suddenly, Hayden felt a tiny bit better. He struck it again. The thick lead borders holding the colored glass in place never gave, only tore at his knuckles, yet he struck at it again and again, feeling bits of glass bow out and fall, the whole window in the area of

Jesus' face curve slightly away from his wrath.

When shortness of breath and the pain and bleeding in his fist overcame him, he stood surveying the destroyed face of our Savior, hands hanging limp at his sides, allowing his blood to drop freely and pool on the altar.

'God has seen worse things done to His son.' The priest's voice echoed around his ears. 'You want to have a fistfight with God, is that it?'

'If He had the guts to come down and face me, yes.'

'You think if God came down to be with you now He would strike you with His fists?'

'I think He already has.'

Now the voice came quiet from just over his left shoulder. 'Let me put it another way, then. Just for the sake of argument, let's say it is possible for you to fight God with your fists. Do you think that you will win?'

Hayden never answered.

After a time he heard the priest's footsteps, walking away, leaving him alone on the altar.

When the priest returned a few minutes later, he handed Hayden a small white cloth towel. 'You're bleeding,' he said. Then he handed back the Bible, which Hayden had dropped earlier. 'I notified the police,' he said quietly. 'Not because it pleases me to punish you, but because I have to file a police report. So the church's insurance will repair the damage.'

'Maybe I could pay you for it,' Hayden said, placing the Bible under his left arm. He wrapped the towel around his right hand, wincing as he felt an imbedded shard of glass dig deeper.

'I think you don't know the cost of a window like this. Unless you're a wealthy man.'

'I'm not.'

'I think you'll need your money for a doctor, to stitch up your hand. And for a good Christian burial for your infant son. It's up to you if you want to be here or not when the police arrive. That's a choice only you can make.'

The priest returned to his rectory, and Hayden sat down in his place in the frontmost pew, the Bible slightly bloody on his lap, and waited for them to arrive.

'How does the defendant plead?'

Hayden glanced over to his court-appointed attorney, to be sure it was correct to speak for himself. The woman nodded.

'Guilty, Your Honor.'

'Guilty with extenuating circumstances, Your Honor,' she added, obviously displeased with the simplicity of his response. 'Mr Reese had just witnessed the stillbirth of his infant son. He was extremely distraught and out of his mind with grief. I'm sure Your Honor can appreciate his mental state.'

'You want me to make an exception for him.'

'I thought it might be appropriate, Your Honor.'

'Well, I disagree.'

The light in the courtroom burned into Hayden's eyes. He felt sick, though he hadn't been drinking. The bailiff reminded him of one of the cops in the hospital, which wasn't helping. He remained silent. His right hand throbbed and ached under a sea of bandage, nineteen stitches later.

'Does the defendant have anything to say for himself?'

'No, Your Honor.' He felt the urging stare of his attorney on the side of his face. 'There's no excuse for my behavior.'

'I'm glad you can see that. I empathize with your loss, Mr Reese. But I will not be part of a system that allows you to make excuses for violent, destructive acts. I will grant you one special privilege. I sentence you to thirty days in jail but I will give you one week to report. I am releasing you without bail. Don't let me down. Go home. Comfort your wife. Bury your son. Then report to this court, ready to serve your thirty days. Do you understand this ruling, Mr Reese?'

'Yes, Your Honor.'

Hayden's attorney put a hand on his arm as they walked out of the courtroom together, her fingers brushing the binding of the Bible, still clenched under his left arm.

'Are you sad, Daddy?'

'Just let your daddy be alone to think, Allegra.'

Hayden sat in the front seat of Thea's Oldsmobile on the freeway, Allegra on his lap, the same seat belt around them both. The window felt cool against Hayden's right cheek. He wrapped both his arms around his daughter and she touched his bandaged hand tenderly.

'Does your hand hurt, Daddy?'

'A little.' The exit for the hospital was coming up. Just ahead. 'I'm so afraid to see her now, Thea. I have no idea what I'm going to say.'

'She loves you, Hayden. That's one thing you never have to doubt. How much Judith loves you.'

'I let her down. I don't ever expect her to forgive me for this. I don't see how she can.'

'People who love each other forgive.'

They pulled up into the circular entrance, Thea parking briefly in the passenger loading zone.

'I think I should wait outside, Thea.'

'You can't put this off forever.'

'It's not about me and Judith. It's just because . . . some of the dealings I had with the staff . . . I just think . . .'

'Okay. You and Allegra wait here.'

So they sat together, Allegra with her tiny hand on Hayden's right wrist, and watched Thea disappear into the hospital lobby.

'What did you do bad, Daddy?'

'I wasn't there for your mommy when she needed me.'

'When Daniel went to heaven?'

'That's right.'

'Why not, Daddy?'

'I don't know, Leggy – Allegra. I don't know. I just couldn't.'

'Did you do your best?'

'I think so. I think I was trying to do right.'

'You always say that's good, then. If I did my best.'

'Thanks, kiddo. Maybe you're right. Thanks.'

'Mommy will forgive you.'

'Think so?'

'She always forgives me when I'm bad.'

'Well, it's a little different with grown-ups.'

'Why?'

'We're supposed to be old enough to know better.'

'Look. There's Mommy.'

So Hayden looked, and saw Judith being wheeled

out to the car by a nurse he had never seen. No Thea. In her street clothes again, the same maternity clothes she'd been wearing when she went into labor, because her husband hadn't been around to bring her a change of clothes.

'Why is she in a wheelchair, Daddy?'

'People coming out of the hospital always come out in wheelchairs. Just to be safe.'

'Can she walk?'

'Just as good as always.'

'She looks sad, Daddy.'

'I know, honey. I know.'

Hayden looked at Judith and Judith looked back, close enough now for eye contact with meaning. He bit his bottom lip hard and raised one hand to wave, but it was his bandaged right, and her face registered her slight alarm, and he dropped it down into his lap again.

Then he undid the seat belt with his left hand and climbed out and set Allegra on the curb. He opened the back door of Thea's car while Allegra ran to give her mommy a hug.

'Daddy says you can walk, Mommy.'

'I can, honey.'

She got to her feet, and Hayden instinctively reached out to hold her arms, as if she would fall without him. The nurse pulled the wheelchair back and they stood that way, face-to-face.

'Where's Thea?'

'Filling out release forms. What happened to your hand?'

'That's not even the worst of it. I'm sorry, Judith. I'm so sorry. I don't know what happened to me. I had no control of myself. I only wanted to be around people I could hurt.' He forced himself to look into her eyes, and paid the price for it. He'd hoped to see anger or defiance, but was not nearly so fortunate. 'I know you needed me.'

'Mommy, do you forgive Daddy?'

'Let's all get in the car now, honey.'

'Allegra, you sit up front with your grandma,' Hayden said. 'Mommy and I will sit in the back.' And he helped Judith in and climbed in after. 'Need help with your seat belt, Leggy?'

'I can do it. Don't call me Leggy.'

'Sorry. You need to make it smaller.'

'I can do it.'

'I just have one question, Hayden.' And it startled him, because she had addressed him directly for the first time. 'Why didn't *you* need *me*?'

Hayden looked out the window and saw Thea striding down the concrete walkway toward the car.

'We'll talk when we get home,' he said.

Chapter Four

1960
Pennies

'Where's Daniel?'

'I don't know, sir. I haven't seen him since Bible studies.'

'You don't know.'

'No sir.'

'I ask you where your brother is and you just don't know.'

'No sir. Sorry.'

Hayden stood on the boards of the front porch, eyes trained down to the faded brown paint. His father stood in the doorway, blocking him, one massive shoulder leaning on the door frame. Unrolling a pack of Camels from the short sleeve of his crisply starched white shirt, he shook one filterless cigarette out, lit it slowly with a cardboard match, cupping his hands around the flame. He towered above Hayden while he waited.

Hayden's father stood six foot six, and Hayden knew he was extraordinarily handsome, the kind of handsome women respond to, even though he wasn't sure yet what a woman looked for in a man, because he'd walked beside his father time and time again down the main street of town, watching the ladies avert their eyes and whisper to one another behind their hands when he tipped his hat and smiled. He seemed to thrill and dishearten them with his looks, all at the same time. He had a square, prominent jaw, a hard line of blond eyebrows with blue-green eyes set deep and wide apart. Thinning blond hair, but he kept his hat on most of the time, a rakish thing with a dip in the front of the brim. His muscles stood out impressively under rolled shirtsleeves.

He stood hatless now. Hayden studied his only physical flaw for comfort, but found none.

'Have I told you you're supposed to be looking out for him?'

'Yes sir.'

'How many times have I told you?'

'Hundreds, I guess.'

'And I ask you a simple question regarding his whereabouts, and you say you just don't know.'

'I'm sorry, sir.'

'Like I don't know that. You're all of sorry and then some, boy.'

'Leave the boy be, Ed.' Hayden's mother's voice, ringing out from the kitchen.

'I asked him a simple question, is all. I want to know where Daniel is because I got something for him.'

'Should've brought something for Hayden, too.'

'Lucy, get off me about that. I don't bring nothing for Hayden because Hayden don't want nothing. Do you, son?'

'No sir.'

'Say it so your momma can hear.'

'I don't want anything, Mom.' Except for him to move away from the door. Let me by.

'I brought Daniel a brand-new, shiny-as-all-hell nineteen sixty penny, just out today. First day in circulation, today. I drove all the way down to the bank to get one for him. Nineteen sixty D. That means it's minted in Denver, Colorado. You know that, boy?'

'Yes sir.'

'I bring pennies for Daniel because he's interested.' He made four syllables of the word – in-ter-es-ted – and shot all four hard over his shoulder into the kitchen. 'Now, Hayden here, he ain't interested in nothing. Are you, boy?'

'No sir.'

'I didn't think so.' He spat a shred of tobacco off his

tongue onto the porch boards. 'Here come the prodigal son now.'

Hayden turned to see Daniel sprinting down the road, Bible clutched in his left hand. He wished again his father would let him by, into the house, so he wouldn't have to watch this.

He looked back to his father, watched his eyes light up as Daniel came closer. 'Now, that boy is an athlete.'

'Yes sir.'

'Lookit him go.'

'Yes sir.' But he didn't look. Just stood with his back to the road until he heard Daniel's footsteps galloping up the old wood porch steps. Then he stood out of the way.

His father's hand shot out and caught Daniel back-handed across the face. Hayden couldn't help but look. Daniel flew backward. Flew. Feet clear off the ground, he sailed over the porch steps and landed on his back in the dirt of their front yard. Hayden heard an 'oof' sound as the air came out of him and the back of his head smacked in the dirt. He rolled over and spat into his hand; a puddle of blood and a perfect white molar landed on his palm.

'How's your big brother supposed to look out for you, boy, if you take off and don't even tell him where you go?'

'I'm sorry, sir.'

Daniel picked himself up, dusted off with his left hand, came back up onto the porch still holding the tooth.

'Bet that's the last of your baby teeth,' his father said. 'Bet you was fixing to lose that soon anyway. Put it under your pilla, see what you get. Look what I got for you.' And he held it out on the palm of his hand, and it was shiny as all hell all right. 'Brand-new nineteen sixty D. Now that one I *know* you don't have.'

'I didn't even know they were out yet, Dad.'

'Brand-new today.'

'Thanks, Dad.'

'I punish you because I love you.'

'I know that, sir.'

'Take your penny.'

And Daniel took it with his left hand and stuck it in his left pocket, where Hayden knew it would stay for days, changing pants when he did. The right pocket was for unremarkable pennies, late forties and fifties, to trade for those older and more valuable. When he found a good one, it would go right onto his collecting board. Unless it was from Dad. Then it would sit in that left pocket for a week or more, appearing in Daniel's palm during the church sermon, and on the corner of his desk in Bible studies, where it could be seen.

'You boys go change out of your Sunday best, and maybe I'll give you money for a matinee. Maybe I'll give you each a quarter, so you can buy some candy to boot.'

And he disappeared from the doorway and Hayden went back down off the porch to fetch Daniel's Bible, thrown halfway into the road. Then they ran upstairs to change.

When he came down in blue jeans, ten steps ahead of his brother, Hayden's mother pulled him aside at the bottom of the stairs.

'Maybe it's not such a bad deal he don't notice you much,' she said, drying her hands on her big pink apron. 'Seeing as he's kinda hard on what he notices most.'

'Sure you don't want to go to the movies?'

'Positive,' Daniel said.

He had his left hand in his pocket, probably wrapped around the new penny; with his right he rubbed the back of his head slightly as they walked down the road. His hair was cut so close to his head that Hayden, half a step behind, could see the redness, and a lump starting to form.

'Where *do* you want to go? As if I can't guess.'

'Anywhere with a cash register.'

'Why do I even ask?'

They stopped at Eli's house. Eli's mother came to the door, called him down from upstairs. A fashionable woman, never tired looking like their own mother. Never seemed to have work to do.

'We thought we'd go by the soda shop, ma'am, and maybe Eli wants to come along.'

'Never knew Eli not to.' She went for her purse as Eli barreled down the stairs two at a time. 'Here's a dime,' she said as he flew by, and he took it on his way out the door.

'Bet you each got quarters,' Eli said when they'd cleared the house and set off down the road into town.

'We do,' Daniel said.

'Shoot. You always do. I'd have to aim a loaded gun at somebody to get a quarter.'

'If we put your dime and my quarter together,' Hayden said, 'we could get one of those super extra giant sundaes.'

'Or go to the movies, and get popcorn and Raisinets.'

'Daniel wants to go to the soda shop. He wants to go through their pennies.'

'So? Let him go his own way.'

'I'm supposed to be looking out for him,' Hayden said.

'Look at that, will you,' Eli said when Mr Perryville brought the sundae to the table. 'Like ice cream mountains.'

'I'm going to climb mountains,' Daniel said. He had

more than a hundred pennies on the table in front of him, all the pennies from the register, sorting them into two careful piles.

'Maybe when you get older,' Hayden said.

'I don't have to wait.' Sure of himself like always.

'Me, I'm ready to climb this one right here right now,' Eli said, and dug the cherry off the center peak with his spoon, and flipped it onto his tongue.

Hayden took a big spoonful of strawberry and just sat there letting it melt in his mouth, knowing he'd have to pick up the pace to eat his half of this mountain before it melted – not an altogether unpleasant challenge. He looked out the window and saw Cheryl Wilkerson come out of the five-and-dime with that girl she always went around with, that plump girl. And he took another spoon of strawberry without taking his eyes off Cheryl.

'Let's go climbing right after this,' Daniel said.

Hayden said, 'Yeah, fine, whatever,' which he would not have said if he'd been paying attention, because he hated climbing.

Cheryl was coming closer now. They were going to walk right by the window. His spoon drooped down toward the Formica tabletop, mostly forgotten.

Eli jabbed him hard in the ribs. 'You like her.'

'Ow. Shut up, Eli.'

'Know what I heard about her?'

'No. What?'

'Something I'm not saying in front of squirt here.'

'It's probably a lie.'

'Four guys don't all tell the same lie.'

'Sure they do. They sit around making it up together.'

She was close now. Close enough to see him. But she was looking over at her plump friend, laughing, flipping her light brown hair around, like it bothered her wherever it landed. She had a beauty mark, just like Marilyn Monroe, only higher, on her upper lip. Just as they passed in front of the window Cheryl looked at Hayden. Right at him. And his face tingled and he hoped she'd look away before it got too red. He felt a little dizzy. Then she smiled, and they were by, past the window just like that.

'She likes you,' Eli said.

'No, she doesn't. She's just being nice.'

'Wait till I tell you how nice she was to those other guys. Look at your face, Hayden, it's all red.'

'Now, how can I look at my own face?'

Daniel looked up from his pennies in disgust. 'I can't believe you guys waste time on girls.'

'Give it two years, little fool. You'll get there.'

'Never,' Daniel said. Hayden gave his head a little push, just put the heel of his hand on the side of Daniel's head, over his ear, and knocked his head aside. Just friendly. But Daniel said, 'Ow. Watch that,' and rubbed the back of his head again.

'What's wrong with him?' Eli said.

'Oh, nothing. He just fell off the porch. Didn't you?'

'Guess I did.'

'That why his cheek's all red?'

'Yeah.'

'But he's rubbing the back of his head.'

'He just fell, Eli. Get off it.'

'Falls off his own porch and now he wants to go climbing.'

'Holy moly, look what I found.'

'What? You got a good one, squirt?'

'Good one? Are you kidding?' Daniel held the penny up high, like the light might be better up there. 'In perfect condition, too. Shoot, I bet I could get two dollars for this.' He lowered his voice on this last note, always fearing the merchants would want their pennies back if enlightened to their obvious value.

'I would think you'd want it for your collection.'

'Well, there you have the beauty, Hayden. I already *got* one of these in my collection. So this one is for sale.' He took an ordinary penny out of his right pocket, added it to the pile, stuck the prize down deep into his left.

'What're you gonna do with all that money?' Eli asked, interested now, as if it were his opportunity just as much.

'We'll see,' Daniel said. 'Eat your ice cream, guys. I'm ready to go climbing.'

They stood in the loose brown dirt at the bottom of the tower, Hayden craning his head back toward the sky. The electrical wires let off a humming noise you could hear from the ground. He looked at the little metal sign. *Danger. High Voltage. Keep Off.* He'd done this a few times, but wasn't getting to like it any better.

'I'm too full with ice cream. You guys go.'

'You are so chicken, Hayden.' Daniel threw into high gear immediately, climbing the base of the tower like a simple metal ladder, speaking from a place a few feet over Hayden's head.

'I'm just full,' he shouted back, because Daniel was pretty high now. 'I'm just full,' he said quietly to Eli, who snorted.

'Maybe. But you *are* a chicken.'

'Thanks a lot, Eli. Nice to have a best friend.'

'You got to admit, your kid brother has ten times the guts you'll ever have.'

'My kid brother has too much guts. Look at that. If he gets up to where those wires are . . .'

'They're wide enough apart.'

'I heard you don't even have to touch them. I heard that power can just arc over and grab you.'

'That's a lie, I bet.'

They sat down in the dirt under the big tree, leaned back against the trunk, watched the little fool go.

'I don't see you getting up there, Eli.'

'I'm full, too.'

'Yeah right.'

'Hey. Last time I went twice as high as you.'

'What do they say about Cheryl?'

'You won't believe it.'

'Because it's a lie.'

'Four guys said so. One was from the Riverside School, doesn't even hang around with the same crowd.'

'Said what?'

'Said she took a walk over the tracks with them, and then—'

'She would not go all the way.'

'I never said all the way. Would you please let me talk?'

'What, then?'

Eli made an obscene jacking motion with his right fist.

'With her hand?'

'You got it.'

'She wouldn't.'

'How do you know she wouldn't?'

'She goes to Bible studies.'

'So? You go to Bible studies. But you'd let her.'

'Guys make that stuff up.'

'Maybe so, but—'

'Holy shit.' Hayden jumped to his feet, ran ten steps, stood under the tower, his neck bent back to the sky. He cupped his hands to his mouth. 'Daniel. Come down, you idiot.' Then, to Eli, 'Look at that fool. He's up past the power lines.'

'Yeah, well, he made it.'

'He's got to pass them again on the way down.'

'He's all the way on top. I don't believe that. Look at him. I never saw nobody climb to the top before. Look at him. Sitting up there waving his arms around, pounding on his chest like he's Tarzan. You're right, that fool got too much guts. He's gonna get himself killed someday.'

'Not on my watch, I hope.'

'When is he not on your watch?'

'Oh. That's true.'

'Look what I bought with my money, Hayden.'

'What the hell is it?'

'I'm telling Dad you cussed.'

'I'm telling Dad you went up to the top of the tower.'

'Okay, never mind. Nobody'll tell nothing.'

They started the long walk home together.

'I don't even know what that thing is.'

It was too big for Daniel's pocket, so he walked with it close to his side, up against his jeans, where it wasn't likely to draw attention. A four-pronged hook of some sort, like four metal fishhooks back to back, only much bigger, and not sharp.

'It's for climbing mountains.'

'You see any mountains around here?'

'I can practice on the tower.'

'That thing can't get you up the tower.'

'Sure it can. You just tie a long, long rope to the end of it here. And you just toss it up. And you wrap the rope around your waist or your leg, and you take up the slack as you go.'

'And then you toss that metal onto a power line . . .'

'Well, you just got to be careful not to.'

'And when you miss . . .'

'Well, the rope isn't metal. The power can't come down the rope.' They walked in silence three blocks. 'Can it?'

'I don't know.'

'Would've bought a rope, but I ran out of money. Tonight I'll put that tooth under my pillow. Maybe I'll get enough.'

'You still got baby teeth?'

'Nah. That was a permanent.'

'Not permanent enough, I guess.'

'Mom'll tell him that, and he'll feel terrible, and I'll clean up. Prob'ly get a dollar.'

'You can get up the tower safer without the metal hook.'

'But this way I learn to be a mountain climber. Ropes don't conduct electricity anyway.'

'I don't know. I told you I don't know.'

They lay in the dark, Hayden thinking about Cheryl, that thing Eli said about Cheryl, and how she smiled at him. Wishing he had his own room, or that Daniel would hurry up and go to sleep.

'That was the best moment of my whole life,' Daniel said.

'I really wish you wouldn't ever do it again.'

'But I have to, though. It was so great. You can't even imagine it, Hayden, I could see the whole valley. I was the king. It's like I owned everything I could see. Tomorrow right after Bible studies. I'll buy the rope. Go out there with me.'

'No. If you're gonna kill yourself, I don't care to see.'

'I won't.'

'You might. Did you ever think the rope could swing? That hook could slide over, or you could lose your footing and you wouldn't fall but you might swing right over into a power line.'

They lay quietly for several minutes. Hayden could almost hear Daniel thinking. 'Okay, then go out with me and hold the end of the rope. So I won't swing.'

'No. It's a stupid idea.'

'Then I'll go alone. Take my chances.'

'Fine. Kill yourself.' He rolled away, wrapped a pillow around his head, squeezed his eyes shut and tried to will himself to sleep. Tried not to think about Cheryl's hand. If only they had two bathrooms in this house, or if only the one they did have locked. 'Okay. I better go, to hold the rope.'

'I knew you would, Hayden, thanks.'

After Sunday mass and Bible studies they went home to change. Their father was standing at the porch rail, smoking and waiting.

'He can't be mad,' Hayden said. 'We're right on time.'

'He doesn't look mad.'

'Got a surprise for you, Daniel,' he called down. 'How'd you like to ride Joe Dawkins's new-broke filly?'

'Really?'

'She's kinda small and her knees aren't all closed up yet, so he wants somebody one fifty or under. That ain't him or me.'

Mom came out onto the porch and stood with one hand on her husband's shoulder. 'Hayden's under one fifty too, Ed.'

'Hayden don't want to ride no green filly. Do you, boy?'

'No sir.'

'He says that 'cause you tell him to.'

'Two boys can't ride one filly.'

'They can if they take turns.'

'I don't want to, Mom, really.'

'Nonsense. This man's got two sons. He's taking two sons riding. Aren't you, Ed?'

'Whatever you say, woman.' He rolled his eyes as soon as she went back inside.

'She doesn't look small to me.'

They stood together in the sand of the pipe corral, all except Daniel, who sat on the rail. Joe Dawkins stood at the filly's head, holding her steady, but she didn't look steady. Hayden could see the wild whites of her eyes looking back at him. His father stood with his hands cupped to give him a leg up.

'Come on, come on, come on, boy. I'm waiting here. You begged me to take you, now get on the horse.'

Hayden placed his sneaker in his father's cupped hands and felt himself swung fast and hard into the saddle, and he landed too rough, and the filly pitched sideways. And Hayden didn't have his balance yet, and almost fell right off again. He clutched at the horn, shaking, until she steadied.

'Don't make him ride if he's scared, Ed. She'll sense it.'

'You scared, boy?'

'No sir.'

'Then hold on tight. You're going for a ride.'

'Wait,' he said, because the stirrups were too long, and his feet weren't set in them yet, but it was too late. His father slapped the filly's rump hard and she startled and took off.

Hayden grabbed at the saddle horn and tried to get his feet in the stirrups. He was off balance, and the filly was headed right for the rail. And he'd end up falling on the rail or under her hooves, he could just see it. He managed to get his feet set, but the stirrrups were long and he had to reach to stay in them, and when the horse veered sharply at the rail one foot went right through, and he pitched off balance again. Only now, if he fell, he'd get dragged.

Joe Dawkins stepped in front of his filly and threw his arms wide. 'Ho, ho, whoa, girl.' He said it soothingly, but she didn't stop like a soothed horse. She planted her feet and threw dirt and went rigid, and Hayden flew forward and landed with his head and shoulders in the dirt, hanging from the stirrup at her left front leg. Which made her dance some more.

'Easy, girl,' Joe said. And Hayden watched her steel-shod hoof dance next to his face. 'Okay, girl. Easy, girl. I got you. Okay, I got her now, Hayden. See if you can work your foot loose.' He pulled himself up and grasped the stirrup, and when his foot slipped out he landed hard on his back in the dirt, and the filly jumped again. And he heard his father laughing over by the rail. Joe let the filly go and held a hand out to Hayden and helped him up. 'You okay, son?'

'I think so, sir.' He clapped clouds of dirt off his jeans.

'You just got off to a bad start. Your Daddy was wrong to set her off like that.'

'I appreciate your saying so, sir.'

Joe put an arm around his shoulder and they walked back toward Daniel and Ed, at the far rail. Hayden's legs were shaking, so with every step he thought they might give, and he'd pulled muscles bad, all up the back of his left leg and up through his butt.

'It's okay to cry, you know,' Joe said. He said it quietly, but apparently it wasn't quiet enough.

'My boys don't cry,' his father called out. 'Now, I can accuse that boy of being many things. But not a crybaby. And also not a horseman.'

'Not everybody gotta be a horseman,' Joe said.

'Yeah, but we don't know *what* Hayden's gonna be. We have yet to find the thing that boy's good at.'

'Just let him alone, Ed.'

'Now watch my little athlete here.'

Joe held her head while Dad gave Daniel a leg up, and Daniel wasn't scared, and the filly knew the difference. No whites showed at her eyes, and Daniel drummed her sides with his sneakers and he galloped around the ring with her, his feet flapping. He never even tried for those stirrups, just held the horn with one hand and rolled with her movements and gave out a big strong Indian war whoop as they flashed on by.

Hayden wondered which was more fun, this or watching Daniel climb a high-voltage tower with a metal hook, and it seemed more or less an even draw.

The following Saturday, while they were sitting in Bible studies, Daniel brought it up again, long after Hayden hoped he'd forgotten all about that foolishness.

Hayden was sitting in his hard wooden desk, looking at the back of Cheryl Wilkerson's head, with his math book on his lap, which he always brought with him, on the pretext of maybe getting homework done on the break. But really he always finished his math homework on Friday night. It just seemed indecent somehow to use the Bible for such a purpose. That kind of thing might lead a guy to seriously burn in hell.

And then this little scrap of paper appeared on his desk. And he unfolded it. It said, 'Today. Right after class. Meet me there. D.' And Hayden closed his eyes and sighed and never thought to doubt where 'there' was. When he opened his eyes he looked over at Daniel sitting two rows away. That pleading face. Hayden shook his head. The eyes only grew more pleading. Daniel had big blue-green eyes, like Dad's, only safer. Hayden knew the question was never going to go away. But he kept shaking his head. Shaking, shaking, shaking. And then he was nodding. And Daniel answered with a satisfied nod, and Hayden looked away.

He looked back at Cheryl. To his amazement, she had turned her head and was looking over her shoulder, straight at him. He froze like that, his gaze snagged on her, and she smiled.

And then Mr Nellis, the Saturday morning Bible studies instructor, slapped the end of his yardstick down on Hayden's desk, hard. It made a sharp noise, and Hayden jumped.

'Hayden. Do you know what we're discussing?'

'The book of Job, sir.'

'And would you care to explain to the class why God destroyed Job's property, and smote his body with sore boils?'

'No sir. I would not be the one to do that.'

Nellis leaned on his yardstick. Leaned in closer, and

seemed pleased. He had black, black hair, and that odd hairline like a widow's peak on his forehead. It made him look wrong somehow. 'You did not complete your reading assignment.'

'I completed it, sir.'

'Then please tell the class why God behaved the way He did.'

'Sir, there's no good reason I can think of.'

Nellis's look changed slowly as he realized where Hayden seemed to be going with this, as he recognized it for what it was, a dissension, and worked himself up to the challenge. And Hayden sat up a little taller himself, and decided he had a right not to understand, and a bully like Nellis could not take that right away from him. They could make him come to this place every Saturday and Sunday morning. Maybe they could even make him read the Book. But they couldn't make him understand.

'Do you suppose God waits to see if you understand His actions before He makes a move? Does He pause and say, "Maybe I better check with Hayden Reese first. See if he approves."?'

Hayden heard the nervous titters of the class in his ears.

'No sir, I doubt He considers me at all. So it shouldn't matter too much to Him if I don't follow on this one thing.'

He glanced up at Cheryl. She was staring at him. He knew everybody was, but he saw only Cheryl. And she smiled again, and he could see her approval. And he knew he was being brave, and his courage wasn't lost on her. Not at all.

'So, you think you know what's right more than God does.'

He returned his attention to Nellis's face. Looked right into his eyes without flinching. 'I didn't say that, sir. I said that in this case God's actions were beyond me.'

'Well, maybe a lot of things are beyond you.'

'If you say so, sir.'

'Maybe you should read the entire book of Job three more times before next Saturday. Or maybe I should just have you keep reading it until you get the picture.'

'With all due respect, sir, you can make me read it all you want. And I'll read it every time you tell me to. But you can't make me understand what I don't.'

'You can stand in the corner in front of the class for the remainder of the session.'

'Yes sir.'

'Leave the math book here.'

'Yes sir.' He couldn't see himself needing it now.

Cheryl Wilkerson shot him a little thumbs-up as he walked by her desk, while Nellis was looking the other way. Hayden stood in the corner, facing the blackboard, legs comfortably apart, hands clasped loosely behind him. Facing crayon drawings and signs made by the younger kids' class. The one in front of his face said, 'Jesus Loves Me.'

Nellis appeared at his left ear. 'I think I may need to phone your father regarding this situation.'

'You do what you need to, sir. He can't make me understand, either.'

After class Hayden found Cheryl waiting for him right outside the church door. 'You were wonderful. That was brave.'

Daniel snorted laughter from behind them. 'Hayden? Brave?'

And Cheryl said, 'Can we ditch your kid brother? Maybe we could go somewhere. A movie or something. Got any money?'

'Yeah, I got a couple dollars at home.' Birthday money from his Aunt Frieda, but he stopped himself before saying so out loud. 'I'd have to stop off and get it.'

'That'd be fine.'

Hayden grabbed Daniel by the collar of his starched white shirt, because the tie was only a clip-on. And he walked him backward until Daniel's back touched the brick of the church.

'Go away, squirt.'

'We had a plan.'

'It's canceled.'

'Until when?'

Hayden looked over his shoulder, and Cheryl was still there, smiling. 'You want to go to the matinee, Cheryl?'

'Heck, if you got two dollars, we can do all kinds of things. We can go out for a sandwich or a soda after.'

'Six o'clock,' Hayden told Daniel quietly.

'Six o'clock? What am I supposed to do until then?'

'That's your trouble, not mine.'

'I'm going up without you, then.'

'Don't.'

'You can't stop me.'

'Just practice till I get there. Get the hang of throwing that hook. And getting up and down. But don't even get near those lines. Stay close to the ground.'

Daniel's face twisted into resentful disappointment. 'All right. But be there at six. Don't be late.'

'If I'm late, don't go up without me.'

'Don't be late or I will.'

'Wait for me.'

'Be there at six.'

'I will. I said I would. I will.'

'If you'll just wait right here a minute,' Hayden said, 'I'll be back before you know it.'

And he left her standing on the porch and ran up the stairs to his room two at a time. His father's car was gone from the driveway, the best break he could possibly have gotten. He smashed his piggy bank onto the wooden floorboards with the heel of his shoe, took the bills, left the shards where they lay.

At the bottom of the stairs he ran into his mother.

'Where's Dad and Daniel?' he said.

'Oh, Daniel talked him into taking him riding again.'

'Perfect. I mean, that's a good thing for them to do.'

'Hayden, who's that young lady on the porch?'

'Cheryl. My friend.'

'Are you two going out?'

'Just to a movie. Maybe a soda after.'

'Well, that's nice, Hayden. You're a handsome boy, I'm not surprised some girl took an interest in you.'

Hayden felt his face redden. He could see Cheryl through the screen door. He was pretty sure she couldn't hear this, but felt suddenly afraid his mother would do something visual to humiliate him. Kiss him, maybe. 'Please don't embarrass me in front of her, Mom.'

And she smiled knowingly, and just said, 'Have a good time.'

And he said, 'Thanks, Mom,' and ran.

*   *   *

'It's early yet,' Cheryl said as they left the soda shop together. 'We could go for a walk or something.'

Hayden didn't have a watch, but he knew it wasn't early. Knew by the sun. Then Cheryl slipped her hand into his, and his breath caught, and he just walked with her, focusing on breathing right. Hoping someone would see. Hoping everyone would.

'That would be nice.'

'We could take a walk over the railroad tracks,' she said. Gave his hand a little squeeze.

Hayden swallowed with difficulty. He knew it meant nothing because he couldn't believe a thing like that, because belief leads to disappointment. That's what his head told him anyway.

'That would be very nice,' he said.

'Open your mouth a little,' she said. And he did, and she kissed him again.

They sat propped up against a big fallen tree, way on the other side of the railroad tracks, where a little stream came down through the culvert pipes and trees rose up tall over their heads. He'd spent time here as a young boy.

He felt the tip of her tongue on his lips, and on his tongue. And a painful feeling in his groin, like something stretched farther than it can really go. A balloon ready to burst. And it was only going to get worse, and he had no idea what to do about it under these circumstances.

She pulled away and they looked at each other in the fading light. 'I'm going to be a virgin when I get married,' she said.

'I can appreciate that. I guess your husband would want it that way.' Only maybe he would be her husband. And he wouldn't care then, what she did tonight with him.

She took hold of one of his hands and guided it up under her pink cotton blouse. Reflexively, he pulled back.

'I thought you said—'

'Touching me there doesn't make me not a virgin. Silly.'

'Right. That's true.'

And she took his hand again and he allowed it to be guided. Up her soft stomach, under her stretchy brassiere. Onto a small firm breast. He let out a little gasp. His pants were way too tight in the crotch, hurting him.

'Okay, that's enough,' she said.

He jerked his hand away. 'Okay.' He sat back against the log and tried to adjust his pants for more room, but only hurt himself worse. 'Ow. Shit.' He pulled his knees up slightly. 'Sorry. I didn't mean to cuss.'

'I don't mind. I don't mind one bit. I like it when

you're bad. We didn't come all the way out here to be good, you know.'

And her face was right up to his again, close enough to kiss in the fading light, and this time both of their tongues explored tentatively. And she broke off the kiss, and pressed her face against the side of his, and he found himself looking over her shoulder into the dusk, in the middle of nowhere.

And he felt her hand on his zipper, and she undid the button at the top of his Sunday pants. And he said, 'Oh, God,' without ever knowing he was about to, and it struck him as a strangely wrong thing to say. When she yanked his shorts down he felt the cool air hit him, shocking, pleasant, strange. And her hand wrapped around him and he pushed once hard into the circle, of her touch and then it was over already, just like that, with a long noise that came out of his lungs and a feeling like everything inside him was exiting at once, bursting out before he ever wanted it to. And then that moment when he hated himself because it was already over, and felt strangely unsatisfied.

'Well, you were certainly anxious,' she said. He wasn't sure if she meant it as a criticism, but it seemed reasonable to interpret it as such. 'Got a handkerchief?'

'Yes, I do. Right here.' He took it out of his pocket and handed it to her. His mother had trained him to carry one. A gentleman always does, she had said. And he had always thought that was silly, until how.

She took it from him and wiped her hand carefully. 'Mind if I keep this? Sort of a souvenir?'

'Not at all.'

He sat up and zipped up, and they looked into each other's faces in the fading light. And she laughed at him.

'What?'

'You just look so damn surprised, is all.'

'I just guess I am.'

'Do you think I'm bad, Hayden?'

'No. Not at all. Not in the least.'

'I am, though. I am bad.'

'Oh. Well. But . . . that's good, though.'

'You mean even when I'm bad I'm good?'

'Especially then.'

And this time they both laughed, together. And it struck Hayden that maybe this was being alive, like everybody keeps talking about. And that next time would go better.

'Walk me home,' she said.

By the time they got back to the road it was almost too dark to navigate. He knew his father wanted both boys home before dark but he couldn't bring himself to care just now. They walked in silence.

Hayden wanted to talk, but had no idea about what. He wanted her to take his hand again, but she didn't. And he wasn't sure that was something he should initiate. So he practiced and practiced what he'd say when he got her home.

She stopped him at the walk up to her house. He wanted to walk her right to the door, but she wouldn't let him.

'I thought maybe next weekend—'

'It's been fun, Hayden. Let's not get complicated.'

'What do you mean, complicated?'

'You know. Complicated.'

'I just want to see you again.'

'That's what gets complicated. You see a boy a couple of times, he thinks he owns you.'

'I just want to see you.'

'You'll see me. You'll see me in Bible studies.'

And she pecked his cheek and rushed up the path and into the house. And Hayden just stood there, alone. Listened to crickets and looked up to see the stars out, very bright, and decided he had better get himself home.

His father leaned on the porch rail with a wide leather belt in his right hand, smoking with his left. Hayden watched him as he approached. Watched moths bat around the yellowish porch light. His father had never struck him, but he didn't doubt this would be the night. And he didn't care. In fact, he welcomed it.

He climbed the stairs steadily, and stood facing his father.

'Where's Daniel?'

'I don't know, sir.'

'I see. It's after dark.'

'I thought he went riding with you.'

'He did. Then he left the house at five. Said he had a plan to meet you. Did he meet you?'

'No, sir, I'm afraid I got tied up.'

'Your momma says you had a date.'

'It wasn't exactly a date, sir.'

'I knew that was too good to be true. You go on up to your room. I'll handle Daniel.'

'Yes sir.'

'Wait. Before you go. You sass your teacher in Bible class today?'

'No sir, I did not.'

'He says you did.'

'I didn't understand something. And I didn't lie about it. But I didn't say anything disrespectful. Sir.'

And he watched his father roll that around behind his eyes, and thought about Daniel, and said a prayer he didn't go out to the tower alone, didn't go up alone. But maybe he shouldn't be praying right now, after the events of the day. Might take a while to get back in

God's good graces. And he felt sure Daniel was okay, of course he was okay, but still he'd feel better when he showed his little squirt face just for good measure.

'I suppose you got a right to speak your mind, if you don't say it disrespectful.'

'That's what I thought.' His back felt straight, and it struck him that he was looking his father in the eye.

'I see a little something different in you, boy.'

'That could be.'

'It's a long time overdue.'

'It *was* a date. Actually.'

'Well, good for you, then. Only it don't get you off the hook losing your brother. You best hope he gets back in one piece. And that I let him stay that way. Now you got church in the morning, so get some sleep.'

Hayden lay in bed for two hours, alone in their room. Then he crossed to the window, looked out over the porch, and saw his father asleep on the porch swing in the yellowish light, the belt dropped by his big wing-tip shoe. And went back to bed.

And decided Daniel must've gone up that tower, but late. Too late. After waiting too long. And gotten himself stuck up there in the dark, which served him right. Let him sit up there shivering until morning. Put the fear of God into the little fool. Last time he'd go near that tower ever again.

He rolled over and tried for sleep, knowing Daniel would come crawling home in the morning.

In the morning Hayden lay awake with his eyes shut tight, thinking, He might not be over there, but that's okay. It's okay if he's not. Because it's early yet, it's a long walk home from that tower and he just might not have made it yet, that's all.

Then he opened his eyes. Daniel's bed still lay empty, neatly made, but that was okay.

When he got downstairs to the breakfast table, they seemed to be butting heads over it. He could hear them before he even got into the kitchen. Could hear his father say, 'Shoot, every boy runs away from home one time or another, don't mean a thing.'

He stepped into the kitchen. His father sat at the table, looking disheveled in the same clothes from the night before. Hayden walked over to the window and looked as far as he could up the road, hoping. Then he sat down to eat.

'Daniel has no reason to run away. How many eggs, honey?'

'I'm not hungry, Mom.'

'Nonsense. You're a growing boy. I'll make you two.'

'Boys come up with reasons, Lucy. It's too soon to call.'

'Won't hurt to have the sheriff keep an eye out.'

'It's too soon. Sheriff'll laugh, is what he'll do. Say, "Shoot, that boy'll just stay away long enough to give you a good scare." And he'd be right, too.'

That's when it hit Hayden, the way things hit unexpectedly, what had probably happened. And it made so much sense. Daniel was staying away to scare him. To punish him for not showing up. Of course.

He looked at his father's face. Unshaven. His eyes red.

His father looked back. 'What're you lookin' at?' he said.

And Hayden didn't look away. Didn't answer and didn't look away. And then a moment later his father looked down at the table, and Hayden knew something that he had never known before, but that he could not quite put words to at the time.

His mother set two runny fried eggs in front of him, and white toast with too much butter. Runny fried eggs made him gag, so he put one forkful at a time onto the toast and ate them together, as fast as possible. And none of it tasted like anything. Might just as well have been eating plastic.

'If he isn't back by dark, maybe,' his father said.

His mother turned from the stove, hands on her hips. 'What do *you* think, Hayden, about this Daniel situation?'

A flash of the events of the evening before snuck

in unbidden, and he looked past his mother out the window, wishing he'd looked down while it was happening, so as to have some kind of mental image of it, burned in. Because the way it was, he might just have dreamed up the whole thing. In the light of morning it felt like something dreamed.

'I have to go with Dad on this. He's just trying to give us a good scare.'

Hayden's father's arms rose, sailed out wide and slow, like to encompass the world or lead a symphony, like what Hayden had to say just proved the whole thing beyond doubt. 'There, now, Lucy. You see? Your levelheaded son here . . . who don't *never* agree with me . . . agrees with me on this.'

'I guess we could give it a little more time,' she said, and turned back to the stove.

Mrs Cash, the Sunday-morning after-church Bible studies teacher, was not only nicer than Nellis but gave shorter assignments.

'Now, you were all supposed to read Jonah this week,' she said, her face still buried in her attendance roll. 'Did everybody read it? Hayden, where is your brother, Daniel, today?'

'Absent, ma'am.'

'Well, I can see that. Do your parents know he's absent?'

'Yes ma'am.'

'Are you okay, Hayden?'

'Yes ma'am. Why?'

'I don't know. You just look kinda funny. Okay. No Daniel Reese. And no Cheryl Wilkerson.'

Hayden looked at the back of her empty seat. Maybe she couldn't face him. Or maybe it had nothing to do with him. But it didn't feel that way. But maybe it was okay, she was absent, because maybe he couldn't face her either.

'God tells Jonah to go to Nineveh,' Mrs Cash said. 'Now. Does Jonah go to Nineveh? Larry.'

'No ma'am.'

'Where does he go?'

'He tries to go to Tarshish. He gets on a ship for there.'

'So, God tells him to go one place and he goes another.'

Hayden looked over at Daniel's empty seat and decided he should leave, right now. Go out there and see. Walk down that road and see . . . what? No Daniel, so no answer. Or—

'Hayden.'

'Yes ma'am?'

'What happens when the storm gets out of control?'

'Jonah is cast into the sea.'

'Are you sure you're all right, Hayden?'

'May I be excused for just a minute?'

'Yes, you may. And what happens to Jonah after he is thrown into the sea?' Hayden heard her say as he pushed through the door, swung down the hall. Shoot, everybody knows that. He is swallowed into the belly of a great fish.

At the end of the hall was a small booth with a nickel pay phone, with accordion glass-paned wood doors. Hayden stepped inside, snugged the doors tight behind him, dug in his pocket for the change from last night's date, and called.

'Deputy Ray Conner speaking.'

Hayden pulled a deep, audible breath of relief. Somebody he knew. Thank God. Somebody he could talk to, like Ray. So he didn't have to hang up and go do this himself.

'Ray? This is Hayden Reese.'

'How you doin', son? What can I help you for?'

'You know my brother, Daniel.'

'I do.'

'I know I'm wrong about this. I just know it, Ray. But maybe you could just check . . .'

'Something happen to him?'

'Well, he never came home last night. And I know I'm wrong . . . I know it's stupid . . .'

'Say what you got to say, son.'

'He was talking about scaling up that electrical tower.'

'Which one?'

'The one two miles down the road, due east of our house. I told him not to do it. I didn't think he'd really do it.'

'You did right, telling me. I'll take a ride over. I won't find nothing, but just to be safe.'

'I appreciate it, Ray. Could you maybe let me know?'

'Where can I call you back?'

'That's a little tricky. I got to get back to Bible class.'

'Tell you what I'll do. Take me a ride by there, and when I see everything's fine, I'll cruise on by the church, honk my horn two short ones. Twenty minutes.'

'I appreciate this, Ray. And just one other thing—'

'Nobody gotta know we talked. I just happened to take me a ride out there.'

'Thanks, Ray. I feel much better already.'

'And Jonah is exceedingly angry.' Hayden looked up into Mrs Cash's face as she spoke. 'Why is that? What does he say to the Lord?' She hadn't said Hayden's name specifically, but she was looking right into his eyes.

'Jonah says, "Was this not my saying, when I was yet in my country?"'

'Very good, Hayden.'

He looked up at the clock again. It had been more than twenty minutes. A lot more. Maybe he couldn't hear a beep from here. He should leave right now. Go home. No, he shouldn't. Because Ray would come by and beep, and he wouldn't hear, and because his parents would want to know why he was home. He would have to sit still somehow, sit here and try his best to listen.

'"And God spake unto Jonah, and He said, 'Doest thou well to be angry?'" What does that mean, everybody? Does anybody know what that means?' Silence. 'I bet Hayden knows.'

'I think it means, are you sure you're doing the best thing?'

'And was he sure? What did he say?'

'He said, "I do well to be angry, even unto death."'

'Very good. Nice to know *someone* is paying attention.'

When he got home, he found three sheriffs' black-and-whites on the dirt in their front yard. One still had its lights flashing around silently. And the doctor's old station wagon was parked across the street, which seemed like a good sign, because the doctor comes when people are sick or hurt. So maybe Daniel only got himself hurt. He listened to the sound of his own heels on the porch steps. Walked into the living room to find three deputies and his father.

'Why is the doctor here?' he said.

His father wouldn't look at him, or answer, just sat on the couch with Daniel's mountain climbing hook in his hands, rolling it over and over, watching it roll.

Ray came over and put a hand on Hayden's shoulder. 'The doc came by to help your mother. He's upstairs with her now. Just gave her a mild sedative, is all.'

And all Hayden's stories he'd told himself, how Daniel only hurt himself, only got stuck up there, only stayed away to punish and scare him, they all just dried up and blew away, leaving a dust bowl inside that he could barely feel.

Ray gave his shoulder a squeeze and said, 'How 'bout we give the boy a minute alone with his father?' And the deputies filed outside, meeting his eyes one by one, holding these tight, sad little smiles with their lips.

Hayden sat down on the couch next to his father.

His father threw the hook onto the coffee table, where it slid and scratched the finish, and he sat with both hands on his thighs. And Hayden sat there next to him, and neither said a word. They just stared at that hook, and at the scratch. And Hayden thought he knew something, how a torch could be passed some-times, and therefore just because his father had never struck him before didn't mean he wouldn't from now on.

And just on that thought he felt a slap at the back

of his neck. His father's big hand. It stung, but not nearly the way he expected it to. And the hand stayed there, and squeezed hard at the base of his neck, like his father was trying to choke the life out of him, only from the wrong side.

He glanced over and saw his father pinching the bridge of his nose with the other hand, like trying to keep something in, and when he pulled the hand down from his face Hayden saw his eyes were wet. Those big blue-green eyes that made boys and women quake for such different reasons, all red rimmed and wet with tears. Only then did Hayden realize that his father's grasp had been intended as a gesture of affection.

Hayden got to his feet, and stood facing him, looking down, watching his father cry. And thought, You son of a bitch. You hypocritical son of a bitch. You taught us so we can't ever forget, and you can't even do it yourself. And he thought, I don't have to cry. I can get through this dry. I'm stronger than you. He didn't say it out loud. He didn't have to. His father's eyes came up, and they exchanged a look, and Hayden knew he didn't have to say it. He walked out of that living room knowing the torch had been passed in a strange and different way, one he never would have expected.

When he got out onto the front porch he overheard a scrap of conversation on the part of the three deputies, now clustered between the cars. Heard one say he'd been talking to Jimmy from the rescue team, and Jimmy said that voltage hit the poor kid so hard it blew his clothes off, and blew the pennies right out of his pockets and welded them onto the steel of that tower, can you imagine such a thing? And Ray, who was standing facing Hayden, looked up and saw him there and told the other guy to shut up.

Hayden sat on the porch steps and Ray came over and sat beside him. For a minute everybody kept silent, and then the two other deputies packed it up and drove away.

'I mighta been wrong to bring that hook back here.'

'What happened to the rope, Ray?'

'Well, now, Hayden, I think if you was to know that, you'd find out you really didn't want to know.'

'That was a joke about the pennies, right? Nothing's that strong. Nothing could do that. Right, Ray?'

'I'm thinking, son, that you might do well not to dwell too heavy on the particulars. You okay here with your dad?'

'Yeah, I am.'

Ray put a hand on the top of Hayden's head and rubbed it back and forth a bit, and then he got up and drove away.

Hayden heard footsteps behind him, and it was the doctor on his way out.

'I'm sorry about your brother,' he said.

Hayden nodded. Then he got up and set off down the road.

Eli caught up with him just a quarter mile out. 'Holy shit, Hayden, I just now heard. Where're you going? I can't believe it. Is it true? Hayden? Where are you going?'

'I have to go see,' Hayden said.

And they walked together half a mile.

'He's not still out there, right?'

'No, I doubt that.'

'Then what do you have to go see?'

'I heard that electricity hit so hard it blew the pennies right out of his pockets and welded them to the tower.'

'Shit. That can't be true.'

'I have to go see.'

'Can I come?'

'I don't care what you do, Eli. I just have to go see.'

They found the site oddly deserted. Stood in the dirt at the base of the tower. Hayden bent down and picked up something he saw in the dirt at his feet. A little scrap of blackened cloth. Couldn't even tell if it was jeans or T-shirt fabric. It crumbled in his fingers when he held it, leaving a dark smudge.

'You're not going up. Right, Hayden?'

'I'm not a coward.'

'I believe you, Hayden. Don't do it.'

'Wait here.'

'I'll never call you a coward again. I'm sorry. Hayden?'

Eli's voice sounded farther away. Hayden did not look down. Just concentrated on handholds and footholds. He should have changed into sneakers, but no use to worry about it now. *I am not a coward.* He wondered how high he would have to go. The buzz of the power lines got clearer, higher up. *Make sure you got a good hold on that next slat before you pull yourself up by it. That's all you've got to think about now. Don't look down.*

He climbed two, three minutes, thoughtless.

He stopped briefly at the big crossbeam. Waited, rested. Breathed. Set off again, never looking down. Not even thinking how far he'd gone, how far he'd have to go. *Get a good hold first. Test that foothold. Don't look down.*

Then he pulled himself up and saw something different in the metal, a kind of blackening, like a fire had blown by here. *I am not a coward.* And he froze and listened to the song of the power lines and wondered if that made this the danger zone. He reached up one more time, pulled up, and right in front of his nose, five of them. Clearly once melted, their edges blurred like rehardened candle wax. And one was shiny as all hell, brand-new copper, heads out, 1960D, and it hit him like high voltage that something really is that strong, and he was close enough to touch it. His arm muscles felt strange and runny and he looked down.

And then he heard a noise. Not a big noise. Maybe a crackle in the line, or a bird hitting it. Or just a branch of the big tree tapping the line in the wind. But it went through him like electricity, because he expected electricity. And he lost his hold and fell.

He could feel himself falling, feel it in his stomach, that dropping-away feeling like a roller-coaster, and it just seemed to go on and on, because he was up so high. When the big crossbeam shot by he reached out and grabbed for it, slapped his arms over it. It slowed him, pulled at his arms like it might tear them clean away from their sockets. Then the momentum pulled his hands right off the beam and he was falling again.

He hit the dirt on his feet, and felt the break in both legs at once, and fell over. And lay there for a second, stunned and awakened by the pain. And when he looked down, he saw that not only was the left broken clean but the bone had protruded through the skin and through his good Sunday pants, both. And he sat half up and looked at it, curious. Strangely white it seemed, and removed from him somehow. Nothing he could quite interpret.

So he just sat there for a moment, looking, feeling

the strangely clean intensity of the pain, distant, and listening to Eli go on and on about something, never catching whole words and sentences of his panic. And then he fell back in the dirt and misplaced the world for a time.

Daniel's service was held two days later, a closed casket ceremony, and Hayden didn't get to go. He had to lie in a hospital bed, with his right leg in a heavy plaster cast, his left pinned and elevated, unable to move much at all, having to call a nurse now and then for a bedpan. Twice a day they'd check the laceration on his leg, and on the day of the service they set a tube in to help it drain, and the doctor said maybe they'd stitch it up next week, when the worst threat of infection had passed.

Eli came to visit him after the service.

'How was it?' Hayden said.

Eli only shrugged, because what do you say about something like that? They sat without talking awhile, and then a pretty young nurse came in and gave Hayden his pain medication with a little cup of water.

'I'll never call you a coward again,' Eli said when she left. His voice glowed with awe. 'You didn't cry. You broke both your legs and sat there looking at that big old piece of bone sticking out and you didn't cry. I couldn't believe it.'

'How's my mom?'

'Okay, I guess. *She* cried.' Eli got up, moved to the door, and looked both ways to assure their privacy. Then he came back and leaned over the bed, 'Hayden, what did you see up there?'

And Hayden nodded. Took Eli by the collar and pulled him in close, to whisper.

'Pennies,' he said.

Chapter Five

1981
Forty Days and Forty Nights

On the seventh day Hayden picked up empty sandbags from the Fire Department in Sausalito after work. And then stood on the beach with a shovel, in his rubber boots and storm suit with the hood up, rain pouring down in sheets around him, drumming and spattering onto his slicker, running off the edge of his hood in front of his face.

He filled the bags one by one, and carried them on his shoulder back to the car, and stashed them in the backseat, watching the back tires tuck higher and higher up into the wheel wells, as though he had two or three big passengers back there.

Then he drove back up the hill to their tiny house, and placed them at angles around the basement window on the hillside, to divert water away.

It was so different, owning a house.

He had barely stripped out of his storm gear, leaving it hanging on a hook in the tile entryway, when Allegra arrived home. She threw the front door wide open and stood there on the covered porch, looking at him, miserable and wet like a cat in from the rain.

'This completely sucks,' she said.

She wore no raincoat, carried no umbrella. Wore no coat at all, in fact, and no hat. Her long straight hair had glued itself to her forehead, and water dripped off her nose, ran off her eyebrows and into her eyes. Her clothing seemed plastered on, clinging to her thin frame, and she shivered slightly.

'Allegra,' he said, and pulled her in and closed the door behind her. 'Why didn't you take an umbrella?'

It wasn't as if no one had predicted rain. It had barely stopped all week.

'Dad,' she said. Just one simple word, conveying his obvious ignorance and her strained ability to tolerate it. 'Nobody in junior high carries an umbrella.'

'You could have worn your slicker.'

'It's dorky looking.'

'I can't believe your mother let you out of the house like that this morning.'

'She was gone already.'

'That explains a lot.'

'Daddy?' she said, suddenly younger than junior high again. 'Will you make hot chocolate?'

'If you'll go take a hot bath and get into dry clothes.'

'Deal. Play you a game,' she said on her way down the hall to her room.

Or two or three games, Hayden thought. Judith had three possible deliveries tonight. They'd likely have plenty of time to kill.

'You're in check,' Hayden said.

'Not again.'

'Sorry.'

They sat on opposite sides of the little chess table, which Hayden had pulled close to the fireplace. The fire, which he'd started while she bathed, had just begun to take hold.

Over her shoulder he could look through the sliding glass doors onto the upper patio, where rain sheeted off the eaves, splattered in puddles on the wood decking. If he looked just right, on the right day, from the right spot, he could see a sliver view of the bay from their upper patio. But today there was only rain, gray sheets clogging the air to infinity, not as far off as infinity used to be. The whole world gray.

'Maybe California dropped off into the ocean,' Allegra said.

'They probably would have mentioned that on the news.'

The steady pounding of the rain on the roof provided the only background noise.

Allegra moved her bishop to block the check.

'Can't do that, honey.'

'Why not?'

'Because of her,' he said, and tapped the top of his queen. Poised also for check, with only that bishop for a barrier.

'Maybe it's checkmate.'

'It's not.'

'Well, I don't see what I can do.'

'That's because you're rushing. Take a minute to think.'

'If I can't figure it out, will you tell me?'

'If you want me to. You always tell me not to help.'

'I just don't want you to let me win.'

'I never let you win. I have far too much respect for you.'

'That must be why I never win.'

'You won once.'

'Once.'

'That's where it starts.'

'Oh, I see it,' she said. She slid her rook over, all the way from the end of the board into the fray, and blocked the check. 'That fire's starting to feel good.'

She took a long sip of hot chocolate while Hayden thought out his next move. 'Is Mom coming home for dinner?'

'I doubt it. She's got three on the way.'

'They couldn't all go into labor on the same night.'

'They could.'

'Well, they could. But I hope they don't. I never get to see her.'

'Maybe tonight we'll get lucky.'

After Allegra had gone to bed, Hayden sat up and watched the eleven o'clock news. The weather forecast called for more rain. Another in a long series of storms lined up like planes on a foggy runway, waiting to move down from the northwest. Waiting their turn to torment the Bay Area. Lots more flooding was expected in low-lying areas.

At eleven thirty he gave up and went to bed alone.

Judith came in at midnight, waking him. She set her beeper down on the bedside table, stripped off her clothes, and threw them on the chair beside the bed, trailing onto the floor, where they would stay until he picked them up and put them in the hamper. She crawled in with him, naked, up against his back. He rolled over to greet her. She kissed his neck and ran her fingers through the hair on his chest.

'I made chicken cacciatore,' he said. 'There's plenty left over in the fridge if you're hungry."

'You know I love your chicken cacciatore,' she said. 'But that's not what I'm hungry for right now.'

'Are we feeling uncharacteristically frisky for a woman who just delivered three babies?'

'Two. But one got complicated.'

'Turn out all right?'

'Yes.'

'Thank God.'

For the sake of the parents, and for his sake. If she had said she'd lost one tonight, this moment would have been ruined. He would have just rolled over and tried, but failed, to sleep.

He felt her hands at the elastic waistband of his pajama bottoms, and he lifted his hip off the bed to allow her to pull them down. His hands explored her back as if in unfamiliar territory.

'To what do I owe this unexpected energy? Not that I'm complaining.'

'I just love you, is all.'

'I couldn't be happier to hear it.'

She kissed him, their mouths fitting perfectly, practiced and comfortable. Then she pulled her head back and looked into his eyes. He wondered what, if anything, she could see in this lighting. No moon tonight, just rain. He could hear it drumming on the roof over their heads, barely see the movement of it through the window, the constant downward sheets. He could feel her breasts pressed against his chest. Her skin felt cool. He could feel the necklace. That same silly little gold-and-opal necklace. It wasn't even pure gold, just gold filled, and the plating had worn off in places. He'd told her years ago she could take it off now. They could afford something nicer. But she never had.

'Something I probably should tell you first,' she said.

'It can wait.'

'Not really.'

'I hope this is not something that might kill the mood. Can't it wait? No, I take it back. Nothing can kill this mood. Go ahead and tell me.'

'I stopped taking the pill.'

Hayden rolled over onto his back, propped his head up on his intertwined hands. His eyes had begun to adjust to the dark. He could see the slight pattern of their textured ceiling. 'Well, congratulations. And here I thought nothing could kill that mood.'

'I'm really sorry you feel that way. It seemed like such a good idea to me.'

'Why would you stop taking the pill?'

'I want to get pregnant again. I was hoping by now you'd like the idea.'

'I don't.'

'So I noticed.'

Hayden sat up, swung his legs over the side of the bed, pulled his pajama bottoms up again, and sat facing away from her, vaguely cold but not quite motivated to fix it.

'I can't go through that again,' he said.

'Ten years is a long time to adjust to something.'

'Depends on the thing, I guess.'

He heard and felt her rustle around behind him, felt her slide over and drape herself across his back.

'I guess I've gotten to thinking that if we wait much longer it won't be as safe.'

'When was it ever safe?'

'If we wait until our late thirties the risks go up some.'

'I don't want one then, either, Judith.'

'But I do.'

'Then I guess we have a problem.'

Her soft skin disappeared from his back, and Hayden noticed he didn't feel any more alone without it. Couldn't feel any more alone.

'I'm not going back on the pill,' she said, from her side of the bed. 'They're starting to gather some negative thoughts now on long-term health risks.'

'Then you shouldn't.'

'Thank you for looking at it that way.'

'I'll get that vasectomy.'

'Please don't, Hayden. Please just think about this.'

Think about it. There's an original idea, he thought. What do you suppose I've had on my mind the last decade or so, Judith? Do you suppose I was only waiting for you to bring it up first? That I never thought to consider it until just this moment?

'I can't go through that again,' he said. And stood.

'But, honey—'

'You're not listening to me, Judith. You're not hearing what I'm saying. I'm not saying I'd rather not. Or I don't want to. I'm saying I can't.'

And because he didn't know what else to do, he walked to the sliding glass door and looked out across the patio into the sheeting rain. And then slid the door open and stepped out.

At first he stood under the eaves, but the rain blew sideways and soaked him, and then, soaked to the skin and cold anyway, he just stepped out and sat in it, on a hard wooden deck chair. Tipped his head back and watched it come straight down in the dark, gusts of wind occasionally bending it on its way.

In a few minutes the cold seemed like less of a problem, and he seemed to lose his motivation to go inside and get dry.

'What have you and Allegra been doing all evening?' Judith's voice from just inside the door.

'Building an ark.'

'Well, that's appropriate. Can we at least talk?'

'Can we? Or may we?'

The door slid shut again.

'Hayden? Are you asleep?'

'No.'

The glowing green dial of the clock said 2 A.M. He'd need to be up in less than three hours.

'Are you ever going back to school?'

'What a strange question.'

'Why is it strange?'

He rolled onto his back and threw one arm out, and she tucked in on top of it, her head on his shoulder. He wrapped the arm around her, brushed her hair back with his other hand. It was shorter now, her hair. For a week or so. And that had been an adjustment for him.

'I'm starting to like it,' he said.

'Like what?'

'Your hair.'

'Oh. Good. So, you just changed your mind about being a doctor.'

'Judith . . .'

'What?'

'I changed my mind about being a doctor *ten years* ago. You've been meaning to ask me all this time? And you just now got around to it?'

'I'm not always sure what I can say to you.'

'You can say anything to me.'

'There's a lot we don't talk about.'

'That doesn't mean you couldn't.'

'I just did. I asked if you were ever going back to school.'

'No.'

'Never.'

'No.'

'So, what are you going to do?'

'What do you mean, what am I going to do? What have I been doing all this time, nothing? I'm working full-time. We got you through med school. I make enough to cover the mortgage. I'm home in time to look after Allegra. We have health coverage.'

'So, you're happy right where you are.'

'Are you ashamed of what I do?'

'Of course not.'

'Are you sure?'

A slight pause. 'Yes. It's just—'

'You had your heart set on "my husband the doctor."'

'Not that, exactly.'

'What then? Whatever it is, just say it. Please. This is making me nervous.'

He felt the thin fingers of her left hand stroking across his arm. The slight coolness of her ring.

'I feel like your life slipped off track ten years ago, and I keep waiting for you to get it back on track again. And now I'm beginning to think you never will.'

Hayden jumped out of bed. All in one motion, right out from under her, half throwing her out of the way with his momentum.

'Did you ever notice, Judith,' he said, pacing at the foot of their bed, 'that we spend a lot of time saying, "In the last ten years," and, "Ten years ago," and we never say what we really mean, which is, "Since our only son died"?'

In the dim he could see her sitting up in bed, still naked, watching him pace.

'Okay. Since our only son died, you seem to have lost your direction.'

'So now I'm just going nowhere.'

'I didn't say that.'

'Who would be raising our daughter at this stage in your career if I wasn't here to do it?'

'All I'm saying is—'

'Right, the bottom line, that's what I'm waiting for.'

'All I'm saying is, you used to want so much for yourself. And now it doesn't seem like you do. I don't know what you want anymore.'

He stood still at the end of the bed and heard a shy little knock at the bedroom door. He slipped into his robe and opened the door for her.

'Daddy, I can't sleep.'

'I'm sorry if we were too loud, honey. Come on. Let's get you back to bed.'

'What are you two fighting about?'

'We're not fighting,' Judith said.

'Don't tell her that.' The vehemence in Hayden's voice surprised even him. Allegra backed up a step. 'Never tell a kid that what they see with their own eyes or hear with their own ears isn't really there. It makes them feel crazy.'

'I'm sorry,' Judith said.

'Come on, Allegra,' he said, and they walked down the hall to her room together.

'Daddy, I'm too old to tuck in.'

'Nobody's too old to tuck in.'

'I guess.' She scrambled in under the covers and Hayden sat on the edge of the bed and brushed her hair back out of her eyes. 'So, what were you fighting about?'

'Your mother wants to have another baby and I don't. And also, she thinks I should still be a doctor.'

'I didn't know you were gonna be a doctor.'

'Well, you were pretty little when I changed my mind.'

'Why did you change your mind?'

'It's too big a responsibility. I don't want to be in charge of people living or dying.'

'You could just do what Mom does. That's not living or dying. It's just babies getting born.'

'That can be living or dying sometimes.'

'Do you like being a janitor?'

'No. Not really. I'd like to get a job doing something nicer. But it got your mom through med school. And it gets me home with you in the afternoons. And we can't afford to give up that health coverage right now.'

'Would you be a doctor if we could afford it?'

'No.'

'Then I don't think you should be.'

'Thank you.'

'And I don't think you guys should have another baby.'

'You don't?'

'No. I think you should spend all your money on me.'

Hayden smiled and kissed her on the forehead. 'I'm going back to bed now. Think you can sleep?'

'I guess so. Dad? Thanks for telling me what's going on.'

'I think that's how this is supposed to work, kiddo.'

Even though nobody else seems to do it that way, he thought on the walk back down the hall.

He shook off his robe and climbed in with Judith. They lay together without speaking for a few minutes.

Then Hayden said, 'I want my family to be

indestructible. I want to live forever. I want to make love, like we were just about to, before everything got all screwed up. Those are my goals for right now, Judith.'

'I don't think I can help you with those first two, but we can still make love.'

'Without you getting pregnant.'

'I'm sure we can think of something.'

Then he just had time for a quick two-hour nap before work.

When the alarm sounded at four forty-five, he lay still and listened to the rain on the roof of their tiny house, and looked out through the glass patio door and watched it come down in sheets.

'It's never going to end,' he said.

'Everything ends sooner or later.'

'Maybe not this time. This time we're all just going to wash away. Or float away. It's never going to end.'

'Everything ends,' she said.

'I just want to take care of you and Allegra. I'm sorry if I'm not doing a good enough job.'

'You are, Hayden. You're doing a great job. I'm just not sure you're taking such good care of yourself.'

'I have to go to work.'

'Okay. I'll be late again tonight.'

'I know.'

Chapter Six ⚡

Say It Like You Mean It

'Please don't embarrass me, Dad.'

'I'm not going to embarrass you. I just think he should pick you up here.'

'Why?'

'Because it's good manners. It shows he respects you.'

'If he has to come in and meet you I'm going to be so humiliated.'

'Okay, then he doesn't have to come in. But he should come by here and pick you up.'

'I have to go get ready.'

'Okay, go.'

Hayden cleared the dinner table. Made up a plate for Judith and left it in front of the brand-new microwave oven, noting the time, reminding himself to refrigerate it if she wasn't home in three hours.

He looked over the sink, out the window, as he washed and dried the dinner dishes, and wished he knew less about the mind of a sixteen-year-old boy.

And that was another thing. The boy was too old for Allegra anyway, who was barely fifteen.

And what was a sixteen-year-old boy with no steady job doing owning his own car, anyway? Parents gave their kids too much, he felt, especially here in Sausalito. No chance to learn to work for a thing, so it would mean something. So that things mattered, having been hard earned.

But he hadn't said any of this to Allegra, because it was her first date, and she was so excited and happy, and amazed that this popular older boy would show an interest in her. Because she didn't know how beautiful she was. And he couldn't ruin this moment for her.

But he had to worry. It was his job. And he had to tell her something. That was his job, too.

This is a hard job, he decided.

When she finally came down the stairs, Hayden held his breath and stared.

She'd put her hair up in back, loose and swirling, and she wore a snug red sweater off her shoulders, her fine, thin white shoulders. And a longish straight skirt and high heels. She did not look like anybody's child. She looked so much like Judith it hurt to look at her, but he did anyway.

'Close your mouth, Dad. I called him. He's going to come by and honk.'

'Good. I want you to take this,' he said, and tucked a ten-dollar bill in her hand.

'Dad. The guy pays for everything.'

'It's called mad money.'

'I'm not going to get mad.'

'Just for emergencies.'

'I'm not carrying a purse.'

'Maybe tuck it in your sleeve or something.'

'This is so dumb,' she said, and folded the bill into a tiny square and slipped it into her bra. Which embarrassed him for reasons he couldn't quite pin down.

'Now.' He held two shiny new dimes on his flat open palm.

'For what? I've got ten dollars.'

'You can't make a phone call with a ten-dollar bill.'

Allegra sighed, rolled her eyes, took the dimes, and slipped them into her shoe. 'It's not very comfortable.'

'I'll feel better.'

'Oh, right, I forgot. Put on a sweater, your father is cold. Step on this all night, I'll be a lot more comfortable.'

'I'm glad you understand,' he said, and kissed her on the forehead. 'I wish your mother was here to see you.'

'Promise me you won't take my picture.'

Those were going to be the next words out of his mouth. Stand right there, I have to get the camera.

'I would never do such a thing,' he said.

Paul Littlefield, Hayden said to himself as she ran down the front walk to his car. A sports car. A 240Z, which seemed excessive as a parental gift, and not the kind of vehicle you want your daughter riding in, but he couldn't fix that now. Paul Littlefield. TJZ056. If she wasn't back by ten, at least he should know the name of the boy, the license number of the car. Any good father would know that much.

He stood at the window and watched the car scream away from the curb, tires skidding. TJZ056.

Maybe a good father wouldn't have let her go out on a school night. At all. Maybe a good father would know what this boy looked like. Where he lived. Maybe he should stop torturing himself. Maybe he should pretend he could think about something else for a while.

But he didn't. He didn't even pretend.

At ten thirty-six the phone rang, and Hayden jumped, and tried to swallow, and his heart seemed to be right up there behind the lump in his throat, or maybe the lump *was* his heart and he'd better swallow it back down.

Don't be the police. Don't be the police. Don't be.

'Hello?'

'Daddy?'

'Thank God you're okay. Where are you?'

'In the city.' Her voice sounded funny.

'In San Francisco? Why did you go so far?' Then he regretted his choice of phrasing, his reflex to grill her straight off when he could simply offer assistance. Reassurance. 'Allegra, are you crying?'

'Will you come get me, Daddy? I lost that ten dollars.'

'Allegra. You sound like you're crying. Are you okay?'

'Please come get me, Daddy.'

'Of course. Tell me where you are. Of course.'

He found her standing on the corner, near the phone booth, a reasonably well-lighted corner, holding the top of her sweater closed with both hands, a black mess of wet mascara running down from both eyes. A child again, with a runny nose.

He jumped out, leaving the car double-parked, and went to her with his arms out, and she let him hold her. She rested her face against his shoulder, bleeding mascara onto his shirt, and he rocked her slightly back and forth.

He wanted to say, Daddy's here, but he knew it wouldn't sound right for a girl her age, so he just rocked her and said it over and over in his own head. Daddy's here. Daddy's here.

Daddy will protect you. Just for this moment, Daddy is able to protect you.

Daddy loves his Leggy.

'Are you okay, honey?'

She nodded against his shoulder. She was still crying. He could feel the sobs shake her shoulders, and he held her tighter.

'Thanks for coming to get me, Daddy.'

'I love you, honey, I'm glad you're okay.'

'I love you too, Daddy.'

She hadn't said that for the longest time. He knew she did, but she couldn't say it often anymore, because she was a big girl and it wasn't cool.

He held the car door open for her, and she climbed in. He pulled around the corner into an illegal parking space, and cut the engine and set the brake.

'Lock your door,' he said, and she did. 'What happened to your sweater?'

'Just a couple of the buttons got popped off, is all.'

'I know this is a hard thing for you to talk about, Allegra. I can't imagine talking to my mother about something like this, when I was your age. But if you could just tell me what happened. So I know what we need to do.'

Hayden noticed his hands shaking. Squeezed the

bottom of the steering wheel to steady them. She's okay, he said to himself, and prayed her story would not contradict him.

'Nothing happened, really. I just got scared.'

'Of what?'

'He wanted to go up into the Presidio and park. He said the view was pretty up there. I'm sorry, Daddy. I should've said no, I guess. I thought he just wanted to kiss. I just wanted to kiss. I'm sorry, Daddy.'

'You don't have to be sorry, Allegra. There's nothing wrong with wanting to kiss a boy. That's normal.'

'It is?'

'Of course it is.'

'Oh.'

'What happened up there?'

'He just started, like, trying to put his hands under my sweater. And up my skirt. And I kept telling him no. I kept saying, "That's enough. That's enough."'

'But he didn't stop?'

'No, he just kept saying stuff like, "What's wrong with you? Everybody does." So I started getting scared. So I just jumped out of the car. And I guess he got mad, because he drove off without me. And then I was gonna take a cab home, but then I looked in my bra and I guess that money got knocked out. Are you mad at me, Dad?'

'Of course not. You didn't do anything wrong.'

'Really?'

'I think you handled yourself well.'

'Can we go home now? I just really want to go home.'

'Sure. Of course.'

Hayden started the car and turned onto Lincoln, headed for the Golden Gate Bridge. Back home to Marin.

They drove without speaking, Hayden looking in his rearview mirror, back across the bay to the lights of the big city. His hands still shook, but his mind, his whole interior landscape, felt tranquil and smooth. Which meant he'd decided, beyond all turning back, what would need to happen next.

'Are all boys like that, Dad?'

'No. They all want the same thing. But some of them know what "That's enough" means. I want you to stay home from school tomorrow.'

'Why?'

'Just sleep in and take care of yourself. You need it.'

'Okay, Dad. If you'll write me a note.'

They rode most of the rest of the way in silence, only her sniffling breaking the still.

Just before he pulled into their driveway she said, 'I thought he liked me.'

'Maybe he does. Maybe he doesn't know how to treat the people he likes.'

*   *   *

Hayden stood on the high school campus with a tire iron in his fist, in the rear parking lot, the one marked for students, in front of a line of more than a dozen student-owned cars. Too many parents giving their kids too much.

The 240Z was parked right up against the concrete walkway at the rear of the school. Fire engine red, with shiny chrome, nearly brand new. TJZ056. He didn't even know what this boy looked like. But he knew how to find out.

He stepped up behind the infuriating vehicle and swung the tire iron twice, breaking out both taillights. Sharp red plastic littered the tarmac at his feet. He moved around to the front and smashed a headlight. That felt good.

He looked up to the building. Students had come to the windows to see. Good. Tell Paul. Tell him to get down here, quick. Some crazy man is out here smashing up his car.

He broke out the other headlight. That felt even better. So he shattered the windshield with three separate, satisfying blows, then hit it a few more times to scatter all that crumbled glass over the seats. He went around behind the car to break out the rear window.

His arm was raised, poised for one additional ounce of satisfaction, when he heard it.

'Hey!'

He looked up to see what he'd been waiting for. The boy. He just needed to wait one second, if he could, to be sure it was the right boy.

'Hey, what're you doing to my car? Are you crazy?'

'Paul Littlefield?'

'Yeah, who the hell are you? What're you doing to my car?'

Hayden laid the tire iron down at his feet. So no one would have to die here. As soon as he did, the boy came in close. Hayden grabbed him by the shirt and threw him back against his own car. Leaned into his face. Bent him back over the roof. For the first time, the boy had the smarts to look scared.

'Paul, do you know what it means when a girl says, "That's enough"?'

'Oh, shit. Is that what this is about?' He had his arms thrown wide, a gesture of surrender. A shock of light brown hair fell across one eye. His features seemed soft and unformed, a pasty baby face. 'She didn't exactly say it like she meant it, man.'

Hayden broke Paul's nose with his first punch. The boy's hands flew to his face, and he cried big unashamed tears, and blood ran down from his hands and stained his shirt.

'Shit, man.'

Hayden hit him again, a hard right to the jaw this

time. And it changed something inside him, in a good way. Something unlivable seemed to disperse, gradually, to become livable again.

'Is that enough, Paul? Or do you want some more of that?'

The boy's hands hovered in front of his face, a weak defense. 'That's enough, man.'

Hayden hit him again, hearing and feeling the satisfying crunch when Paul's jawbone gave. Then he slammed his fist hard into the boy's lean stomach. Hayden stepped back slightly, to allow Paul to double forward and vomit onto his own shoes.

'You know, Paul, you just didn't say that like you meant it.'

When Paul straightened up he looked briefly into Hayden's face, eyes full of a deeply satisfying fear. Then he tried to run. Hayden took hold of the back of his shirt, spun him around, hit him one last time. One last powerful shot to his left eye. The best shot he had in him. The one that would have to do.

The kid just teetered there for a moment, Hayden holding tight to the front of his bloody shirt. Then Hayden realized the only thing holding Paul upright was that handful of shirt. So he knew then that he'd done enough. It was a clean line, one he could live with. He had hurt the kid enough. He let go of the shirt and stepped away.

He expected Paul to crumple. Instead he stood strangely stiff, eyes wide but unfocused. Just hesitated, like something the wind is about to blow over, then fell back ramrod straight and landed with the back of his head on the concrete walkway.

Hayden looked up to see a crowd of teachers and students watching. More than a hundred. Many of whom he knew.

He looked down to see a pool of the boy's blood spreading on the concrete around his head.

On visiting day, Hayden lined up with twelve other orange-jumpsuited men. They filed silently into the visiting area, a long narrow room with shiny metal stools bolted to the floor, facing a Plexiglas window.

Hayden had never thought to question who his visitor would be. Never expected anyone but Judith. But when he sat down and looked through the glass, it wasn't Judith. It was her mother, Thea. And for some reason he felt even more ashamed.

He picked up the telephone from the partition wall on his left. 'Thea.'

'Are you well, Hayden?'

'As can be expected. How's Paul?'

'Not out of the woods yet. But they think he'll pull through. But they're worried now about brain damage. Permanent brain damage.'

'I didn't mean to hurt him that bad.'

'I know that, Hayden. Everybody knows. You had almost two hundred witnesses. They all say it was something about the way he fell. But it doesn't help much. Apparently when you beat somebody unconscious you're responsible for how they fall.'

Hayden nodded slightly. Chewed at the inside of his lip. 'Yeah. My attorney explained that to me at great length.'

'I'm sorry we couldn't afford somebody better.'

'Well, it's not worth losing the house over. He thinks we can plead it down to something reasonable.'

'Even with all the priors?'

'There aren't that many.'

'Four.'

'I thought it was three.'

'No, it's four. There was that church incident. And the man in the supermarket. And your last boss. And what was the other one? Oh, yes, that thing that happened in traffic.'

'I guess I forgot that one.'

'This won't be county jail time.'

'No. I know, I'm not looking forward to the pen, believe me.'

'Did the attorney say how long he thinks it might be?'

'He's thinking I could come up for parole in twenty-six months. If the kid doesn't die.'

'It doesn't look like he will.'

'Good. Then twenty-six months maybe.'

'I'll tell Judith.'

'Why didn't she come, Thea?'

Hayden had to wait an uncomfortably long time for his answer. He watched her face, but her eyes wouldn't meet his. He wished he could do this without the glass. That he could touch Thea's hand, or she could touch his shoulder. He wanted somebody to touch him.

'The boy's parents are suing you for damages, Hayden.'

'Oh.'

'They're going to take everything.'

'The house?'

'Of course, the house. Everything. Everything you two have worked for.'

'She's really upset, I take it.'

'That would be understating the case. And she doesn't want Allegra to ever have to come to a place like this. Not to mention a place like the penitentiary.'

'I'm not going to see Allegra for over two years? She'll be seventeen when I get out.'

'I'm sorry, Hayden. It's the way she feels.'

'That doesn't seem fair.'

'She wants to protect the girl. Just like you do.'

Hayden leaned his forehead onto one hand, a half-hearted attempt to cover his face. In preparation for something that might prove difficult to say.

'I wish you could have seen her, Thea. All dressed up to go off on her first date. She was so full of hope. Like that whole part of her life was just opening up. Because somebody liked her. She met a boy who liked her. She was just all lit up like a Christmas tree, Thea. I wish you could've been there. And then I go pick her up and she's standing on a street corner all alone, crying, with the buttons torn off her sweater. Standing there all alone, feeling completely used. Just used and put aside. I couldn't take it.'

'Oh, Hayden. Poor dear Hayden.' Thea put her hand against the glass. And it felt so loving to him, such a strangely affectionate gesture, and he loved her for it. He wanted to put his own hand up there to meet it, but, his muscles seemed frozen, and the whole moment made his stomach hurt. 'We all love you, Hayden. You know that. And nobody ever doubted your motives. It's just the method that gets a little out of hand. You're so angry, and Judith is hurt because you never take her into your confidence. She's been married to you for fifteen years and she doesn't even know what you're angry about.'

'Tell her I'm angry because people don't treat each other right.'

'That won't satisfy her.'

'No. I know it won't.'

'She feels like you never talk to her. She's so upset that you went ahead and had that vasectomy. I think she's more upset about that than the house.'

'It's my body, though. I mean, I would never tell her what to do with her body.'

'She felt you could've discussed it.'

'We did discuss it. We talked it to death. She's not mad because we didn't talk about it. She's mad because she couldn't talk me out of it.'

'Maybe so. But it hurt her.'

'What's going to happen to them, Thea? While I'm . . . away. If they lose the house?'

'Well, I'm sure Judith can afford an apartment. She makes a good living.'

'Eventually she's going to come see me. Right?'

'I would hope so.'

'I have to tell you something, Thea. I can't admit it in court but I have to tell somebody. About Paul. About the way he fell. When you beat somebody unconscious they go limp. His body went stiff.'

'Meaning what?'

'I don't know exactly.'

'What are you trying to tell me?'

'That I hurt him worse than I meant to. This kid was sixteen, Thea. He was skinny. I might have had a hundred pounds on him. I might have been almost twice his size. I hit him as hard as I could in the head. I don't know what I was thinking.'

'You're saying he had brain damage before his head hit the pavement.'

'I don't know. I'm not a doctor. As Judith keeps reminding me. I just know something was already wrong.' They sat still and quiet a moment on opposite sides of the glass. 'I had to admit that to somebody. Uh-oh. Our time's up already. Tell Judith I love her, okay?'

'She knows.'

'Tell her anyway.'

'I will.'

Nine days later Hayden was placed on a bus in chains. He stared out through the barred windows all the way to the state pen. La Casa Grande, the man in the next seat called it. He watched the drivers of neighboring cars avert their eyes.

He served the first five months of his time there learning to survive. Wondering at what point exactly he had let his life get away. Looking back, trying to pinpoint the moment.

He never quite succeeded in narrowing it down. The more he looked back on his life, the more it seemed like something that had never exactly belonged to him.

He spent the first five months of his time there without visitors of any kind.

Chapter Seven

Jonah Was Thrown

'You *have* been getting my letters. Haven't you?'

'I'm sorry I haven't written back. I've been busy. It's been hard, working and taking care of Allegra. And we had to move. I'm sorry.'

'But Thea's been giving you the letters.'

'Of course.'

They sat on opposite sides of a hard wooden table, in a drab gray room with twenty-four other hard wooden tables. A guard in each corner. He hated to be seen here, like this, and yet was so relieved she had finally come.

Maybe she was right about Allegra. Maybe this was no place for her. Maybe the shame he felt, sitting in front of her in his prison work shirt with a number on the pocket, maybe it would be amplified to an unbearable level if Allegra were here, hurting on his behalf.

But he missed her so much. Still, he didn't dare bring it up.

Judith had not yet looked him in the eye. Not once.

'Before you leave here today, give me your new address.'

'You've been working out,' she said.

And it made him self-conscious for some reason. His prison shirt was short-sleeved, and he saw his own arms the way she must see them. He'd bulked up some, yes. What else was there to do?

'I guess I have.'

'It makes me nervous.'

'Why?'

'You were strong enough before.'

'I never raised a hand to you.'

'I never said you did. I just said you were strong enough already.'

'Don't forget to give me your new address.'

'No.'

'No, you won't forget?'

'No, I'm not going to give you our new address. Hayden, I came here to tell you something. It's important. It's hard, okay? This is hard for me. Try to just listen. Don't say anything for a minute, okay?'

So he just shut down inside. Turned off all the lights and sat in the dark in himself, in that place where there's no further down to go. All the way at the bottom of that deep well, where you hope for nothing, so nobody can really hurt you or take anything away. 'I'm listening.'

'You told me once that when you were growing up, you had to take a lot of religious schooling.'

'Right.'

'Remember the story of Jonah?'

'Yes.'

It made his stomach hurt to remember it.

He'd worked with a man named Jonah once, and it made him sick, every time the name was spoken. Every time. And he knew if he thought hard about it he'd remember why, what that bad connection was. So he never thought hard about it. He just quit the job instead.

Now, when it came out of Judith's mouth, he resented her for using the Bible against him, and for choosing a chapter that could make him sick.

But he didn't say any of that. He just listened.

'Remember when he was on that ship? And everybody on it was going to die. But it was *his* fate. They were just along for the ride. It was his fate. It was his fight with God. So he volunteered to get off the ship. Remember that?'

'You should study the Bible before you throw it in my face, Judith.'

'I did. I read the story.'

Hayden picked at a spot on his jeans, a torn place, and decided he wasn't going to look at her face again. Not if she was going away. He never wanted to look at her face knowing he was seeing it for the last time.

He looked instead at a guard in the corner, who looked back suspiciously. Apparently that was inherently wrong, to look at the guard. Apparently the men look at their wives or girlfriends every moment they can. Five months here, and still so much to learn.

'You read it wrong,' he said. 'Jonah was thrown off that ship. He didn't volunteer.'

'No, he did, Hayden. I just read it. Yesterday. Thinking about coming here and talking to you. He said something like, "I know it's for my sake that this great tempest is upon you."'

'Judith, one of those verses is titled "He is thrown into the sea." Jonah did not jump. He was thrown.'

'Well, whatever, Hayden, the point is, he could see it was his fate, and he was bringing everybody else down with him.'

Hayden made the mistake of looking at her face then. Into her eyes, raised to his for the first time. They didn't look cold or hard. Not at all. But he knew his own did. And he knew his own eyes were an accurate reflection of him, of the land on the inside.

'So you've decided to move away and leave no forwarding address. Is that what you're saying?'

'We lost everything, Hayden. Everything we worked for. Fifteen years of work down the drain. And now I'm trying to build up some kind of life again, and I don't want to lose it all again. You're not a very safe person to take a boat trip with, Hayden.'

'What about Allegra?'

'That's where I'm asking your cooperation. I'm asking you to be something like Jonah.'

'I have a right to see her.'

'Legally, yes. And I'm sure you could track us down easily enough. But I'm asking you not to.'

'So you're throwing me out of your life.'

'I think I'm asking you to leave voluntarily.'

'What if she grows up and wants to see me?'

'That's up to her. But she's not grown now. She's at an impressionable age.'

'You'll tell her where to find me?'

'If she's an adult and she wants to find you, yes.'

'How will you know where I am?'

'If you let Thea know where you are, then we'll always know.'

'Are you sure about this, Judith?'

But when he asked that, she started to cry. He

298 CATHERINE RYAN HYDE

never looked up to see, but he could hear her. Crying.

The visiting period ended before she could say whether or not she was sure.

Standing in the lunch line, a twenty-year-old boy tried to elbow in front of Hayden. And that felt worth fighting over, which seemed an odd decision in retrospect because Hayden wasn't hungry and hadn't intended to eat.

Hayden dropped his lunch tray and knocked the young man down, and squeezed his throat until his face turned purple and his eyes bulged, and banged the guy's head again and again on the concrete floor, listening to inmates cheering and chanting in a circle around him, excited by the violence. All sounding supportive. All on his side. Even though they never had been before.

And he couldn't even remember, when he felt the stick strike the back of his neck, what had initially happened to start it. He just remembered looking up at the fluorescent light fixtures and being sprayed in the eyes with pepper spray, even though he wasn't trying to get up.

And being led away blind.

When he could finally see again, he found himself in a dark concrete room, about six feet square, with a concrete bench and a metal-ringed hole in the concrete floor that he assumed was intended as his toilet. No windows, and the inside of the door was lined with concrete.

Many hours later an eye-level slot in the door slid open, and light spilled in. Light. He'd forgotten to appreciate it all his life. A pair of eyes looked through the slot, and Hayden realized he couldn't remember what he'd been thinking about all that time. A dinner tray appeared in the slot at the bottom of the door, and Hayden thought he could smell liver. He wasn't hungry anyway.

The eye-level slot remained open for a moment, so Hayden stood in front of it, both hands on the door.

'I'd like to see a priest,' he said.

'Probably not.'

'Why not?'

'That's a privilege.' Arnie Masur. Hayden knew the guard by his voice. Knew he could do a lot worse than Arnie.

'Cigarettes are a privilege. Workouts are a privilege. I don't see a bunch of guys lining up to talk to a priest.'

'Well, I'll ask. But don't get your hopes up, Hayden.'

The door banged open. It may have been as long as two days later, but without light, without windows, Hayden found it hard to gauge.

Two guards stood waiting for him with chains.

They chained his hands to his waist, and his ankles to each other, and walked down the hall with him, one on either side, walking slow to accommodate his short steps.

He was led into a room something like an interrogation room, with a wooden table, a chair on either side. A barred window. The light made Hayden blink. Made him squint, but he liked it. He tried to memorize it, daylight, to remember later in the darkened box.

A cage comprised half the room. Not barred, but built of a heavy metal mesh, like welded wire, with a three-legged wooden stool the only amenity.

The guards placed him inside and closed the door with a heavy metallic clang, without bothering to remove the chains.

He sat alone and wondered how long he'd be here, and why, and how he was supposed to go to the bathroom if that need should arise.

About half an hour later the door opened and a priest came in, in a gray suit and clerical collar, with an overcoat draped on his arm. Fortyish, with a ring of rusty hair over his ears. Sad and tired looking.

He took a chair from beside the small wood table, pulled it close to the cage. The sound of the chair legs on linoleum hurt Hayden's ears, a screech like a scratched blackboard.

'I'm a Catholic priest,' he said. 'It was only when I got here and they gave me your records that I realized you're an Episcopalian. I didn't know that. I just knew somebody wanted to see me. They don't tell me much.'

'It doesn't matter,' Hayden said. 'Did you bring a Bible with you?'

'Yes.' He reached into the pocket of his overcoat and extracted it. White leather covered, with gold leaf at the page edges.

'Thank you for coming in to see me. Will you look up the book of Jonah?'

The priest opened the Bible. Lifted the front cover, flipped a few pages, and scanned down the contents page with one index finger. Which seemed odd to Hayden, who could have found it without looking it up.

'Here we go,' he said. 'What do you need to know?'

'I had a disagreement with someone. She tried to tell me that Jonah volunteered to get off that ship. I said they picked him up and threw him in. I want to know who was right. It's important to me.'

'I don't think either one of you is completely right or completely wrong. See, it says right here. Wait just a minute. Oh, here it is. Jonah, chapter one, verse twelve. "And he said unto them, 'Take me up, and cast me forth into the sea; so shall the sea be calm unto you: for I know that for my sake this great tempest is upon you."'

'But they threw him in, right? They picked him up and cast him into the sea. I learned that. I remember that.'

'Eventually they threw him in. But it was his idea. See, they cast lots. So they might know for whose cause this wickedness was upon them.'

'And when Jonah's came up, they threw him in. But you're saying he gave them his permission first.'

'Not only did he tell them to, but they didn't want to. Not at first. Wait, let me find this again. Oh, here it is. Jonah, chapter one, verse thirteen. "Nevertheless the men rowed hard to bring it to the land; but they could not: for the sea grew more and more tempestuous against them."'

'So they tried not to throw him overboard. Even when he said they should.'

'Correct.'

'So she was right.'

'Yes. But they did throw him. When they saw they would not survive any other way. What's this about, then? Did you just bring me out here to solve a bet or something? Or is something seriously wrong?'

Hayden leaned forward against the metal grating, feeling sick. It made him sick to talk about Jonah. And to talk about himself, which he might be about to.

'My wife came to see me. She says she wants me to be something like Jonah. To jump ship before we all drown.'

'Maybe you *should* be more like Jonah. Maybe everyone should.'

'You think she's right.'

'I don't know. I don't know anything about her. Or about you. Or the situation.'

'She's taken my teenage daughter and moved to a new place. She doesn't want to tell me where. And she doesn't want me to try to find out.'

'Do you plan to honor her wishes?'

'I don't know yet. I can't seem to make sense of the whole thing in my head.'

'Can you think of any good that might come of not honoring her wishes?'

'I can't predict the future, Father.'

'No, none of us can. But I understand this must be difficult for you.'

'We've been married fifteen years, Father.'

'A terrible adjustment for you.'

'I don't know where I'll go or what I'll do.'

'How much longer do you have to serve your sentence?'

'Twenty-one months minimum.'

'Then at least you have plenty of time to think.'

Hayden pressed his forehead to the metal grate, closed

his eyes. Blocked out the view of the priest's face, a face that hurt at least as much as it helped, if not more.

He wanted to talk to this man further, because when the priest left, they'd throw him back in that dark box. He didn't know for how long. They hadn't even told him how long. There's such a thing as too much time to think.

'After fifteen years she shouldn't throw me away so easily.'

'How do you know it was easy?'

'Well . . .'

'Did it seem easy for her?'

'No.'

'So it may have hurt her to do it.'

'But she did it.'

'She may have felt she had to. There are two different kinds of leaders, my friend. Two different ways to lead. Nobody really knows which kind they are until they're in battle and pinned down, and it's clear there will be losses. Say you're in battle and you have five men under you. And you care for them all. You want that no one should be lost. But you find you have to sacrifice one of your men.'

'No good leader sacrifices one of his men.'

'That might not be true. Without that sacrifice maybe everyone will die. That man and the others as well. Then what?'

'Nobody should be sacrificed.'

'Well, that's the kind of leader you are, then. You've identified yourself. Your empathy for that man is so great that you will die. And he will die anyway. And the others will be lost. Maybe your wife is the other kind. If she can save you, maybe she will. But if not, she won't die with you. What good would it do?'

'I don't know. I just know I wouldn't give up.'

'A lot of people won't. A lot of people will let a drowning loved one pull them under.'

I'm not drowning, Hayden wanted to say. But of course, he couldn't. The chains on his wrists and ankles wouldn't let him. The marks on his face from the metal grate would call him a liar.

'Jonah was an angry man,' Hayden said. 'As long as I'm being compared to him, I just thought I'd mention that.'

'He was angry about the gourd. When the gourd withered and died.'

'He was angry before the gourd. He was angry about everything. He was angry about God's decisions. He was angry at God.'

'And I believe God questions him about that.'

'He does. He says, "Doest thou well to be so angry?" He asks Jonah twice.'

'You know your Bible well.'

'Yes, Father. I was given no choice. Do you know

what Jonah said to God in reply? Without looking, I mean.'

The priest closed the Bible, sat with it on his knees. His overcoat had fallen onto the scuffed, dirty floor, but he didn't seem to notice.

'Without looking, I couldn't tell you verbatim. So, you tell me. What does Jonah say?'

'He says, "I do well to be angry, even unto death."'

'Ah. Yes. Well. Maybe you shouldn't be *too* much like Jonah, then.'

'I believe that lot's already been cast.'

The priest stood, picked up his overcoat, and moved toward the door.

'Father? Please don't go yet.'

'Was there something more?'

But Hayden couldn't answer. Couldn't tell the priest he was afraid to go back into the darkness. Afraid to be alone again. That he would rather be stabbed to death out in the prison yard in the sun than sit alone in that cool concrete box, in the dark, trying to find watermarks for time inside his own head. Alone with thoughts that would catch him and violate him and walk away remorseless.

The priest stood waiting at the door. Hayden shook his head.

He wanted to say God had abandoned him. That even though he didn't believe in God, he felt it was wrong of God to abandon him here. But he knew what the priest would say. The priest would say Hayden had abandoned God. And he would be right.

'Thank you for coming in, Father.'

'I wish you well.'

Seconds later the guards came and returned him to his confinement. Removed the chains, banged the steel and concrete door shut. Left him alone in the dark. A close, heavy dark, like the belly of a great fish.

Book Three

ONE FULCRUM MOMENT

Chapter One

1996
The Dead Guy in 219

Sometime, perhaps a few moments or a few weeks before he opened his eyes, Hayden lived a series of strange dreams.

He dreamed about water. A wall, a sea of it, roaring down a mountain, coming right at him.

He dreamed that he opened his eyes from a dream and saw Judith sitting next to his hospital bed. But in the way of dreams, she was only about thirty, as she had been when he'd seen her last. And when he opened his eyes and looked into hers she called him Daddy. So he closed his eyes again.

A moment or a week later he dreamed he was drowning in an ocean, a black, black sea, his eyes open to utter blackness, and a terrible heavy pain of no oxygen in his chest. Then he broke the surface, and sputtered, and coughed, and the pain was unchanged and un-changeable, and it was his. There was no waking from this pain.

He opened his eyes to a bright hospital room with three other beds, one of which was occupied, and a nurse who bent over to pick up something she'd dropped. When she stood again and met his eyes, Hayden knew he'd startled her.

'I'll get Dr Stanley,' she said, and hurried out.

When his coughing had subsided, Hayden felt tubes in his nose and throat. A strange ease in breathing, as if he barely had to try.

Hayden's roommate addressed him. The voice sounded like that of an older man, but it hurt too much to turn his head to see. 'Welcome back to the living,' the voice said.

As if it were a cause for celebration.

The familiar doctor came into his room at 9 A.M., in a white lab coat, and silvery hair, and tanned skin like well-worn leather giving way to white teeth and bright eyes. Very much alive. The woman who'd operated on him. Who'd said he wouldn't last forty-eight hours. He wondered how long it had been so far.

'Well,' she said, 'if it isn't the miracle man.'

'I scared that nurse,' Hayden said. Weak but clear.

'So I keep hearing.'

'I was never supposed to wake up.'

'Oh, I don't know if I'd put it quite like that.' She stood at his bedside, removed a small chrome penlight from her lab coat pocket, and shined a narrow beam into each of Hayden's eyes.

'That's why it scared her. I was the dead guy in two nineteen.'

'Let's just say we wouldn't have been surprised to lose you, and leave it at that.'

'How long have I been here?'

'About ten weeks. Now tell me a few simple things. Do you remember the events that led up to your injury?'

Hayden blinked and tried to concentrate. But it seemed easier to think about the ten weeks. Ten weeks.

'I don't remember what happened to me. No.'

'Can you tell me your name?'

'Hayden Reese.'

'When were you born?'

'December twentieth, nineteen forty-six.'

'Ah. A mere lad. Can you tell me who the president of the United States is?'

'Actually, no. If I've been here ten weeks, then I missed the election.'

'Excellent point. Nice to know your brain is sharper than mine. Do you remember who the president *was*?'

'Bill Clinton.'

'Still is.'

'Thank God. Why would I have trouble remembering?'

'Lack of blood, lack of oxygen to the brain. The freshest memories get lost.'

'Do they ever come back?'

'Sometimes yes, sometimes no. We'll have to call your daughter,' the doctor said. 'Tell her you're awake.'

'My daughter?'

'Yes. She came to visit you while you were in your coma. Nice young woman. We all liked her.'

Isn't that lovely? Hayden thought. You all know Allegra. Isn't that just one more thing we don't all have in common?

Later that evening the nurse he'd startled came in with his sleeping pills. Actually, she came in with everybody's sleeping pills. Everybody's evening medication, dozens of little paper cups on a white plastic tray, which she set down on Hayden's bedside table.

Three nurses ran by the open door of his room. As he turned his head gingerly to look, he noticed that the old man in the next bed had fallen asleep.

'Cardiac emergency,' the nurse said, though Hayden had not asked.

'It's okay,' Hayden said. 'Go. I'll be fine.'

'They don't need me for a cardiac emergency.'

'Then why did that nurse call your name?'

'I didn't hear her call me.'

'Just now,' Hayden said. 'Just as they ran by the door.' Hayden did not know this nurse's name, and so hoped she wouldn't ask specifically what name he had heard.

The nurse ran from the room, leaving Hayden alone with the tray of medication, every single pill of which he downed, using up every one of those little cups of water.

Hayden tried not to open his eyes. Squeezed them shut and tried to pretend he might never have to, that it might have worked, that he might only be dreaming he was alive.

When he gave up and opened them, more out of curiosity than anything else, his familiar doctor stood over his gurney in what appeared to be a recovery room. He thought he might actually feel a little worse than before, but it was hard to judge.

'It just pisses me off,' she said, 'when some un-grateful son of a bitch tries to undo all my good handiwork. I just hate that. If you're trying to get on my bad side, congratulations. Why do I even try to save people?'

'I'm sure you meant well,' he said. He had to push

to release the words. Still, they came out a spidery whisper, reminding him he wasn't a man anymore, or at least, not a complete one. And it hurt to push them out. But he did anyway. 'I might have thanked you at the time. I was so scared to die. Now I found something that scares me more.'

'Listen,' she said. She leaned over to help him see her face. Her plastic hospital badge said *Dr M. L. Stanley*. Her breath smelled slightly of alcohol and tobacco, and made him want a cigarette desperately. 'We've heard some stories about you. Big tough guy. Likes to throw his weight around. Real big and strong. But it's only on the outside. Right?'

'You've got no right to—'

'Just shut up,' she said. 'Don't try to sell me a line. You're big and strong on the inside, too, go ahead and prove it.'

She spun on her heels to leave, and he knew that right at the moment he wasn't big and strong on any side. And he wasn't sure he could speak loudly enough to stop her.

'I just want to get out of here,' he said.

'If you mean the hospital, don't worry. The county is a lousy host, and you're on the bottom of the sliding scale. If you were speaking in a broader sense . . .' She stopped to allow him to say otherwise. When he didn't, she said, 'Sorry. That's not my department.'

She slammed out, allowing the door to shut with a bang.

Ten o'clock that evening she came into his room, saw that he was awake, and pulled the curtain to keep from disturbing his roommate. She turned on the little reading light above his bed. She sat in a chrome and plastic chair at his bedside.

'Sorry I couldn't get in sooner. It's been a long goddamned day. I just now finished my rounds, if you can believe that. Sorry I blew my stack.'

'I suppose you were justified.'

'Are you a drinking man, Mr Reese?'

'I'd rather you call me Hayden. When people call me Mr Reese it reminds me of my father. If you knew my father you'd know why I don't say that like it's a good thing.'

'If you call me Marian. Are you a drinking man, Hayden?'

'I have my moments, Marian. Now I suppose you're going to tell me I can never drink again.'

'No, now I'm going to pour you one.' She took a small, flat pint bottle out of her lab coat pocket and poured two fingers for each of them into clear plastic water cups. 'One won't hurt you. Might do you good. It'll damn sure do me good. Tell anyone and I'll deny it.'

'Thanks,' he said, and took it from her in his right hand. And took a long pull. 'My left arm isn't working too well.'

'I can imagine it isn't. It relies heavily on those chest muscles. That jigsaw puzzle I tried to piece back together for you. You're looking at a nightmare of physical therapy, Hayden. I can't say I envy you.'

'I still can't feel my left leg.'

'You have a piece of shot in your spine.'

'Am I going to walk?'

'Oh, hell yeah. You'll walk. Even if you don't get that feeling back, you'll walk. People walk on one leg all the time. With help. Crutches. More physical therapy. The nerves will regrow. To what extent I can't tell you. Maybe if you're really diligent and lucky both, you'll be able to walk with just a cane.'

'Why do I have a sense that there's worse news?'

'All kinds of it.'

'I had a feeling you were trying to brace me for something.'

'Why? Because I poured you a bourbon?'

'Yeah. Because of that.'

'Nothing to do with it. I just don't like to drink alone. You only have half a lung on the left. You'll never have great wind. There was a pack of cigarettes in your jacket pocket.'

'So, you'll probably throw those away.'

'We did, ages ago. That is one luxury you can never afford again. Now. Here's the real bad news. You have more surgery in your near future. Now that we know you're still with us, we need to do some bone grafts. Build up that chest wall again. A lot of it will be steel. You'll never have a good experience with a metal detector, ever again. You're full of shot as it is, and the surgery won't help. Expect delays when you're traveling. For the rest of your life you'll have to show up at airports an hour early. I hope you're fond of strip searches.'

'Well, I never was before. But I guess that'll be as much excitement as I get from now on.'

'Oh, stop feeling sorry for yourself. I have no patience for that.' She paused. Sipped. 'It's not minor surgery. It'll set you back some. But it's got to be.'

'It's not like I have any choice in the matter.'

'You're a stubborn, disagreeable son of a bitch, aren't you, Hayden?'

'It's what I've been told. More than once. More than twice, actually. And you know the old saying. Three men call you a jackass, buy a saddle.'

'You're supposed to feel privileged to be alive. You've got two pieces of shot lodged in your pericardium.'

'I don't know what a pericardium is.'

'Let's just say it's as close to your heart as shot could get and still allow us to have this conversation.'

'So I just barely squeaked by.' He didn't mean that as a question. Just something he'd known all along but decided to say out loud, just to hear how it sounded.

Dr Marian laughed. A throaty but pleasant sound, with her head tilted back to let it out. Then she leaned in and spoke low, a tone befitting a secret. 'If we'd been crass enough to bet on you like a racehorse, Hayden, I'd have lost my shirt when you opened your eyes. I know I shouldn't tell you that, but what the hell. You seem to know it anyway.'

Hayden slugged down the last of his bourbon, enjoying the burn in his gut, the glow of it. He'd had his morphine recently, and felt comfortable, if thickheaded, and the company seemed good all of a sudden.

She took his glass and poured him one more finger of bourbon, one of her own fingers to her lips to swear him to secrecy. 'You're quite a legend around here,' she said. 'Stories get around. We've heard a few of your exploits. Probably the tip of the iceberg, I'll bet.'

'Probably. Aren't you sorry you put me back together?'

'Not at all. I have a special weakness for irrational men. In fact, if I was a girl of fifty again . . . well, enough of that. Here's the worst of the news. You're never coming back a hundred per cent, physically speaking. Expect limitations. You're going to have to find a new way to solve your problems. The brawn bit isn't going to cut it anymore.' She threw her head back, downed the balance of her bourbon, collected both cups before standing up to go. 'Have to clean up the evidence,' she said. 'And listen. This surgery I'm about to perform on you is a lot of hard work. Don't you dare try to undo my hard work again. Don't think we won't be watching you.'

'I don't,' he said. 'One more thing before you go. It's about my daughter. Or anybody else who might want to come visit me. I don't want to see anybody. Is that clear? I am not taking visitors. At all. I don't want to wake up with visitors in my room and have to tell them that myself. I want everyone who might ask told that I'm not seeing anyone. Period.'

Dr Stanley stood with one hand on the curtain surrounding his bed, looking at his eyes in a way he found disconcerting. 'I hope you'll change your mind about that.'

'I'm sure you do.'

She drew the curtain all the way back and let herself out.

Hayden breathed deeply and closed his eyes.

'I'll trade you.'

The voice startled him. But it was only the old man in the next bed, who he'd thought was asleep.

'What do mean? Trade me what?'

'Pardon me for eavesdropping. You want to die? I've got terminal cancer. I'll trade you. You can have it. And I'll hobble around on a cane with my chest all tore up, and short of breath, and I'll do all that nasty physical therapy. But at least I'll get to be with my wife and daughter.'

'If I had a wife and daughter,' Hayden said, 'maybe I'd feel the same.'

'Doesn't matter,' the old man said. 'We can't trade anyway. I just couldn't help making the point.'

In the morning Hayden woke to find the bed beside him empty, and carefully made.

A few minutes later a nurse came in with a wheelchair and a small portable oxygen tank.

'Dr Stanley wants you to spend some time outdoors.'

'Why?'

'Because you go in for surgery tomorrow. She figures it's your last chance for a while. You've been in bed too long.'

'Amen,' Hayden said, and tried to sit up. And realized this was going to hurt.

Hayden sat in a robe and slippers in the wheelchair, on a borderless concrete patio facing the front hospital lawn, still out of breath from the exertion of rising. But it did feel good to be outside. The portable oxygen tank had been wheeled out with him, and it sat beside his weak left arm.

He looked up at the dark, heavy sky and felt afraid for reasons he couldn't pin down. Not afraid of the storm that was obviously coming. Just afraid. Then he heard Dr Stanley's voice behind him, which made him feel even worse.

'Go on inside, Nurse. I'll bring him in after a while.'

'Need a light?' the nurse said.

'Don't be a smart-ass.' Dr Stanley stood next to the wheelchair, on Hayden's right. When the nurse disappeared she said, 'Besides, I've got a Zippo.' She lit a cigarette and stood at Hayden's side, looking off at the view, as if to see what he saw. 'Got an impressive batch of storms lined up, waiting to hit us. Or so they say. Is this cruel? Smoking in front of you?'

'Yes.'

'Well, too bad. You're a good excuse for a cigarette break.'

'I thought doctors were too smart to smoke.'

'This is County General, honey, it ain't the Mayo Clinic.'

'How long do I have to be on this oxygen?'

'Until after the surgery. You need a chest wall to breathe efficiently. Most people don't know that. Damn, this is an ugly part of the world. Don't you think?'

'Sometimes the mountains are a nice view.'

'If you like electrical towers.'

A spasm of coughing racked him, and Dr Stanley switched her cigarette to the other hand and moved downwind of him, but it wasn't the smoke at all. He just coughed. He just often did.

'Damn, I'll bet that hurts,' she said.

He didn't even care to address it, it hurt that much. He wanted to move on to something else. 'I *don't* like them.'

'Don't like what?'

'Electrical towers.'

'I was being sarcastic. Nobody does.'

'I think maybe I like them less than most.'

Before Hayden could think of a way to change the subject, Jack came through the front hospital doors and walked past them on his way to the parking lot. It surprised Hayden to see him. Jolted him right down through his stomach. Neither man acknowledged the other.

'You know that man?' Dr Stanley asked.

'Some.'

'He's been paying your bill.'

'I'm surprised. He doesn't have a lot of money.'

'It's not the fortune you might think. Sliding scale and all. But it still isn't cheap. He came in on the first of last month and covered it. Didn't give his name or anything. And that's where he was just now. Paying it again. I thought maybe he was family.'

'Hardly.'

'Too bad. You'll be needing some family. Four or five days after surgery I'm compelled to throw you out of here. But you won't be ready to live alone.'

'Can't I stay until I can take care of myself?'

'Well, that depends. Are you one of those eccentric millionaires with wads of money stuffed into your mattress?'

'Sadly, no.'

'Well, as I might have mentioned already, the county is a lousy host. I'd love to take you home with me, honey, only my husband is not only old and boring but possessive. He gets in my way a lot on these things. What about your daughter?'

'I couldn't ask that of her. I don't even know her.'

'She called. Asked if you were awake. One of the nurses told her you're not taking visitors. What about the guy who shot you?' she said, indicating Jack's path to the parking lot with a flip of her head. 'Think he's guilty enough to pay your way a little longer?'

'How did you know—'

'I'm not stupid, honey.'

'I sensed that.'

'So, do you remember now? What happened?'

'No. But I remember what led up to it. I can put two and two together as well as you can.'

'You could *get* to know your daughter. She seems to want to know you.'

'I'm getting tired of taking advice,' Hayden said.

'I don't expect you've ever been very good at it. But here's one last piece of advice you don't want. Okay, fine, you've got a big trauma here. I'm not trying to be insensitive to that. Well, actually I don't ever *try* to be insensitive, it's just in my nature. I know it's a difficult adjustment. But, goddamn you, Hayden, just start adjusting. Just fucking *start*, will you? And the first order of business,' Dr Stanley said, 'is to ingratiate yourself to *somebody*. And fast.'

Hayden chose not to address that. So he just sat a minute, and breathed in every trace of her smoke possible, and looked out across the hated electrical towers to the mountains framed by low, heavy black storm clouds.

'What happened to that guy in the next bed?' he asked.

'Thought you said you could still put two and two together.'

'I was just talking to him last night.'

'What did he say?'

'Well, that's kind of personal.'

'Okay. Whatever.' She crushed the butt of her

cigarette under her right heel. 'Does it put any of this in a better perspective? Never mind. That was probably too personal.'

She wheeled him back inside.

Chapter Two

Veterans Day

Laurel came into his room without knocking, not ten minutes after he'd gotten settled into bed. He wished he could tell her not to do that, but it was a dicey thing, this being her house and all. And that was just the problem with being in anybody's house: no control. But there was no real place for her to sleep at his house, and no phone in case he needed her, and it wasn't fair to ask her to come driving over all the time anyway.

A hard rain pounded on the roof.

She came in holding a bedpan in her left hand.

Hayden shook his head. 'No. No goddamn way. You think I'm going to have you cleaning up after me like a baby in diapers?' My God, he thought. Of all the people. Could you maybe just leave me any pride at all? One little scrap of dignity, maybe?

'You got another way to settle those needs?'

He pointed to the bathroom off his bedroom. Peg's old room, before Peg moved out to live with a twenty-one-year-old named Josh. It had happened while Hayden was in the hospital. This time Laurel had just let her.

'What's your mode of transportation going to be?'

'You let me worry about that. I'm still a grown man, you know.'

'I never said you weren't, I just—'

'And another thing. I know this is your house and all. But I'd really appreciate it if you'd rap on the door before you come in here. Not to make it sound like I don't appreciate all you're doing.'

Laurel rolled her eyes. Threw the bedpan on the big overstuffed chair in the corner, which seemed odd to Hayden, who'd expected her to take him at his word and take the damn thing back to wherever she'd gotten it. 'I'm getting a glimpse of what it's gonna be like living with you.'

'It won't be for long.'

'What do you mean? The minute you're on your feet you're out of here?'

'Of course. What did you think?'

She looked a little stunned. Almost like she might lose her balance. She came over and sat on the edge of his bed.

'Well, Jack is out for good now. I meant that. We already filed the papers.'

'Look, Laurel. I told you before this ever happened.'

'You said because of Jack. Because I took Jack back.'

'Then you said, "Maybe I want to change my mind now." And then I said, "Maybe I don't want you to."'

Laurel jumped to her feet, as if to distance herself from the words. Her disorientation was finding its way into anger, he could tell. Finding a familiar, comfortable home there. 'I thought you didn't remember any of that.'

'Parts keep coming back to me. I keep remembering that part, I don't know why. But not what happened right before it or right after it. And something else, too. Something somebody told me. Can't think who it was, though. Something about love. How any idiot can fall in love but the trick is to love somebody who'll actually do you some good. And how most people don't ever get that last part right.'

'You don't think we could do each other any good?'

'We never did before.'

She just stood over his bed a moment, staring at him. Right into his eyes. Just armoring up more and more behind that defense of hers. Letting it build up to where it could serve her. 'Okay, fine. That's the way you feel, Hayden, fine.'

She walked out, slamming the door sharply behind her.

Hayden thought awhile about how it might've been smarter to make sure he really could get to the bathroom first. Then he could have told her all that afterward.

He decided to give it a try. He rolled onto his side and lowered himself off the edge of the bed, slowly onto his hands and knees. His left arm wasn't so good, and his left leg was all but useless, but it would hold him up if he got it folded firmly under him. So there he was on his hands and knees, stable enough, and not needing any help from anyone. So he crawled there. It had an eerie feel to it, crawling, like this was what he'd been reduced to. Then, on the other hand, he'd a hundred times rather crawl by himself than get there any other way with anybody else's help. Most particularly Laurel's.

It wasn't all that hard to lift himself up onto the toilet, because his good right leg was plenty strong enough. He just had to be careful to get a good grip on the edge of the sink for balance. Then, once there, he realized he didn't really need to go, but he did what he could anyway, so he wouldn't have to come back anytime soon.

On the crawl back to bed he heard a rap on the door. Before he could even open his mouth to say the direct opposite of 'Come in,' whatever its direct opposite might be, the door swung open.

'Get the hell out of here!' he yelled.

He must have sounded convincing, because she jumped back and pulled the door almost shut behind her. Just holding the knob, using the door like a shield. Listening, maybe, but not where she could look in. Hayden just froze there on the floor, like an animal crouching for cover where no cover exists.

'Are you okay, Hayden? You need help?'

'I do not need help,' he said. 'I am doing fine. I need privacy. Got that? Privacy. And what the hell good does it do to rap on the door if you just go on to throw it open the next second?'

'I'm sorry. Fine. You want privacy? Fine. You want to be left alone? I'll leave you alone.'

And she did.

A few hours and a good long nap later the door flew open with no knock.

'Goddamn it,' he said, because for all she knew he could have been on his hands and knees again. Could have been in any one of a number of positions in which he wouldn't care to be viewed. And yet he hadn't meant to yell at her. Not again. Not this time.

But he hadn't yelled at Laurel, because it wasn't Laurel coming into his room. It was Scott.

'Thought I made it clear I wasn't seeing visitors.'

Scott stood over his bed in full uniform, cap and shoulders wet from the rain, tapping his fingers against his big side-handle baton. 'Real goddamn good to see you too, buddy. But this ain't a social call.'

'Am I under arrest for something?'

He heard a hopefulness in his voice as he asked it. Scott must've heard it, too.

'No, why? Would you like to be?'

'Yes. Please. That's one good place I could be right now. Get all the help I need, only not from anybody I used to sleep with.'

'Sorry to disappoint, buddy. I came to see what your plans were about Jack.'

'What about Jack?'

'He's out on bail. We was kind of waiting to see which way the pendulum would swing. Murder, attempted murder. Could've gone either way for a while. Lord, that was one nervous man, let me tell you. Now I'm ready to charge him with attempted murder. Only it could go easier or harder on him, depending how you testify.'

'I don't want to press charges against him.'

'You don't have to. It's the People versus Jack. One way or another, he does time.'

Hayden looked up at Scott's face. Thought about looking up at the same face as they loaded him into the ambulance. It seemed strange and sudden, that he should remember that now. Those moments were meant to be gone, and yet that one came back. He thought about how it hadn't seemed to matter, back then, that Scott was seeing him laid out like that. Maybe the shock. Maybe he just didn't have enough blood in him, at the time, to care.

'It was an accident.'

'Excuse me?'

'Jack came by to shoot some ground squirrels for me. Place was overrun with them. I got in the way, like an idiot.'

Scott scratched his head a moment. 'You're sticking to that story?'

'Thought I would, yeah.' A long silence. 'I beat him senseless and he didn't press charges against me.'

'I didn't ask you why.'

'Well, I'm telling you. It's not like it would put me back the way I was before. Besides, he didn't do it to *me* when he had the chance.'

'Yeah, well I also remember *why* he didn't. And I'm just hoping your thinking doesn't go along those same lines.'

Hayden didn't answer.

'Well, you take care, buddy. When you stop being so stubborn over visitors I'll come back see how you're doing. Right now I gotta go make Jack's day.'

'Scott—' Scott stopped with his hand on the door-knob. 'You seen George around town anywhere?'

Scott leveled him with a strange look. Like something might be badly wrong with Hayden, and if he just looked closely enough he might see it. 'You still forgetting things?'

'No, I remember most stuff. Why?'

'Because I don't know anybody named George. And not to upset you, buddy, but I don't think you do, either.'

'My dog.'

'Oh. Ugly Dog. Why didn't you say so? I didn't know Ugly Dog had a name. He's with Peg. They've gotten plenty attached since you been gone.'

'He always liked her better anyway,' Hayden said.

Hayden rapped on the floor with the handle of the broom Laurel had given him for just that purpose.

A moment later he heard her footsteps on the stairs. Just for a split second they hurt him, those footsteps. Like remembering too clearly when she was his lover and how much he would've wanted to hear those footsteps coming up to his bedroom. At one time it would have been all of that and more, and it made him sad, like something precious had been lost. And then he didn't want her to open the door, because he didn't want her to see him like this; but it was too late for that.

'What is it this time?' she said.

'What did you do with that newspaper I had right here beside the bed? Did you straighten up in here while I was napping?'

'Yeah, I did. I threw it in the recycling. It was old.'

'I know how old it was. It was from Veterans Day. I was saving it.'

'Why?'

'Could you just go get it out of the recycling, please?'

'Hayden, you're not even a veteran.'

'I didn't ask what my draft history was, Laurel, I asked you to go fetch me back that paper. Please.'

'What part? I might've used some of it to wrap the trash. The Disposall's on the fritz again.'

'It was right on the front page. It has a picture of the napalm girl. You know, that little naked girl running down the road. And a picture of a Vietnamese woman. At the Veterans Day celebration. At the Vietnam Memorial. And it has an article with it.'

'Hayden, I'm kinda busy, tryin' to get the house cleaned up.'

'Please, Laurel. It's important.'

She stamped out, slamming the door.

Ten or fifteen minutes later her footsteps pounded back up the stairs, hard and angry. They did not make him feel what he'd felt the last time.

She came in without knocking, with a hammer in one hand, a nail in her teeth. Something like a big framed picture under her arm. She glared at him without speaking. Then she pounded the nail into the wall beside his bed and hung it up. He had to wait for her to move aside so he could see what it was. When she did, it was that article he'd wanted to save. Kim Phuc, the napalm girl from that famous Vietnam-era photo, come to Washington to tell the men who dropped the napalm on her – and on her family, some of whom died – that she could forgive. First a little girl, face twisted with pain, then a round-faced, friendly woman, smiling with dignity and grace. And forgiveness.

He looked at it without speaking, took in the way it looked, hanging there beside his bed.

'There,' Laurel said. 'You finally happy now?'

He wanted to say, Actually, yes. That was perfect, just what she'd done. Even though she had done it with rage. Even though she hadn't meant him to be pleased.

But before he could form the words in his head she said, 'Your daughter called again. What the hell am I supposed to keep telling her if you won't talk to her?'

'Get her number. Tell her I'll call when I'm on my feet.'

'Why'd you say your daughter was dead if she wasn't, anyway?'

'To avoid answering a bunch of questions. Like the ones you're asking me right now.'

'Does this mean you got an ex-wife alive somewhere, too?'

'Not exactly,' Hayden said.

Which was true. She was not exactly his ex-wife. Because they had never exactly divorced.

Hayden expected Laurel to ask what that meant, but she left without saying more. So she must not have wanted to know.

When he woke next it was night, dark, still pouring rain. He woke to the sound of it hammering on the roof, and to yelling downstairs. A fight.

He didn't want to turn on the light to look at the clock, so he just peered at it from as close up as possible. It was only about eleven.

He lay on his side listening. One ear in the pillow. One voice was Jack, though he'd more or less known it would be. He only made out every other word or so.

'My house, my goddamn house.' Then Laurel saying something about the divorce settlement. 'It ain't all yours yet,' and then, 'I ain't the one shot him.'

It went on like that for a while.

Hayden sat up in bed and turned on the light, be-cause, he thought they might stop if they knew he was awake. And the bedroom door was ajar, the way it always was at night, in case he had to call for something.

He always wore a T-shirt in bed, because it was such an ugly thing, the part the T-shirt covered. So ugly and hard to look at. For him or for anybody else.

So for just a moment he felt almost whole, sitting up in bed, covered, almost able looking, when Jack stuck his head in the door.

'Sorry about the yelling,' he said. 'Sorry you had to hear that. Some stuff I gotta say right to your face, though.'

He stood in the bedroom doorway, in the spill of light from Hayden's little bedside lamp, holding his cap in his hands. Rolling it around and around. It had some kind of printing on it, but in that limited light Hayden couldn't see what it said.

'Not that I hate you really one bit less than I ever did. But I'm sorry what happened. I'm sorry it came to that. No excuse for that, whatever you mighta done. But – I just can't get used to you being here in this house, though, is all.'

'I'm going home tonight.'

'You are?'

'Yeah. This isn't going so good. And it's over, anyway, with me and her.'

'Well, she told me that but I didn't believe her.'

'Do you believe me?'

'Not really.'

'Well, it's true.'

Jack had nothing to say back to that, and Hayden didn't know – or really care – whether Jack believed it now or not. So Hayden just sat there in bed, and Jack just stood in the doorway, rolling that cap around in his hands.

'What's that hat say, Jack? I can't read that far.'

Jack looked down at the cap as if stunned to see it there. 'Oh.' He held it out for Hayden to see. It said, FRIENDS DON'T LET FRIENDS DRIVE FORDS.

'Well,' Hayden said, 'once upon a time we could've got into it real good just over the hat. But I'm a little tired and sore for fighting right now. I'm going to ask Laurel to drive me home tonight. I need to be in my own place, anyway.'

'One other thing, Reese. Just listen to this. Just shut up and listen. Don't say nothing to me, because this is hard and I don't like saying it one bit.'

Hayden waited. He didn't say anything. He just sat and watched Jack slap the cap back onto his head, as if that might be a good down payment on going somewhere else.

'I appreciate not having to go to jail. I was looking at some time. It's a break for me. You know what I'm trying to say.'

Hayden thought he might, but he didn't supply the words for him.

'Thanks.'

'You're welcome.'

'Aw, now, I told you to shut up and not say nothing.' He flew out of the room, stamped down the stairs. 'Laurel? The man would like to go home now. He said so himself. I didn't tell him to say so. He just did.'

Then the sound of the front door slamming.

Laurel's footsteps on the stairs, which hurt more this time than they ever had, ever could have before. Because this was the last time. He wouldn't hear them again.

'You're joking, right?'

She stood in the doorway with her hair coming down from where she'd pinned it up. All that soft reddish-brown hair. It made him think about crying, almost see it as a possibility. But of course he didn't cry.

'No. I'm not kidding. I need to go home now.'

'You're not ready to be on your own.'

'I'll be fine.'

They faced each other like that in silence. Ten seconds, twenty. Looking at each other's face. Hayden could hear Jack's truck pull out of the driveway.

'Okay. I'll drive you in the morning.'

'I was thinking tonight. I was thinking now.'

She stared at him a moment longer. As if maybe tears were somewhere in the back of her mind, too.

Then she said, 'Fine. I'll just get my coat.'

Chapter Three

How to Spot a Hero

Not even seven o'clock the next morning, Hayden opened his eyes to see Peg sticking her head into his little cabin.

It seemed like every time he opened his eyes, there was a door with a head sticking through it. It was making him deeply weary and he just could not figure out how to get it to stop.

It was cold in there, and her holding the door open didn't help. He pulled his one thin blanket tighter around himself.

'You awake, Hayden?'

'I guess I am now.'

She let herself in, with George at her side. George had put on some weight and a thin haze of hair. He came over to Hayden's bed, sniffed him briefly, then walked away again like he hadn't found anything of interest there.

Peg seated herself on the edge of his bed.

'I came to take care of you.'

'What about this guy you were living with?'

'Ah, he's a big loser. All he ever does is go out drinking with his friends. He was never as good to me as you were. Now, what can I do for you?'

'Go away and let me sleep.'

'No, really.'

'Really. I didn't sleep well last night.'

'I could walk down to the market and get you something?'

Hayden rubbed his eyes. Sighed. 'Actually, there is something you could go get me. I left something important at your mom's house. It's on the wall above the bed. It's just a newspaper article but it's in a frame on the wall.'

'Boy, that's a long walk, Hayden.'

'I sure would appreciate it, though. So long as we got a break in the rain and all. I'm afraid if you don't go get it, she'll throw it away. She doesn't understand that it's important.'

'Okay. George and I'll walk over and get it.'

'Thank you. That's a big help.'

And it was. But it was also an hour-and-a-half round trip on foot. So Hayden got to go back to sleep.

*   *   *

Hayden sat up on the edge of the bed, just for a moment thinking he could stand. Not quite awake yet to those changes. Their reality, having been briefly absent in his sleep, had not yet been fully redelivered.

A hard rain pounded on his roof. God, it was still raining. When wasn't it raining? Was it ever going to stop?

The door swung wide, making him cold. Somehow it had gotten to be winter. Peg stood in the doorway, dripping wet. Miserable looking and soaked to the skin, her red hair dark and plastered to her cheeks and forehead.

For a split second Hayden was just going to walk to her. Just go over there, put his arms around her, and dry her off. Then it all came settling back again.

So he just sat there on the edge of the bed, and they looked at each other. George came into the room and shook himself, spraying dirty water everywhere. A splash even made it onto Hayden's cheek.

Peg crossed the room, handed him his framed article. The cardboard of the frame back had soaked through, so now the newsprint was damp. But it was still readable, which he figured was the important thing. Peg flopped into Hayden's favorite chair.

'I'm sorry, Peg,' he said. 'I should've given you the keys to my truck. Can you drive a stick shift?'

'Sort of.' Her voice sounded funny.

'Sort of. That gives me a sense of confidence.' Before he could even finish the sentence Peg burst into serious tears. And he couldn't even go to her. 'What, Peg? Did something happen?'

'You don't forgive me,' she said. 'I knew you didn't.'

'Forgive you for what?'

'For what? For what? How can you say that, Hayden? I'm the one got you shot.'

'No, Peg. I'm the one got me shot.'

'But if I hadn't told him—'

'Then it would have happened somewhere else at some other time.' He looked down at the napalm girl, grown. Her smiling face. 'Is that what you thought this was about? Not being able to forgive you?' Isn't that just like a kid, Hayden thought, or for that matter, any human being. I'm the center of the universe, so this must be all about me.

'What's it about, then?'

'I don't know. She's just my hero, is all. Remember when I said you had lousy taste in heroes? Well, she's a real one.'

'Why? What'd she do?'

'Forgave.'

'Is that hard?'

Hayden laughed. A bitter, cynical-sounding thing by the time it hit his own ears. 'Is that hard? Yes. That's hard. Revenge is easy. Lashing out is easy. Tearing up the world. But as far as letting it be what it is . . .'

'I don't understand the half of what you're saying, Hayden. Are you fevered again? So . . . you *do* forgive me?'

'Peg, I got a whole list of people I can't forgive. Myself included. You are not on the list. Could you come over here? Because I can't just get up and walk over to you.'

She sat on the edge of his bed, childlike, and he put an arm around her. Eased her head down onto his shoulder, feeling her wetness soak through his clothes.

'Oh, I almost forgot to tell you,' she said. 'Mom says to say your daughter called again. She said it's real important.'

Peg slept on the cot, set up in the kitchen. Hayden refused to crawl in her presence. So his only alternative was to teach her to help him get places. A strange sort of leaning process, which didn't involve putting weight on his left arm or armpit, as crutches would have.

And after he'd convinced her she could not stay in the bathroom with him once she'd gotten him there, it worked out fairly well.

She'd just gotten him there one afternoon around lunchtime. He was standing with his good right hand braced on the wall for balance. Wearing just a T-shirt and Jockeys, because if he wore pants it was too hard to get them undone with his left. Standing there relieving himself in private when he heard a knock on the door.

That's unique, he thought. Somebody actually knocked. Must not be from around here.

He heard Peg open the door. Someone's footsteps coming in out of the rain. Peg's voice. 'Oh, I don't think he'll bite you.' Hayden wondered what made her so sure.

Then another voice, a woman's. 'If it's not rude to ask, who are you?' It caught him somewhere funny, that voice, and he knew he knew it, but it wouldn't find its place in his head. He'd have to open the door to put a face with it. But there he was, only partly dressed.

Then he heard Peg say, 'I'm his girlfriend.'

'The hell you are,' he bellowed, and opened the bathroom door, suddenly prioritized right out of caring how dressed he was or was not. 'Who the hell are you telling that to, Peg?'

He looked out, half expecting to see Allegra, wondering what Allegra would look like. Would he know her just to look at her face? Had some part of him known she'd show up here if he avoided things long enough?

It was not Allegra. It was Judith.

Hayden stood with the bathroom door wide open

and out of his reach, looking at Judith, who looked back. Even if he'd wanted to move closer, he couldn't have.

Her hair had gone silver, and she'd let it. A good choice on her; it served her well. It was short, radically, stylishly short, her hair, and her skin had gone somewhat wrinkled with the sun, but she was no less stunning. More, if anything. She had taken age and somehow twisted it around to serve her. Some people can do that.

And it didn't seem fair to Hayden, to be paralyzed and exhausted and recovering from major surgery at a moment like this, when even under the best of circumstances he'd be left feeling that she was too good for him, and always had been.

'Well, then, *you* tell *me*,' Peg said, more than a little miffed. 'Who exactly are *you*?'

'My wife,' Hayden said. To spare Judith having to say it. 'This is my wife, Judith.'

Peg stood frozen a moment. Then she seemed to unstick herself. She came as far as the bathroom door, as if wanting to say something to Hayden privately. But when she spoke, it would have been loud enough for the neighbors to hear, if Hayden had had neighbors.

'Well, she looks damn good for roadkill.' Peg stormed away again, grabbed his keys off the table by the door. 'I'm taking the truck, *honey*.' She put a cloying emphasis behind the word 'honey.' 'Come on, George. We're out of here.'

And they were.

Hayden stood with his right hand braced on the sink, watching Judith, who watched back. 'What are you doing here?' he said.

'You wouldn't return Allegra's phone calls.'

'Then why didn't *she* come?'

'Now she thinks you don't want to see her. It's really important to her that you come to the wedding, Hayden.'

'I'll come. I'll come to the damn wedding. I just need time to get on my feet.' Then he realized that must sound strange to her, because he was on his feet, in the most literal sense. And until he attempted to move, how could she understand his situation?

'Hayden, the wedding is Saturday.'

Though he took as long as he reasonably could to get around to it, sooner or later he had to ask Judith's help. Sooner or later he had to admit that Peg had gotten him into the bathroom and, if he were to get out at all, Judith would need to get him out.

'She's not my girlfriend,' he said.

'She's obviously in love with you. But it's none of my business. How do I do this?'

Just for a moment Hayden appreciated Peg, and missed her, because he had Peg all trained.

Judith joined him in the tiny bathroom. An awkward moment, to say the least. He noticed she didn't wear her ring now, and then wondered why he had ever expected her to. His own was in a drawer somewhere, lost but disturbingly unforgotten.

'I haven't done anything to encourage her to be. I need to get you on my left. And I need to lean on you without putting my arm on your shoulder. I can't put any weight on that arm.'

She snugged in to his left side, circled his waist with her arm. He tried to take a step, but she didn't stay close up against him the way Peg knew to do. He had to swing his whole hip, the whole left side of his body, to get his left leg forward. Then he nearly lost his balance, but she steadied him. He braced his right arm on the door frame, resting briefly, wishing he could do this with somebody else. Anybody else.

'So,' she said, 'that's not the woman you got shot over.'

'That's not even a woman, Judith. That's a sixteen-year-old girl.'

'It's none of my business. I'm sorry.'

He ventured another step. It worked somewhat better. He could feel her muscles tremble slightly from the exertion of bearing his weight.

He said, 'That's her daughter.'

'Whose daughter?'

'The daughter of the woman I got shot over.'

Three more steps to a kitchen chair. He rushed them. Nearly stumbled on the last, but was able to right himself on the chair back. He eased into a sit.

Judith sat across the table from him. 'I guess your life has been more interesting than mine.'

'You say that like it's a good thing.'

She smiled briefly. Then the awkwardness took over again. It made Hayden feel light headed. Or maybe that was the strain of walking over here. Or both. He wanted to be somewhere else but couldn't imagine how to get there.

Judith finally broke the silence. 'Why wouldn't you call her back?'

'I don't even know where to start with that.'

'Start anywhere. Start at the truth and work your way out.'

'I'm not anxious for anybody to see me in this condition.'

Judith nodded in a way that looked almost apologetic. 'Yeah. I wish I'd called ahead. I'm sorry. But you don't have a phone here. Or so I've been told. I guess I misjudged your condition when I walked in the door. You kept saying you'd call her when you were on your feet. And when I first saw you, I thought you were. On your feet. Walking around and living with a young woman. I guess I should know you better.'

'What should you know about me? I haven't seen you for fifteen years.'

'Some things don't change.'

He looked up at her face, but it hurt him, because she was fifteen years older, which meant so was he. Which meant fifteen years that he'd missed. Been cheated out of. And also because it was the same face. At the essence of it, it was.

'I can't go to that wedding now. Couldn't she postpone it? Until I can at least walk on crutches?'

'She already postponed it. While you were in the hospital. We'll rent you a wheelchair.'

'I don't even have a decent suit. Out here who needs one?'

'We'll rent you a tux.'

'Stop having all the answers, Judith. Couldn't she postpone it one more time?'

'No, I'm afraid not. Not this time.'

'Why not?'

'If I tell you, promise not to get mad?'

'No. But what can I do about it anyway?'

'Allegra and John are expecting their first child. She already bought her wedding dress. If she waits any longer, she won't fit into it.'

'Why did you think that would make me mad?'

'Well, you know. Your little girl. You haven't had a long history of liking her boyfriends.'

'I never met any of her boyfriends. Just that one young man who assaulted her. Did they want this baby?'

'Very much. Just not so soon.'

Hayden smiled a little in spite of himself, thinking about Allegra's premature arrival in their lives.

'Do they love each other? Is he a good man?'

'Yes and yes.'

'Then stop worrying about what I think.'

A silence fell. The rain began again, pelting the roof, tapping at the windows. Judith rose, walked to a window to look out. Such a simple gesture, crossing to a window. Hayden missed that.

'Has it been raining here long?' she asked.

'Forever.'

'Reminds me of that time we had to sandbag our house in Marin. Remember that?'

'Yes. Where do you live?'

'Not two miles from that house.'

'Where does Allegra live?'

'Less than two miles from me.'

More silence. The silence was becoming a force to contend with. The surprise of her coming through the door had glossed over so much. So many things that were now coming to settle.

Judith said, 'Do you have a radio here?'

'In the closet, but I don't think the batteries are good. Why?'

'You need a radio. They're expecting flooding around here. I heard it driving in. You have a creek to the west of you, right?'

'To the west *and* the east.'

'You need a radio.'

More silence. Hayden wondered what he would do if the creeks really rose. What if Peg didn't come back? He wondered if it might get as bad as 1989, when the water rose to an inch below his front door before receding again. Or worse.

Judith said, 'It's important to her, Hayden. She wants you there.'

'I put up a wall, Judith. Between me and her. Between me and you. I had to. It was the only way I could go on.'

'What am I supposed to tell her?'

'I don't know. The truth?'

She came back and sat with him. Pulled her chair close, leaned forward, and took both of his hands. Her hands felt cool. 'Come back with me, Hayden. Two nights at John and Allegra's house. Then I'll bring you to the wedding. Then stay over one more night and I'll bring you home. So you'll be in a wheelchair. We're your family, Hayden. Why would we care?'

She looked up at him as she finished speaking. Dropped his hands and sat back, slid her chair back, in fact, at what she saw on his face.

'How could you say that to me, Judith? How dare you come back here after fifteen years and tell me I'm your family?'

'You're right. I'm sorry. But she's still your daughter. I told you, if you always let Thea know where you were, that I'd tell Allegra. If she ever wanted to see you, I'd tell her. Well, this is it, Hayden. She wants to see you.'

Hayden sat a moment with his head in his hands.

'I'll have to write a note for Peg,' he said.

The windshield wipers on Judith's BMW swished back and forth double-time against the splattering rain.

They drove fifty miles in silence.

Then Judith said, 'I look pretty good for roadkill? What does that mean? Is that an expression in these parts?'

'Yeah, it is. We talk that way out here in the sticks.'

'What did she mean by that, Hayden?'

Hayden sighed, breathed smoothly, tried to lose himself in the dark rain, tried not to cough. It didn't work. A spasm of coughing burst out of him, and he winced, and tried to calm it. Tried to cough without jarring his chest, which was impossible, but he tried. His pain must have shown on him. When he looked over at Judith he could see a reflection of it on her face.

'Don't tell me, let me guess. It still hurts when you cough.'

'I told everyone . . . when I first moved here . . . that my wife and daughter had been killed in a car accident.'

'Oh.'

'It was easier than—'

'You don't have to explain.'

So he didn't.

After a few miles Judith stopped for gas, and to call Allegra and John, because they were out of cell phone range. She stepped back into the car dripping wet, and they drove north again.

Judith said, 'They're making dinner for us. We'll all have dinner at their house. When we get in.'

'Okay.'

'And they'll be ready with a wheelchair.'

'They can rent a wheelchair on this kind of notice?'

'They already did. You know how Allegra is.'

'No, I don't. How is she?' He wasn't just trying to be argumentative, or bitter. He really didn't know, couldn't even imagine what kind of adult she might have become.

'Optimistic,' Judith said. 'She refused to believe you wouldn't come.'

*   *   *

She ran out to the driveway to meet the car. A short-haired, attractive blond woman, someone he knew he knew.

If he'd seen her on the street he might not have thought, Allegra. But if he'd seen her on the street he might have thought, Judith. Might have breathed that name out loud, knowing all along it could not be. That she was too young to be. That it was an almost, any-way. Not a completely. But that's what he might have said.

She opened the passenger-side door for him. John came out of the house behind her with a wheelchair. They'd already rented a wheelchair. So sure he would come, while he would have sworn he wouldn't.

And Hayden realized he was scared. Deeply scared. He could feel his heart pounding around in his sore, vulnerable chest, and he could hear the same beat in his ears. The closer she got to addressing him, the louder it pounded.

'Daddy,' she said. And it felt strange, to be called Daddy by a grown woman.

He looked up into her strangely familiar, strangely unfamiliar face.

'Allegra,' he said. 'You grew up.'

Chapter Four

Shrinkage

'Could you pass me the rolls, John?' Hayden asked quietly. He felt somewhat sheepish about asking, because they were almost within his reach. He'd used up three days' worth of wind and muscle strength and energy just getting through this day. Even using his hands to butter the roll once he got it felt like a strain.

John was a dark, thoughtful-looking man, a few years older than Allegra, with wire glasses and intelligent eyes. Hayden could already see that John was afraid of him. And it struck him that he wasn't free of his past fights just because he had none in his future.

'So, Daddy, when do you start your physical therapy?'

Allegra's attempt at small talk. He wanted to say, Stop it. Stop pretending nothing happened. Stop ignoring the fifteen-year chasm. He might have if they'd been alone. But Allegra and John had worked hard on this dinner and, more to the point, needed some reassurance that the wedding guests could get along.

'About another two weeks, I think.' He'd have to get signed up for all kinds of public assistance first, but he didn't want to say that.

'Its going to be a little wedding, Dad. You won't literally have to walk me down the aisle. It's just a tiny little chapel and we'll take our places up front. And that's it. There'll just be a few people in the pews. Mostly close family. We've invited all our friends to the reception. But the wedding is just for immediate family.'

'So, who's going to be there?' Hayden sat in a moment of silence, then looked up in time to see a glance exchanged between his estranged wife and his estranged daughter. 'What? Who's going to be there?'

'John's parents and grandparents,' Allegra said. 'You and Mom. Thea . . .'

'Good. I always liked Thea.'

'John's sister and two brothers.'

'Is that it?'

The look again. '*You* tell him, Mom.'

'Tell me what?'

Judith blotted her mouth on a cloth napkin and set it on the table, though she wasn't nearly done eating.

'Hayden, after we were apart, I took Allegra to meet your parents.'

Hayden put his fork down and felt dinner sitting on his stomach, suddenly feeling heavy and undigested. 'How did you locate my parents?'

'I knew their last name and the town you grew up in. It wasn't all that hard.'

'Like it wouldn't have been hard for me to find you and Allegra. Except I knew you didn't want me to, and I voluntarily respected that.'

'I told you he'd be upset, Mom.'

'Hayden, we just visited them. I just thought they should know they had a grandchild.'

'And now you've just invited them to the wedding.'

Hayden and his sudden family sat in silence for a few beats, and then Hayden lapsed into a painful coughing fit and John rose and took his own plate to the kitchen. A moment later Allegra got up and began to clear the table. With his food about half eaten, Hayden volunteered for his plate to be taken. He didn't want the rest anyway.

'Both of them?' he said after a time.

'Yes,' Judith said. Flat, prepared, unapologetic.

'My father is still alive?'

'Yes.'

Allegra stuck her head in from the kitchen. 'Pie, Daddy?'

'Sure, okay,' he said without thinking.

'He's changed a lot, Hayden,' Judith said. 'Just so you know. I just want to prepare you. He had Alzheimer's, even when we first went to see them. He's worse now.'

'What did he say about me?'

'Nothing. He doesn't remember you.'

'Are you sure that's Alzheimer's? Maybe I just didn't make a lasting impression on him.'

'Grampa Ed is really sick, Daddy.' Allegra set a slice of pie in front of him on the table; Hayden knew he didn't want it.

'I'm tired. I'd like to go back to my room now. John, could you help me with that?'

Hayden knew he hadn't the strength in his left arm to wheel himself, and worried that if he wheeled with just his right, he'd end up going around in a circle, which seemed an uncomfortably apt metaphor for this moment. He wasn't sure quite how this wheelchair thing worked.

'I'll take you,' Judith said.

He didn't want her to, but he didn't speak up.

'Just leave me over here by the window,' he said.

'There's something I want to tell you now that we're alone.'

But they'd been alone all afternoon. Hayden

wondered what she needed to say and why she couldn't have said it sooner.

He sat at the window in the dark, hearing her voice at his back, looking out at that strangely familiar bay view. He felt something rub against his leg, and a cat jumped into his lap.

'Well, I'll be damned,' Judith said.

'I didn't know they had a cat.'

'He doesn't usually come out when there are strangers in the house.'

'Maybe he knows I'm not a stranger.' Hayden stroked the cat behind the ears and worried that maybe he *was* a stranger. 'This looks a lot like the view from our old house.'

'Except you don't have to stand on tiptoes in the shower or lean off the porch rail to see it.'

'I'm sorry I lost us that house,' Hayden said, and then sat stunned, wondering where that had come from.

'Water under the bridge.'

'What did you want to tell me? Now that we're alone?'

'That I'm a coward. I should have let you see her.'

'You were strong enough to do what needed to be done.'

'No. I was a coward."

Hayden still couldn't see Judith, which felt right. He could feel her there, behind him, and he stroked the cat under the chin and listened to him purr, and a moment later felt Judith's hand rest lightly on his shoulder.

'You were never a coward,' he said.

'Yes, I was. I knew if I saw you we'd end up back together. That's why I asked you to stay away. You were a good father. I never should have taken that away from you.'

'You never sent me divorce papers. For the first few years I was waiting for them. Every day, when I went out for the mail, I expected to see them there. But you never filed. Why didn't you ask me for a divorce, Judith?'

'That's what my last boyfriend wanted to know. We broke up over that.' Hayden wanted to say, So he was your last boyfriend. So you're not seeing anyone now. But of course he stopped himself. 'I'm amazed that Tigger likes you,' she said. 'He doesn't like much of anybody. Do you think you can ever forgive me for that, Hayden?'

And he sat for a few moments facing that familiar view in the dark. Thinking, preparing to say things he could never have allowed in the light, in sight of her face. 'Truth?'

'Yeah.'

'Truth is, I don't know much about forgiveness. I'm just starting to play with that idea.'

'Maybe you could practice on me.'

'Maybe.'

'Maybe you could work up to Ed.'

'No. I draw the line at Ed. I'm really tired, Judith. I'm not sure you understand how tired I am.'

'I'll leave you alone to get some sleep then. Need help getting into bed?'

'No.'

He might, but couldn't take it from her.

'You were a good father. You'll be a good grandfather.' She kissed him on the back of the head, on that spot where his hair had begun to thin. And let herself out.

Almost an hour and a half later the door creaked open, allowing a sliver of light from the hallway.

'Daddy?' A thin whisper.

'I'm awake, honey.'

'I kind of knew you would be.'

She came in and sat in the straight-backed chair by his bed, and Hayden pulled himself into a sitting position, his back against the padded headboard, and turned on the bedside lamp.

She sat in a long nightgown with a blue robe over that, in fuzzy slippers. Looking like someone he knew, like his little girl, only bigger. She had something on her lap that looked like a boxed chess set.

'I see you've met Tigger,' she said, pointing at the orange tabby cat, who repositioned himself between Hayden's calves.

'He introduced himself, yes.'

'He doesn't like anybody usually.'

'So I hear. Is that a chessboard?'

'I thought it might be like old times. Are you up for a game?'

'Sure. Of course I am.'

And for the first time he could remember, Hayden experienced a strange burning feeling behind his eyes that might have been tears. But the strangeness of the sensation shocked him right out of the moment again, and they never materialized. Just left him feeling it had probably been his imagination.

She spilled the chess pieces out onto the bed, and folded out the board, and they worked together to arrange them. They ended up with the white pieces on Hayden's side, so he started.

'So, are you and Mom going to be okay at the wedding?'

'I think so.'

A long silence while he decided how to move, what to move. Then her answering move came almost immediately, and presented an immediate pressing threat, and he realized he was already on the defensive. And he realized it had been fifteen years since they'd played, and that she'd been practicing all this time. Realized, in a way he perhaps never had before, that her life had gone on without him and he'd missed it.

'What about Grampa Ed?'

'That could be a problem.'

'What can we do?'

'Would it ruin your wedding completely if I choked him to death?'

'Daddy. Don't even joke about it.'

'I'll just have to be on my best behavior then.'

They played in silence a few minutes, and Allegra put him in check, and the moment he got free, put him in check again. And he knew he was on the run now, and it was only a matter of time. But he didn't mind. Not from her.

'Daddy? Why do you hate Grampa Ed so much?'

'Truth?'

'Truth.'

'Even if it might hurt your feelings?'

'Go ahead.'

'Truth is, right at this moment I don't know you well enough to talk to you about that.'

'Okay.'

'Did that hurt your feelings?'

'It's okay. It's true. I'm glad you said it out loud. I think that's checkmate.'

'I think you're right.'

'I'm sorry.'

'Why should you be sorry?'

'I don't know. I didn't think I'd beat you.'

'You're supposed to grow up and beat me.' She began to scoop the pieces together, to load them back into the folding chessboard box. 'Wait,' he said. 'Don't clean up so fast. One more game.'

'Okay. One more game.'

And she beat him that game too.

'When are they coming?' Hayden asked.

'Tomorrow night.'

'They're staying here?'

'I'm afraid so.'

'Then I need to stay somewhere else,' he said.

She gathered up the chess pieces with a smile that looked tight and sad. But she didn't argue.

'I put fresh towels in the bathroom for you,' Judith said.

Hayden stood with his right shoulder on the door frame for balance, a crutch propped stiffly under each armpit. The crutch on the left proved almost unbearably painful when he leaned his full weight on it, pulled on those resected chest muscles, so he tried not to lean hard on it. But he had to practice.

'Thanks for hiding me out,' he said.

'You still have to see him tomorrow.'

'I'll deal with that tomorrow.'

'Maybe you should get back in the wheelchair now.'

Hayden glanced at it, sitting alone and static in the corner of her guest room, under the window. 'I don't have much more time to get used to these crutches.'

'It's too soon. Go to the wedding in the wheelchair.'

'I can't.'

'Why? No one cares.'

'I can't.'

'Fine. You can't. I'll be upstairs. I'd like to think you'll call if you need any help. But I know you too well.'

And she disappeared.

Hayden crutched his way over to the window and looked out. Saw only the hillside, a small overgrown garden. Green, all green. He swung his way slowly around the room, wondering at that fine line between getting used to crutches and wearing himself out. Waking up sore and overtaxed. He knew the line was out there somewhere, but wasn't sure he'd know it when he saw it.

His room had a brown leather sofa on one side, a desk in the corner. A double bed on the other side that seemed out of place. It looked more like an office, with a bed moved in at the last minute. Not everybody has a spare downstairs bedroom.

He stopped on the way by the window again. Wished

he could see the bay, something that looked like Marin. He felt his bearings turning muddy, half lost. He was never quite sure where he was these days.

He set off around the room again, his jaw set now, wincing. Doing it anyway. Allegra would tell them he was here. His mother would ask, When is Hayden getting in? Where is he staying? When can we get together? And even though Hayden had told Allegra not to give away his whereabouts, she would. Because she was a lousy liar. Always had been.

Maybe Hayden should be there, facing him. Maybe this was too much like hiding.

He pitched forward, wearing down now, and felt himself overbalance. Tried to throw the right crutch forward to catch himself, but its rubber tip snagged in the thick carpeting and he just kept falling. Landed hard on one crutch, bruising his ribs, jarring his wounded chest painfully, knocking out what little wind he had left. He lay still for a few moments, waiting for the pain to subside. Working on shallow, even breaths. Wondering if the noise would bring her downstairs.

He tried to get up, but it was hard to get his good leg underneath him, and he felt so weak. He looked up to see Judith standing in the bedroom doorway.

'Can I help?'

'I can do it.' She turned immediately to go. 'Judith?

Wait. That was just one of those old reflexes. I could use some help.'

She got his wheelchair from the corner, wheeled it close, and set the brake. Together they levered him up and around and he fell heavily into the leather sling seat, sorely out of breath.

'Thank you,' he said, and took the brake off. Tried to roll over to his temporary new bed, but his left arm had no remaining strength at all. So she helped again.

'Why are you doing this, Hayden?'

'Do you have any idea how tall my father is?'

'No. How tall is he?'

'Six six.'

'He doesn't seem that tall.'

'Well he is.'

'What's that got to do with—'

'Do you have any idea how helpless I would feel sitting in that chair staring at his belt buckle?'

'Hayden, he's not that threatening.'

'Not to you, maybe.'

'You need help getting into bed?'

'No. I just need to rest a minute.'

'Good night, then.'

'I wish the wedding wasn't tomorrow. I need more time.'

'You're so twisted up about this, Hayden. Won't it be better to just get it over with?'

'Yeah, I guess.'

Judith stopped in the doorway on her way out. In the dim light she didn't look much different than he remembered. He felt for a split second that he could lose his bearings in time as easily as he'd lost his recent bouts with place.

'I'm sorry I invited him. If I had it to do over again, I wouldn't.'

'If we had it to do over again, Judith, just think of all the things we'd change.'

When he looked up to the doorway again she was gone.

Hayden sat up in bed, turned on the light. It was only nine thirty. Why had he thought he could sleep? Exhausted and sleepy were two entirely different entities.

He picked up the phone, beside the bed. Called information for the number, then dialed half of it. Hung up the phone. Picked it up again and dialed all seven numbers. It rang four times, then Allegra picked up.

'Hi, honey. Am I calling too late?'

'No, we just got back from the airport. Are you okay over there?'

'Fine. Did you tell them where I was?'

'They haven't asked yet. I just said you're meeting us at the chapel tomorrow.'

'Good. Allegra? Can I talk to my mother for a second?'

'Sure. Hang on, Daddy.' She must have set the phone down then, because he could hear her, but distant. Hear her calling. 'Grandma Lucy?'

An unfamiliar voice came on the line and said hello.

'Is that you, Mom?'

'Hayden?'

'Yeah, Mom. It's me.'

'Where are you, honey?'

'I'm over at Judith's, Mom.'

'I was hoping we'd see you tonight.'

'I'm not sure I'm really up for that. Maybe I could just see *you*. I'd like to talk to you. I really would. I could send a cab for you. It's only a couple of miles.'

'Well, I really can't go off and leave your daddy, hon. He needs a lot of help all the time. We could both come. I sure would like to see you. My God, hon. It's been years.'

'I don't think I can see him tonight, Mom. I thought maybe I could just see you alone for a while.' Believe me, Mom, if I thought I could see you without seeing him I wouldn't have stayed away all these years.

'I really can't go off and leave him.'

'Yeah, you were always loyal to him.' The other reason I didn't come visit. 'I'll see you at the wedding tomorrow.'

She said, 'I sure look forward to it, Hayden.' She
didn't say, Are you okay? I heard you almost died. But
maybe she hadn't heard that. How did he know what
she had heard?

'Good night, Mom.'

Hayden hung up the phone and turned off the light
again and sat in the dark. That feeling came back, that
itchy, aggravating feeling of something behind his
eyes. But he pushed it away and thought, I never could
talk to her. Why should I be surprised?

He thought he would never sleep. But when Judith
climbed into bed with him it jostled him awake. At
first he just held still, as if she were an intruder, a thief,
and his best shot at survival might be to play dead or
asleep.

But after a moment he felt strangely, stiffly awake,
and it seemed too much like acquiescence to say
nothing at all.

So he said, 'What in God's name are you doing?'

And, she said, 'I don't know. I just got tired of
lying awake wrestling with myself about it. I'll go if
you want.' But he didn't tell her to go. She tucked up
against his back. 'I always hated sleeping alone. I never
feel safe.'

'You couldn't have felt too safe with me.'

'At night I did. I'm not trying to make a move on you.'

'I know.'

They lay still and quiet for a moment, and the sense of affront dissolved, and it felt natural to have her up against his back, something he'd always known. It still seemed familiar.

She must have felt something similar, because she said, 'You never used to wear pajama tops.' He sighed and didn't answer. 'People change, I guess,' she said, as if to save him the trouble.

'It's such a mess.'

'What is?'

'My chest. I don't even like to look at it myself.'

'Can I see?'

'No.'

'I didn't think so. You always wanted to keep things from me. Anything you thought I wouldn't like about you. You always wanted to spare me your messes. But it's part of what always kept us apart from each other, I think.'

'We weren't always apart from each other.'

'In some ways we were.'

Neither spoke for a time, and Hayden wondered if they were supposed to go back to sleep this way. But he felt entirely awake. Judith broke the silence in a quiet voice.

'Lucy told me a lot about your childhood.'

'Like what?'

'She told me how hard Ed was on you. And on Daniel.'

'Did she tell you what happened to Daniel?'

'Yeah.'

'She shouldn't have.' But to his surprise he felt strangely relieved. As if something heavy could be set down now. 'I should have told you myself.'

'Yeah. You should have.'

'When you're married to somebody you should trust them with that sort of thing.'

'I'm glad you finally see that.'

'Think you can ever forgive me for that?'

'I know I couldn't have at the time. But we're a lot older now. We've had a lot of time to think.'

'I'm not sure you can think your way through forgiveness.'

He rolled over slowly, painfully, and lay facing her. And could barely make out the lines of her face in the light from the window. She wore a nightgown cut low, scooped down to show her collarbone, the bones of her intact, unscarred chest. And as his eyes adjusted to the dark he saw the necklace. He couldn't believe it was the same one, so he reached out and took it in his hand; he held it close to his face to see.

'Yeah, it is,' she said.

'Isn't all the gold plating worn off by now?'

'I think it was all worn off by nineteen eighty-five.'

'Why do you still wear it? Never mind. Don't answer that.'

'Maybe it would be better if I went back upstairs.'

'No, don't. Please stay.'

She rolled over and he tucked up behind her, threw his weak left arm over her, and they lay that way together. Hayden couldn't seem to get beyond that strange sense of alertness to her presence. He never got back to sleep.

They set off along the coast together at 7 A.M., in Judith's BMW. Hayden was in his rented tux, with the crutches leaning on the seat beside him and the wheel-chair folded up in the backseat.

'Just as a fallback,' she said. 'That's not a pun.'

'How long a drive is this place?'

'More than an hour.'

'Are my parents driving up with Allegra and John?'

'I would think so. I don't know. I just know I'm supposed to bring you.' They drove in silence for a few minutes, then Judith said, 'I'm really sorry.'

'About what?' His guess would have been the fiasco of inviting Ed, but he wanted to be sure.

'I should have just stayed in my own room. See, I knew this would happen. As soon as I saw you again.'

And they lapsed back into silence. Hayden looked

out the window for a few minutes, ran his fingers along the sharp creases of his tuxedo pants. 'Why should you be sorry?'

'It isn't fair to you. You can't throw a guy away for fifteen years and then try to take him back again.'

'I had no idea that's what you were trying to do.'

'Well. Not *trying*.'

'I don't think we're in any danger of getting back together.'

The silence cycled in again, and Hayden noticed it felt less comfortable each time it came around.

A moment later he looked over at the side of Judith's face. Stung himself for a moment on her looks. She wore a deep green dress for the wedding, and a trace of makeup, and gold earrings that he recognized from years ago. Along with that face. Only the dress was new.

And he knew by the look in her eyes and by the grip of her hands on the wheel that he had hurt her feelings. And he found himself surprised, both that such a simple statement would hurt her and that he still knew her well enough to tell.

Hayden stood balanced on crutches on the hilltop near the car, surrounded by a thick stand of cypress trees. The ground under his feet seemed unusually soft, a sandy soil, and the walking wouldn't be easy. And he was already exhausted from dressing himself. And the cross on the chapel roof made him feel edgy.

Judith came around and stood close in front of him and put a hand on his collar. He expected her to adjust it, but she didn't. Just put one hand on it.

'You look handsome,' she said.

'Thank you.' He wanted to tell her she looked pretty, but he knew he couldn't bring those words out just now.

He swung his weary weight slowly, carefully, to the front entrance of the chapel, and stood before the open doors, a riot of flowers catching his eye inside. And found himself confronted with three wide wooden steps, which might just as well have been Mount Everest.

Judith wheeled him up the ramp and in the side door, the delivery door, into a storage room, and they left the chair there. And she put one hand on his arm as they made their way inside. Hayden knew it must be hard for her to walk so slowly. Didn't know whether her hand was there for his balance, to prevent another crutch accident, or if she just wanted to be close, for old times' sake. Like last night.

'We're the first ones here,' she said, and helped him into a seat in the frontmost pew.

A few seconds later John's parents and two brothers

arrived, and greeted Judith, and Hayden tried to stand to meet them, but they told him to please not bother, to just be comfortable. And he shook all their hands from a seated position, and heard all the names he was about to forget, and then they all disappeared, including Judith, to bring more flowers in from their car.

Hayden sat alone looking at the painted plaster statue of Mary beside the altar, arms out wide, looking up toward the sky, and wanted to ask her what she thought she saw.

A hand appeared on his shoulder. 'Hello, Hayden.'

'Thea,' he said, without even looking, because he knew the voice. And he felt glad, gratified, which was a feeling he had not completely expected. She came around and sat beside him.

'Good to see you again, Hayden.'

'You look wonderful.'

'No I don't. I look old.'

She looked older. But good. A welcome sight. 'We're all fifteen years older, Thea. You didn't corner the market on that.'

'Oh, I suppose. Have you been well?' Her voice changed as she said it, her face changed to evince concern, weighing heavy in her eyes.

'Is that a trick question?'

She laughed. Hayden was just about to say, We'll

talk. We'll get together and talk for hours. We owe it to each other. After all, Thea was the closest thing to a mother he'd had in years.

But the thought was disturbed by the arrival of two more guests. An elderly couple. They hobbled through the door together, her hand on his arm, as if he'd tumble without it. He walked stooped, the man, his spine pitched forward, his face blotched unpleasantly by that skin condition that produces patches of missing pigment. A slight ring of thin white hair over his ears, cloudy eyes that seemed to look at nothing. The woman looked ten years younger, but that was still old enough.

'Are those John's grandparents?' Hayden asked Thea.

She just watched him stare for a moment without answering. Then she said, 'Hayden, those are your parents.'

'Help me up,' he said, though he did not entirely believe she was correct.

He teetered there on his crutches, looking past them as they approached, searching out a familiar face. Judith or the kids. He looked over at Thea and she smiled at him. A sharp pang of nicotine craving struck him unexpectedly.

'Hayden?' His mother's voice. He knew it not from the past but from the phone call last night.

'Yeah, it's me, Mom.'

They stood right in front of him now, and Hayden looked down to see the top of his father's mottled, bald head. Which seemed impossible and wrong. His father looked up, eyes strangely cloudy and without color. And spoke.

'You a friend of the bride?'

Which embarrassed Lucy. 'Ed, it's Hayden.' She shouted the words close to his ear.

'Who?'

'Your son.'

'Oh, oh. Right. Of course.'

'I have to go help Ed sit down, honey.'

'Sure, Mom. We'll talk later.'

And he stood quiet and still and watched them walk away, and heard Ed say, 'Who was that again?' Watched them settle in the front pew on the other side of the aisle. Watched his father's eyes, staring off into nothing.

'Could you do me a favor, Thea? Could you go get my wheelchair? It's in the storage room in the back.'

While she went off to get it he settled carefully onto the wood pew, and looked at his mother, who smiled apologetically. And looked back to see Thea arrive with the chair, and they were a welcome sight, both of them. He wouldn't have to try to get up again. He couldn't remember what had possessed him to attempt this day on crutches. So painful and tiring and without purpose.

Judith came back and sat beside him. 'The kids are here. They'll be right in. Good move,' she said, indicating the wheelchair near Hayden's right knee.

'How did my father get so short?'

'He's just stooped.'

'No, he's not *just* stooped. Even if he could stand up straight he'd be a couple of inches shorter than me.'

'Well, old people shrink, Hayden. They lose bone mass.'

'My father shrunk.' He chewed that over in silence for a moment. 'That's not a bad deal.'

'I tried to tell you there was nothing to worry about.'

'Yeah. I guess you did.'

After the ceremony, Hayden sat in the comfortable sling of his wheelchair in the sandy dirt, at the edge of the slope, with the wheels safely locked. Looking off to the ocean, listening to the happy murmur of guests at his back, clustering in front of the chapel.

A minute later someone came to stand with him, to share the view.

Hayden was pleased to see it was John.

'You okay, Hayden?'

'Fine. I'm happy for you two.'

'You don't look happy. Was it hard seeing your father?'

'Yes, it was. But not for the reasons I thought. I'm sorry, John. You don't need to know all this.'

'No, it's okay. I'm listening.'

He squatted down beside Hayden's chair, and Hayden stared at the identical fabric of their tuxedo-covered legs.

'All my life I've hated my father. It's been like a drivetrain for me. I'm not sure what I'll do without that. I don't know what's supposed to power me without it.'

'You can still hate him if you want.'

'Not really. Look at him. There's nothing left to hate.'

They both glanced over their shoulders. Watched Ed shuffle away from the crowd, and Lucy go after him and steer him back again.

'I don't think hate would even stick to him,' Hayden said. 'Nothing to hang it on, you know? Probably roll right off him again.'

'Yeah, I guess you're right.'

'I'm fine, John. Really. I just need a moment alone.'

And John obliged him that.

He sat looking at the view, thinking, If I'm not

Hayden Reese, a man who hates his father, then . . . what? Then who am I? Hayden Reese, a man who . . . what? Does what? Thinks what? Is what?

Before he could think it out clearly, Judith arrived to wheel him back to the car.

Chapter Five ⚡

But You Can't

Hayden sat up sharply in bed, jarred free of sleep. Coughing. Thrust suddenly out of a dream that upset him but that he couldn't quite re-create.

It was there, right there somewhere. Right at the edge of his consciousness. He thought he felt a breath of it, and it seemed to involve those woods on the other side of the railroad tracks, where the culvert ran through and trees rose up over his head.

But when he reached in for more, it flew away.

He sat up with his eyes squeezed shut, waiting for the pain of the coughing to subside.

Then he opened his eyes and looked around. Tried to remember where he was. A vague familiarity, but nothing he could place.

Judith's spare room. It came to him with time. He

looked behind him in the bed to see if she had joined him in the night, but he was in this alone. The bedside clock said it was not yet 11 P.M.

He struggled into his wheelchair and rolled over to the desk. Picked up the phone. Dialed directory assistance.

'What city please?'

'I'm in Sausalito. I need a number for a cab company.'

'Which one, sir?'

'I really don't care which one,' he said.

Hayden wheeled up to the house with the crutches across his lap. Listened to the sound of the cab fading away down the street, and wondered if he should have asked the driver to wait.

He abandoned the chair in the driveway and made his way to the door on crutches.

The house stood dark, silent. Empty looking. He prayed he could get someone up to answer the door. It wouldn't be John or Allegra. They were gone already. Away on their honeymoon. Only his parents were still here. Hayden prayed the someone who answered would be her, not him.

He stood with his right shoulder leaning hard on the big wood door, and knocked. Waited. Then grew more desperate, more impatient, and felt more abandoned here, and alone.

He rang the doorbell, several long, insistent rings.

'Who is that at this hour?' he heard her say through the door.

'It's me, Mom. Hayden. Let me in, okay? I need to talk to you.'

The door swung open.

She stood in her robe, her hair half styled from the wedding day, half smashed by her pillow. She looked old. Older than her seventy-four years. And tired. Not just tired because it was late at night. Tired more because it was late in a hard life. Hayden tried to see her as familiar. As his mother. But he seemed to remember her only from the wedding.

'Hayden. What is it, honey, that couldn't wait till morning?'

'Mom, I need to talk to you. It's important.' He came inside, slow and careful on his crutches, wincing at the pull of muscles in his left armpit. He wasn't physically up to this yet. It had been such a long day. He was so tired. 'Is he still asleep?'

'Oh, Lord yes. He always could sleep in a boiler factory. Now he's so deaf. What is it, honey?'

Hayden lowered himself carefully onto the couch.

'Mom, I have to tell you something. I should have told you years ago. The only thing worse than what I'm about to tell you is that I kept it a secret all this time.'

'What, honey? What is it?' She turned on a light

beside the couch to see him better. Looked into his face and her eyes welled with sympathy. 'I thought we weren't going to see you again before we went home. I'm glad to see you, honey, but Lord, it's so late.'

'Please listen, Mom. Please let me tell you this. It's important.'

'Okay, honey. Okay. I'm listening.'

'It was my fault.'

'What was?'

'I was supposed to go out there with him. To hold the rope. I told him not to go up without me. But I said I'd be there. I said I'd meet him out at that tower. Six o'clock. But I never showed. I went off with that girl instead. It never would've happened if I'd been there like I said.' Hayden paused, waited for her to react. Then he couldn't bear the waiting. 'I understand if you hate me. If you never want to speak to me again. But I had to tell you, Mom. I couldn't keep holding on to that.'

'Oh, Hayden.' Her hand came out to touch his face. Liver spotted and bent. 'Oh, honey, is *that* your big secret? Honey, that's nothing.'

'How can you say that? Don't you understand what I'm trying to tell you?'

'It's just nothing, honey. I can't believe you held on to that all this time.'

'I don't think you hear what I'm saying. It was all my fault.'

'No, honey, it wasn't. You said so yourself. You said you told him not to go up without you.'

'Yeah, but—'

'He was an impulsive boy, Hayden. He never did what he was told. He never listened to us, either. It's not your fault he was too rash for his own good.'

And she looked into his face again, and her own face twisted strangely. Hayden thought she was going to cry, but she didn't. She laughed.

Hayden sat still and felt alone and vaguely insulted. That had been his big secret. It *was* big. It wasn't so damn funny. And she seemed to see that, to read that in his eyes or on his face. And she stopped laughing, and the sympathetic look returned.

'Hayden, honey. I blamed myself, too. For a long time. For years. I thought, I was his mother. I should've known where he was. What he was doing. I should've taught him better. What would hurt him. What to stay away from. But I taught him fine, really. He knew what would hurt him, he just went for it anyway. You can't know where your kids are all the time. It was thirty-six years ago, Hayden. Lord, honey, it killed me too, but sooner or later you got to get back to what you were doing before it happened.'

They sat quiet for a moment, Hayden staring down at the crutches leaned across his legs. His left leg felt a little tingly. A buzzy sort of numbness. Marian had said it might, and that it would probably be a good sign. Some feeling might come back. Not all. Be happy for whatever you get, she had said. But he couldn't think about that just now.

'He was my responsibility.'

'He was not. He was our child, Ed's and mine. It was our job to look after his welfare, not yours. You were just a boy yourself.'

'Dad said I was supposed to look out for him.'

'Well, honey, your father said a lot of things. He said it was the Russians put fluoride in our drinking water. Remember that?'

Hayden remembered. And it made him laugh. Just a chuckle at first, but a lot of steam and pressure came out alongside that chuckle, and it got seated and kept going. Turned into almost a giggle. And Lucy caught it, too.

'That always seemed so funny to me. I could never figure out why the Russians wanted us to have strong teeth.'

And they laughed together for a minute, and then sobered suddenly, at almost the same moment.

'Ed had some funny ideas, all right,' she said.

It struck Hayden that they were discussing him as if he were dead.

'What else was he wrong about?' Hayden hoped it would be a long list. Instead she thought too long before answering.

'Well, he always thought Daniel could do every-thing, and you couldn't do anything.'

'Are you sure he was wrong?'

'Positive.'

'What did I ever do better than Daniel?'

They sat together quietly for two or three beats, and then Lucy said, 'You survived.'

'I don't know if that's a talent.'

'It is. The most important one. It requires good sense. God forgive me for saying this, I loved that boy. But he never did have an ounce of good sense. You were always the responsible one. You thought things out before you did them. Lots of good things about you. I tried to remember to always tell you, at the time. Because I knew Ed never would.'

'Why did you stay with him?'

'Where else would I go?'

'How could you stay with him all these years?'

He looked up at her face and thought she looked hurt. And wished he hadn't asked, wished he had just limited this to himself, not turned it around onto her.

'I made up my mind after what happened. I decided if he ever raised his hand to you, I'd take you and go.'

'But he never did.'

'No, he never did. Seemed like his hand went down after that. And yours went up. He was kind of pathetic from then on. Especially after that time you beat him so bad.'

'I really did that? It's funny, I remember that. But for some reason I always think I'm remembering wrong. Like something I wish I'd done. Not like something I really did.'

'Oh, you did it, all right. Hit him with a chair. Broke his collarbone and gave him a concussion. Then you walked out of the house with just the clothes on your back and I didn't see you again for three years. That time when you were nineteen and you came to visit while he was at work. Never told me where you were all that time. Never came again after that. He was so beaten down by then. Seemed kind of cruel to run out on him after everybody else did. Besides, I loved him. I know that may be hard for you to understand but I was in love with that man. No matter what he did, the feeling never seemed to go away.'

'It's not hard to fall in love,' Hayden said. 'The hard part is to love somebody who might actually do you some good.'

That stopped the conversation pretty well in its tracks. Hayden sat quiet and began thinking maybe he should call a cab. Go back home to Judith's. Why he thought of it as home he couldn't say.

'Nobody said things like that in my day,' she said, just as he was about to struggle to his feet. 'It was more like a lottery. You just fell in love. And then later you found out what you'd gotten yourself into.'

'I think most people still do it that way.' The urge to rise, to leave, seemed to abandon him like breath spilling out in a long sigh. 'I just keep thinking, If I could just go back to that moment, and go meet him out there this time. Think of everything that would be different now.'

'But you can't, though.'

'Such a stupid thing. Such a stupid, unimportant moment. At the time. And then, by the time you find out how important it is, it's over, it's too late. Everything balances on that moment, but you don't even get to know that till it's too late. If he just could've survived that. Somehow. Sometimes people do. There was that kid in southern California a couple of years ago. Lost an arm and a leg to those burns but he made it somehow.'

'Why would you want Daniel to go through all that?'

'So he could forgive me.' He waited, but she didn't answer. 'People do that, you know. Forgive each other for really big things. The kind of things you'd never think they could get beyond. It happens.'

'I don't think you need Daniel to forgive you, honey. I think you just need to forgive yourself. I can't believe you haven't done that yet. Thirty-six years, Hayden.

That's a long time to suffer. Don't you think you've paid enough?'

'Sometimes I tell myself I have. It's all words, though.'

He braced his crutches in place and levered to his feet.

'Why not sleep here, honey?'

But he didn't really want to see Ed in the morning. He could. He knew he could, if he had to. But why subject himself to that? And Judith would worry if she woke up and found him gone.

'Could you just call a cab for me, Mom?'

'Okay, if that's what you want.'

And she went off to make the call, and Hayden got a head start on the trip back to his wheelchair. Which he assumed, hoped, was still sitting alone in the driveway waiting for him.

Such a long trip. Such a long day. His mind rolled back to the wedding earlier that morning, and it seemed like something that had happened weeks ago. Such a long, tiring day.

And the crutch hurt so much under his left arm. He wondered if this was what physical therapy would feel like, but he knew it would be worse, much worse. But he made it to the chair.

He sat in the driveway in the still night, looking up at the stars, and decided it didn't matter. It didn't matter that it would be hard, that it would hurt. What mattered was that he had survived, that he was fifty years old and he was still here. Which was a lot more than Daniel could ever say.

Lucy came up behind him.

'They said it'll be fifteen minutes for the cab.'

'That's fine, Mom.'

'Should I keep you company?'

'I'm okay here by myself.'

'It's kind of cold. But I'll stay here if you want.'

'Go back to sleep now. I'm sorry I woke you up.'

Hayden heard the soft sound of her slippers on the asphalt driveway. Walking away.

And because he didn't expect to see her again, he said, 'I love you, Mom.'

And she said, 'I love you, too, Son,' and went back inside.

When the cab turned down Judith's street, he wondered how he'd get back in. He'd thought of leaving the door unlocked for himself, but he hadn't done it. Not safe for her. Not fair to leave her in that position. He'd have to knock and wake her up.

But as the cab pulled into her driveway, Hayden saw that the problem had repaired itself.

The lights were on in the living room and Judith was awake, sitting in the window, looking out like a parent waiting for a teenager to get home from a first date.

In her nightgown she came out to meet him, and helped him into his wheelchair, which was much appreciated. He was so tired and sore from those damn crutches.

'What woke you up?' he said when they were back inside, safe, and finished with this difficult day at last. 'How did you even know I was gone?'

'I'm not sure why I woke up,' she said.

Which Hayden took to mean that she had come downstairs again to be with him. But he could be wrong. And he didn't want to embarrass her if he was right. So he just said, 'I'm so tired.'

'Can I help you get undressed and get into bed?' After the uncomfortable pause, she said, 'It's not like we don't know each other.'

'Sure. I need the help.'

She wheeled him into the downstairs bedroom. 'If you want to sleep with your shirt on, I'll understand.'

'No, it's okay. You wanted to see that.'

'You sure?'

'You said I never showed you my messes.'

'If you're sure.'

She pulled the covers back and helped him swing over onto the bed.

He sat upright and unbuttoned his shirt, took it off, and lay down on his back and undid his jeans, and she helped by pulling them off, along with his socks and shoes. And he made a quick choice to leave the underwear just as it was, and pulled the blankets up over himself. But only over his bottom half, so as not to appear to be hiding his scars from her.

She came and sat beside him and touched the ruined skin of his chest lightly.

'Thank you for letting me see,' she said. 'Does that hurt?'

'Just a little. I mean, you're being gentle enough.'

'Trust me with one more mess,' she said, and got under the covers with him and turned off the light.

'What do you mean?'

'Tell me who you were so mad at.'

'I don't know what you mean.'

'You were so angry. All those years. Tell me why.'

'I thought my mother told you.'

'She told me what happened. I want to know why you were so angry. You must have thought someone was to blame.'

'Somebody had to be. It happened.'

'I don't know. Some things just happen. Act of God.'

'I'm not sure I believe in God,' he said, and reached for her in the dark. Took her hand and pulled her over closer.

'Are you making a move on me, Hayden?'

'Look, don't take this the wrong way,' he said, putting

his arm around her shoulder, needing that closeness suddenly, 'but I haven't got the energy.'

She put her head down on his shoulder, her finger-tips tracing the patterns of scar tissue on his chest. 'I thought you did believe in God,' she said. 'In some form, anyway. It always seemed like you were looking for something to believe.'

They lay quietly together for a while before he answered.

'I used to think the power lines were God. Well, I mean – not the lines, but the power. You know they always describe God as a power. I know it sounds weird.'

'Not really. Not after what happened.'

'Electricity is such a strange thing. I mean, it's always there, it's all around us. But you can't see it. But it can take your life just like that.' Hayden snapped his fingers in the dark. 'I guess I kind of deified it when I was younger. Once you see what it can do, that makes more sense.'

'So, whose fault was it?'

'I still don't know what you mean.'

'You must have blamed somebody to be so mad.'

'I blamed myself.'

'Do you still?'

'Not right at this moment. I guess not.'

'So, who are you blaming now?'

'I don't know. That's the problem.'

'You're the one who always thought everything had to be somebody's fault.'

'I'm still not sure what you're driving at.'

'Never mind. Is it okay if I stay?'

'Please do.'

He rolled over, out from under her, and she tucked up to his naked back, and threw one arm over him, and they lay together in the dark, Hayden wishing he could sleep. He was so exhausted. If only he could get some sleep.

'I told that little asshole not to do it,' he said, surprised that he'd said it out loud. It hadn't really been premeditated, to voice it. But as long as he had . . . 'Now he's out of here and I'm the one who has to live with it.'

He waited to see what she would say. When she didn't respond immediately, he said, 'I can't believe I just said that.'

'I can't believe it took you so long.'

'You can't be mad at somebody who's dead.'

'Sure you can.'

'You can't blame a dead person.'

'Sure you can. You can and you should.'

'It doesn't seem right.'

'It seems right to me.'

'I can't believe how tired I am.'

'It's been a hard day.'

But he closed his eyes again and knew he couldn't sleep.

He felt Judith brush against him as she rolled onto her other side. Felt himself respond to that. Unexpectedly. He rolled up against her back, and then she felt it, too.

'That exhausted, huh?'

'I didn't ask for that to happen.'

'I could do all the work.'

'Is that what you want, Judith?'

'It's not like we never did before.'

'It's not like we ever thought we would again.'

'We're still married. Technically speaking.'

'We can't pick up where we left off.'

'I never said we could. God, why would we even want to? Considering where we left off.'

'I'm not the same man you married.'

'I noticed that. But you see, you're also not the same man I left.'

He drew away to give her more room, and she rolled onto her back. And then he rolled over on top of her. Feeling the familiar way their bodies fit together. Different in some ways, the same in others. More the same, the way he remembered. She wrapped her arms around his back.

'I could be on top if this is hard for you.'

'We'll see how long I last like this.'

She kissed him. A tentative kiss, with their tongues barely, shyly touching.

When he pulled his face away, he felt it coming around again, for the third time in as long as he could remember.

That burning behind his eyes.

That strange, irritating sensation.

But her hands exploring his back and sides distracted him from that strange burning, and he forgot to put a lid on it. Forgot to hold it in.

And he felt one tear let go. Heard it, in fact. The slight tap of it, hitting the pillow near her head. Wondered if she had heard it, too.

Then a second one, from the other eye. It welled up and fell and he listened for the tap, but didn't hear it. Wondered if it had fallen on her face.

And wondered whether this was how crying was supposed to go, how it was supposed to feel. Why it should be a big deal, one way or the other.

'Hayden,' she said, 'are you crying?'

'I think maybe so.'

'Hayden. When did you learn to cry?'

'I think this is my first lesson right now.'

Chapter Six

He Is Delivered from the Fish

Judith woke him in the morning with coffee in bed. And he sat up, still bare chested, to drink it.

'When do we leave?' he asked.

'Think first. Make sure that's really what you want.'

Tigger, Allegra's cat, jumped up on the bed, because he'd been brought to Judith's house for the length of the honeymoon.

Hayden sipped at his coffee and listened to the thoughts and questions tumbling around in his head. But he couldn't bring himself to ask why she wanted him here, what made her so sure that was a good idea.

So he just said, 'Why did she name her cat Tigger, I wonder.'

And Judith said, 'She didn't. He used to be my cat. I named him.' She sat cross-legged on the end of his bed in her robe, bare legged and barefoot, her hair freshly combed, no makeup. Not that she needed any. 'I always identified with Tigger. The character, not the cat.'

'You're not a very bouncy type.'

'I have my moments. I think I identify with Tigger because he doesn't even know what he is. I mean, he's a Tigger. But apparently there aren't any others like him. And he doesn't even know what Tiggers eat. And he doesn't know what he can do. So he assumes he can do anything. Bounces up a tree and then figures out he can't climb down.'

'I never knew you felt like that.'

'There's a lot we don't know about each other. We could find out, though.'

And the thoughts and questions began to tumble again. It took him a while to sort them all through. None of them seemed like something he could say.

So he just said, 'It's impossible.'

'What is?'

'You and me. It's impossible.'

She looked hurt, like he'd taken all the bounce out of her. She didn't look her age suddenly. More like someone young and hurt. 'It's not impossible,' she said, somewhat belligerently. 'It's just highly improbable.'

And Hayden laughed, and Judith joined him in that.

'Okay. It's highly improbable.'

'Want breakfast?'

'Not really. I'm not very hungry.'

'Okay. If you're sure it's what you want, I'll drive you home.'

'I'm sure,' he said.

About two miles into the headlight zone, they encountered a roadblock. Hayden saw it in the distance. Wanted it to be manned by somebody he knew, somebody local, Scott or one of his deputies. But it looked more like the highway patrol.

They were cruising along in Judith's BMW with the top down. The day was perfect, the sky blue, the air clean-smelling and crisp, and it wasn't until he saw the roadblock that it even occurred to him to wonder what the weather had been doing while he was away.

Judith rode the brake slightly. Eased the speed way down.

'What the hell,' she said.

'Maybe there was flooding.'

'Oh, yeah. I forgot about that.'

'We should have been listening to the radio,' he said.

Hayden could understand why Judith would forget. But how could he have? She'd told him the creeks were on the rise. And yet he'd gone off and never thought to listen to the news, or watch the weather channel, or call home. But he couldn't beat himself up too badly for it, because he understood why. It was Allegra, suddenly his daughter again. And this sudden son-in-law, John. And seeing his parents again. And finding out he was about to be a grandfather. And Judith in his bed, suddenly acting like his wife again. It just hadn't left any room in his brain for the weather. Especially not the weather somewhere else.

Judith stopped in front of the roadblock. The highway patrol officer came over and stood with his arm on the top of the windshield.

'Sorry, folks. This highway is closed.'

'I'm a local,' Hayden said. 'I live up there.'

'Some ID, please?'

Hayden dug his wallet out of his back pocket and passed his driver's license across Judith.

The officer frowned at it. 'Well, brace yourself,' he said, 'because it hit hard up there. I'm going to let you through, but you drive careful now. You're going up there at your own risk. Lot of mud and debris on the road. Go slow. You see a patch of mud, don't know how deep it is, don't go into it. Rescue personnel got too much to do, can't be hauling stuck cars off the road.'

Hayden just stared at the man, willing his brain to work faster. Better. 'I was only gone three days,' he said. It sounded weak and foolish when he said it, but that's what he was able to manage.

'Well, sir, we got sixteen more inches of rain in that three days. Twenty-two up in the mountains. They're calling this a fifty-year storm. All that water got to go somewhere. So it came downhill. You folks go slow and careful, you hear?'

'We will, Officer,' Judith said.

'Have a nice day, now.'

Hayden snorted, but Judith pulled around the road-block smoothly and fairly quickly, and they were gone and away before that came out. Before it could be heard.

'What if you've taken a lot of damage?' Judith said. 'What will you do?'

It was a question Hayden couldn't answer, and so did not wish to be asked. He made no reply.

'If you've had water in the cabin, it'll be a huge job cleaning it out. There'll be mud everywhere. 'You won't be able to stay there.'

'Let's just wait till we see.'

'I'd stay and help you if I could, but I have appointments tomorrow. I can't afford any more time away from my practice.'

'Scott'll help me,' he said. Unless Scott was too busy with all the other emergencies. 'Peg'll help me.' If she's speaking to me.

When they pulled into his long driveway, already everything was wrong. His bearings were all wrong.

Because there were no landmarks. No mailbox where it should have been. Was it gone? Or was he wrong about where it should have been? Because, with that coating of silty mud on everything, maybe he could be wrong about where things should be.

They rounded the bend of his driveway, and he braced himself for the worst. Or thought he did, anyway. Braced himself to see a tree through the roof. The cabin taken right off its foundation. Two feet of mud oozing out the front door. But he saw none of that. He saw, instead, a scene for which he was not prepared. A smooth, unfamiliar, undeveloped piece of land. Mud everywhere, debris, mostly tree trunks and limbs. A yellow Frisbee half stuck in the mud. A dead calf washed away from some unlucky rancher miles upstream. A 300- or 400-pound tree limb snagged on the edge of what he gradually realized to be the foundation of his cabin.

Judith said, 'Hayden. Didn't the cabin used to be . . . ?'

'Yes,' he said. 'Right there.'

'Well, I know this is a stupid question, but – where did it go?'

'Downstream,' he said. 'I would venture it went downstream.'

'You sound calm about this.'

'I do, don't I?'

'Do you feel calm?'

'I don't know what I feel, Judith. I'm a little numb right now.'

They sat quietly for a few minutes. Hayden leaned his head back on the headrest and looked up at the brilliant blue sky. It seemed wrong, somehow, for all this to hit him on such a beautiful day. He felt Judith reach across the seat for his hand. He allowed her to take it and hold it.

He thought first about Kim Phuc, the napalm girl. Washed away downstream. Silly, because he could get another copy of that. In the library, or at the back-copy office at the paper. But it had been his, stored safely in his house, and it didn't seem right that it should be gone.

Then he thought about the photos of Jenny. All gone now, and he'd never get to take another. Years would pass and he wouldn't remember what she looked like, not really. Not clearly.

Then he thought about his wedding ring, in some drawer somewhere in that cabin. Was the drawer still in the chest somewhere, and was the chest of drawers still in the cabin? Or had every element come apart from itself? Was that ring sitting all by itself under ten inches of mud, and if so, in what part of the state?

Judith broke the still. 'I don't get it' she said. 'Water has that much force?'

'Sometimes,' he said. 'I've heard it can. I think usually it's more what's *in* the water. Whole uprooted trees. Cars washed off highways. They hit garages and barns and then the debris of that is racing downhill, too.'

'I wonder how high the water got.'

'You don't need to wonder. There's your high-water mark. Right there.' He pointed to the base of the closest electrical tower. 'The bottom of that tower. See where the mud has coated it?'

'Oh. Yeah. God. Thank God you weren't in there.'

He thought about that for a minute. Peg gone. Scott would have gotten him out. Right? Peg would have put petty issues aside. Wouldn't she? 'It's not that it was a lot of stuff. Or that it was good stuff. It's just—'

'It's just everything you owned.'

'Right. Except . . .' He pointed to his suitcase in the backseat. The few things of his she'd packed before leaving this place. He figured his worldly possessions amounted to about that of a weekend traveler.

'It was a spartan life,' she said. 'You really lived all alone out here for fifteen years?'

'Except for the various times I was in jail, yes.'

'Not many of the comforts of home.'

Whose home? he thought. But he felt no need, no desire to quarrel with her now. 'I thought it was pretty fancy for a fish belly.'

'A what? Is that another expression you use out here?'

'You forgot.'

'What did I forget?'

'I was Jonah. Remember?'

'Oh. God, I wish you hadn't reminded me. That's such an awful memory. It makes my stomach hurt to think about that.'

His, too, if he'd let it. If he'd thought about it. Instead he let his mind mull over a more general area of his water karma. The way he'd dreamed of all that water while he was in the hospital. Watching it roar down-hill, drowning in it. Probably not prophetic. Probably just a sign that his lungs were filling up. Still, the water thing. It didn't seem to want to leave him alone.

Judith broke the silence again. Broke his strange, state-of-shock thought patterns. 'What happened to Jonah, anyway? After he got swallowed by the whale? I can't remember anymore.'

'Actually,' he said, 'the Bible doesn't say it was a whale. It says, "A great fish."'

'Well, a whale is pretty great.'

'But it's not a fish.'

'Maybe they didn't know that back in biblical times.'

'Maybe not.'

'What happened to him? I can't remember.'

'The fish spit him out.'

'That's it? Just like, ptooie?' And she exaggerated the motions of a spitting fish. 'Like a bad taste in his mouth?'

'Not exactly. According to the Bible, the Lord spake unto the fish and it vomited Jonah onto dry land.'

'Ah, He spake. Right. Then it didn't spit. It vomited. There's a difference.'

'Yes, I suppose there is.'

They sat quietly for a few minutes, looking at mud and electricity, and the strange absence of what had been. Looking not so much at what he saw but at what he expected to see and did not. 'That's how I feel right about now,' he said after a time. 'Like something that got vomited up.'

'Physically, or otherwise?'

'Both, I guess.'

'Physically, you have to give it some time. You haven't even been out of the hospital two weeks. It'll get better.'

'I'm sure it will. Jonah only had to be in that belly three days, you know.'

'Meaning?'

'I spent almost fifteen years in this place.'

'I can understand you're still angry with me.'

'I didn't say that. I just said fifteen years is a long time.'

'Well,' she said, 'I guess it is. But maybe fifteen years to us is like three days to God. You know how God is.'

He didn't. Not really. But he didn't bother to say so.

'Well, I guess you'll have to come home with me after all,' she said.

'Yeah,' he said, without even thinking, or worrying, or hashing, or negotiating, or asking questions. 'I guess I'll just go home with you.'

They wound their way slowly and carefully back through town. Trash Dumpsters had been hauled in and set by the sides of the road, for locals to discard their carpeting, their soaked books, their furniture, things that had been worth a great deal to them, usable, just a few days before.

They talked about getting something to eat, but figured they'd have to get well clear of the damage zone first. Hayden thought about telling her to stop and let him off. Just go on without him. But he decided to share his reservations with her instead.

'What the hell am I going to do up there?' he said.

'Recover,' she said.

'Then what? What do I do for money? Just live off you?'

Judith chewed at the edge of her lip a moment. 'First you'll apply for social security.'

'At age fifty?'

'You're permanently disabled.'

'Oh. Right.'

'Do you own that land?'

'Yes.'

'If you sold it, you'd have a little money to start over.'

Hayden saw the diner up in the distance on his right. Saw somebody who looked like Jack sweeping water out the front door. Stroke after stroke of thick, muddy water. All the tables and chairs had been stacked out in the parking lot.

'Pull in here,' he said.

'I don't think we'll get a good meal here.'

'Just pull in. Okay?'

She did.

Hayden sat without moving for a moment. He kept his eyes on Jack as he spoke to Judith. 'So, I'd be living in your house?'

'We could play that by ear. The kids have that extra room if you'd be more comfortable there.'

'Just what they need. A chaperon.'

'No. A baby-sitter. Which is exactly what they need. Remember when we first had Allegra? How did we survive that, Hayden? Do you remember?'

They both said it at the same time. 'Thea.'

That was hard to argue, even for Hayden.

He pulled his crutches out of the backseat. Judith started to get out, to come around to help him.

'Don't,' he said. Then, afraid he had come off sounding short, he said, 'I just need to say a few words to this guy before we go.'

She waited silently as he levered himself onto his crutches, bracing on the car door, leaning his back against the car to gain balance. She watched without helping. And Jack did the same. He'd stopped sweeping now. Just stood with both hands leaning on the broom, watching.

Hayden made his way over to Jack slowly. Careful not to overbalance, trip, otherwise end up on his face in the mud and gravel in front of this man.

He stopped less than a foot from Jack. Stood tall.

'Hayden.'

'Jack.' He hoped Laurel was somewhere else. At home, or off in the city. But he didn't ask.

'We thought you were dead, Hayden.'

'Now, why would you think that?'

'Have you been up to your place?'

'Yeah. Just now.'

'Then you should know.'

'I guess I don't kill so easy,' Hayden said. 'I was away at my daughter's wedding. I left a note telling Peg where I'd gone. Maybe she never got it, though.'

'That or never said so.'

They stood without speaking a moment. Not an awkward moment, really, just strangely respectful somehow. Everything looked and felt weightier and more important than it might have in different company.

Jack said, 'I'm awful damn sorry what happened to your place.'

'Looks like you got your hands full with your own losses.'

Jack glanced over his shoulder at the diner and sighed. 'It's here, though.'

Just for a minute Hayden felt sorry for Jack, and lucky that his cabin was gone. It seemed easier, somehow, to walk away and start life all over again than to pick up the pieces one by one.

'Well,' Hayden said. 'Anyway. I'm leaving here. Going back up to the Bay Area. Just let folks know, okay? Tell them I'm alive but I'm gone.'

Jack looked past him to the car. To Judith. But he asked no questions. 'Peg's still got your truck, though.'

'Tell her to keep it. I don't have a clutch foot, anyway.'

Jack seemed to absorb that for a moment, as though it took time to drop it into place. Like it might have to dawn on him slowly that Hayden's lack of clutch foot was Jack's own doing, his fault. Like the ramifications kept stacking up and surprising him. But he didn't address any of that. Just said, 'Well. Good luck to you.'

Hayden nodded. Turned and slowly made his way back to Judith's car. Before he'd managed three clumsy steps, Jack said after him, 'I'm sorry.'

Hayden stopped and turned around, took in the look on Jack's face.

Then Jack said it again. 'I'm sorry.' And Hayden knew he wasn't referring to flood damage.

'It's forgiven,' he said.

'How can it be?'

'It's forgiven.'

Sometimes you just have to take a man at his word. Not ask questions he can't answer himself.

When he'd managed to ease back into Judith's car, he felt relieved to be leaving this place.

'Who was that?' she asked as she pulled back onto the highway.

'Oh, that. That was just Jack.'

'Jack.'

'The guy that shot me.'

'Ah. I'm glad you didn't tell me that beforehand.'

They drove in silence for a few miles. A few long but fairly comfortable minutes. Past the sign that marked the end of the headlight zone. The sign that reminded Judith to turn her headlights off, which she did.

'So, you just told him you forgave him.'

'I did, didn't I? You know, for the first time in my life I'm halfway thinking I understand why God dumped all that shit on poor Job. Kind of makes you understand what's what. Kind of lets you see what's important and what's not. You know? Look for a place along here we can get something to eat.'

She helped him out of his clothes, all of them. And helped him into bed. Then she climbed in after him, her own clothes half strewn on the chair and half falling off onto the floor. Straddled him almost playfully, the way she had often used to after a long day at the hospital or the office, when they both should have been too tired.

It felt strange to Hayden, how little seemed to have changed. It seemed the intervening years should have transformed all this somehow. Made it something it hadn't used to be, or vice versa.

He ran his hands along the outside of her thighs, up to her hips. Her body had changed some, but not the feeling it produced in him to touch her.

'Are we crazy?' he said, sounding only mildly curious.

'I'm not sure,' she said. 'I'm not even sure if I care.'

'You have patients in the morning. Shouldn't you be getting some sleep?'

She leaned over him, and her breasts and the necklace fell onto his chest, but lightly. 'I need the love more than I need the sleep,' she said.

And he took her at her word on that.

Hayden and Judith sat on the floor in the living room, in front of the fireplace, eating Chinese food right out of the paper cartons. Hayden held the lemon chicken carton under his chin because he was, by his own admission, hardly a master of chopsticks. He was game, but clumsy.

The phone rang.

Judith jumped up and answered it, not so much because they still considered it solely her phone but because it was easier for her to jump up.

'Thanks, John,' Hayden heard her say. 'You all right?' A pause, then, 'You're sure?' Then, 'Okay, good. We'll be right down.'

She hung up the phone and took the lemon chicken

carton out of Hayden's hand. She reached down to help him to his feet.

'Get up, Grampa. It's time.'

Hayden's brain went numb, tingly and slightly cold.

'What? No. Can't be.'

'Is.'

'She's not due for another two weeks.'

'Tell that to your new granddaughter.'

'But she wasn't supposed to—'

'Babies are like that, Hayden. They almost always change your schedule. You almost never change theirs.'

Hayden took the hand Judith extended, positioned his good right leg underneath him, and rose to his feet.

'Don't be nervous,' she said.

'Right. I just won't be nervous.'

'Well, you'll be nervous, but . . . I just mean, don't be nervous.'

On the way to the hospital, Hayden rode in silence. Judith glanced over at the side of his face.

'You're nervous,' she said.

John had his camcorder in the labor room, already taping the proceedings.

Allegra was laughing at him about it when they arrived.

'Turn it off,' she said. 'Please. Turn it off. There's nothing exciting about a fat woman in bed. No one will want to see that.'

'Ha!' John said, turning the camera on Judith and Hayden as they entered the room. 'See? The grandmother and grandfather arrive. If that's not exciting, what is?'

'Yeah, we're a thrill a minute,' Judith said.

Hayden felt uncomfortable being filmed, but had no idea how to say so.

John stepped closer and zoomed the lens in for a close-up of Hayden's face. 'What do you want to say about this moment for posterity, Granddad?'

Hayden's mind went blank. His mouth opened, but no words came out, nor did he expect any to. He wasn't even sure why he'd tried.

Just then a strange sound came out of Allegra, a sort of muffled scream. John dropped the camera on the bedside table and helped her through the contraction, breathing with her the way they'd been taught in Lamaze class.

Hayden watched, a feeling of pain and pressure growing in his chest and gut. He hadn't fully prepared himself for this. His Allegra in agony, and nothing he could do to help her. No chance to take the pain away, no way to even ease things for her. All he could do was watch.

Just when he thought he couldn't take another moment, the contraction subsided.

Everyone breathed normally again.

John took up the camcorder and, once again, trained it on Hayden's face. 'So? Anything to say?'

'Not much,' Hayden said. 'Just that I'm glad I get to be here for this.'

Hayden stayed in the labor room with his family for a little better than two hours, feeding Allegra ice chips from a spoon and wiping her forehead. Feeling the pressure grow, the pain of watching her hurt. But he wasn't going to give in to it. He would get through this.

Finally Allegra said, 'Are you okay. Daddy? You look terrible. Are you in pain?'

'Only because you are,' he said.

'Oh, Daddy.' She squeezed his hand. 'Take a break if you want. Wait out in the waiting room. I won't mind.'

'You're sure?'

'Of course I'm sure.'

'Well, maybe just for a minute.'

He struggled to his feet.

Just as he reached the door to her room, he heard her say, 'I'm glad you're here for this, too.'

*　　　*　　　*

Judith came out to the waiting room to find him. She was holding John's camcorder. Hayden didn't like that. There was something on her face he didn't like, too, but he couldn't have put it into words.

'There you are,' she said. 'Hold onto this, okay?'

He rose to his feet. She tried to convince him not to bother, but he did it anyway. He took the camcorder out of her hands. Held it by the strap with his right hand, so he could lean on the cane with his left. He hated the weight of it in his hand, dreading what it might represent.

'Why isn't he taping?'

'Things are getting a little complicated. Please don't worry, Hayden. Oh, of course you'll worry. I'm sorry. Stupid thing to say. But don't worry more than it's worth. Okay? It's just that the baby is coming really fast, and she's managed to turn herself around. Seems she's dead set on coming out right now, and backwards. We thought it would be better if John just concentrated on helping Leggy. Allegra. Where did that come from, huh? Anyway, please don't worry, Hayden. Babies are born breech every day.'

'But if she turns around like that, isn't she more likely to get tangled up in—'

Judith put a finger to his lips. 'Don't borrow trouble, Hayden. That usually doesn't happen. Babies are born breech all the time. I know this is hard for you. Just breathe, okay? Don't do that shallow breathing thing. Breathe deeply. I'll keep you posted.'

Then she was gone, leaving Hayden in the waiting room more or less alone. At least, not in the company of anyone he trusted or knew. He stood leaning on his cane for a minute or two, knowing how he would have handled this in the past, wondering how he would handle it now.

Hayden left the camera at the nurse's desk for safe-keeping. Then gradually, very gradually, he made his way outside to wait. It was a process requiring patience and planning, and yet there was something clean and reassuring about it. It was, after all, walking. His left leg was still partially numb, and he had to drag it behind him as he took each step. With his right hand he felt for a wall or doorway, gently insuring his balance. With his left, he leaned hard on the cane and swung the lower left portion of his body forward. His left leg more or less followed.

Not so long ago he'd had to ask a doctor if he would ever walk again. Now, slow and inefficient though it was, he was able to walk out to the street to pass the difficult time.

The rainy weather front that had stalled over the city most of the day had moved off, leaving the streets slick, the sky splotched with patches of clearing. A strong moon shone through, occasionally obscured by drifting clouds. The night air felt clear and cold in Hayden's lungs.

He closed his eyes.

A moment later Judith appeared at his side.

'What are you doing out here?' she asked.

'I suppose it's the opposite of storming into the delivery room. As far as I can tell, anyway. Shouldn't you be inside overseeing things?' His voice sounded calm to his own ears. Maybe he was calm. It was hard to be sure.

'She's in good hands, Hayden. The people taking care of her now should be the most impartial ones. They don't need me in there.'

Judith stood close to his left side. She felt close enough to hold him up, so he let her. He switched his cane to his right hand and put his left arm around her shoulders, leaning on her in the most literal sense.

'Besides,' she said, 'I figured you needed me out here.'

'You're right. I do.'

They stood a few moments in silence.

Looking off down the hill, Hayden watched a stream of headlights on the freeway. He watched the occasional car slip by on the street in front of the hospital, the tires making shushing sounds on the wet pavement.

A small black-and-white cat ran through the hospital parking lot and out into the road. The headlights of a passing van lit its shape as it scurried across, dangerously close to being hit.

Judith spoke – absently, Hayden thought. 'Look out, cat.'

It carried Hayden's mind away to an old, uncomfortable place. A memory smashed its way into his head and stayed. It made his stomach hurt, but maybe his stomach had been hurting already, just waiting to know if his daughter – and granddaughter – would be okay.

After a minute, Judith said, 'What?'

'Nothing.'

She didn't question his response, but a moment later he questioned it himself.

'I'm sorry. That was the old me, wasn't it? "What's wrong, Hayden?" "Nothing." I'm sorry. Watching that cat almost get hit reminded me of something. Something I didn't think much about at the time. Have you ever done that? Where you look back on something that didn't seem to mean much when it happened, but looking back it means plenty, and all of a sudden you see the whole thing a lot more clearly?'

'I believe that's happened to me on more than one occasion, yes.'

So Hayden told her all about the baby possum.

'I was so upset with the momma for letting it go,' he said, when she'd heard the essential details. 'I was willing to get hit by a truck to save it. I mean, she did everything but die herself to get it off the road. But somehow I thought that wasn't enough. She only let it go to save herself. But she let it go. I bet if you'd been there, you'd have told me why I got so upset about that.'

'Maybe,' Judith said. 'Other people's lives always seem easy to dissect.'

'I can't believe this is happening, Judith. I promised myself I'd never be in this position again. I even had a vasectomy so I wouldn't have to go through this. I didn't think about grandkids. I didn't think it would be just as hard. This scares the crap out of me, Judith.'

'I know it does,' she said. 'I know. I think it's nice that you told me, though.' After a brief silence she said, 'You don't have to answer this if you don't want, but at a time like this are you tempted to pray?'

'To who, though? To what?'

'I don't know. I hate to use the word "God," because it's so loaded for you. How about if we just say, "God or something along those lines"?'

Hayden laughed.

'What's funny?' Judith asked.

'I was just thinking, it took all these years to convince me that God isn't something along those lines.'

He motioned upward with his chin. He didn't look up, didn't even know if there were power lines above his head. But it was okay, because she knew which lines he meant.

'Okay, never mind about defining who or what. Just . . . other than the obvious . . . what would you ask for if you could?'

Hayden felt something move in his gut. Something like fear or resistance or hope. Or a combination. The sort of thing he'd gone most of his life without feeling and wasn't quite sure what to make of at this late date.

'I can't talk about that out loud right now.'

'Okay,' Judith said. 'Okay. I'll go look in and see how things are going. Watch that window.' She pointed up to the waiting room on the second floor. 'I'll come to the window when I want you to come back up.'

He stood leaning on his cane for a few minutes, then took four steps over to a streetlight and leaned his back against the post. He stood facing the hospital, looking up into the empty window. He closed his eyes for a minute or two. When he opened them, the window was still empty. He looked up at the sky, watched clouds blow across the moon. He concentrated on wave after wave of fear. It felt cold and tight, and there was nothing he could do to change it. There was nothing he could do to change anything.

He looked at the waiting room window again, and Judith was there. He felt something especially cold grab at his stomach, chill his intestines. His legs felt shaky and weak, and for a split second he thought he might go down. He reached his right hand around to the lamppost to steady himself, looking down briefly as he did. When he looked up again, Judith was giving him a sign. Thumbs-up.

He stood watching for a moment, enjoying the sight. He couldn't see the expression on her face, but he could imagine her smiling.

He slowly, carefully made his way back inside.

Hayden sat in a sturdy plastic chair in Allegra's room, and John placed the baby in his arms. He supported her tiny head with his weak left hand, wrapped his good right arm underneath her for purchase. He looked down into her face. Her eyes were squeezed shut and her hands moved as if reaching blindly for something. Her skin looked nearly translucent, and she had a whisper of silky-looking dark hair. He wished he had a hand free so he could touch it.

'We were worried about you, little girl. Congratulations on earning your name.'

'How did she earn her name?' John asked.

'Kim is a hero's name.'

'I wondered if it had some special significance.'

'Just that it's a hero's name,' Hayden said, not wanting or needing to say more on the subject.

He looked up into his son-in-law's face and realized John looked haggard and worn. His eyes looked tired, his hair uncombed. Hayden knew John was probably happy, but also that he was probably scared. It's scary, suddenly being responsible for a new life. Hayden knew the feeling well. He found himself wondering what he could do to help John. For the moment, probably nothing. But in the next few years, maybe a lot.

'I know I've asked this about a hundred times,' Hayden said, 'but are you sure I should be the one to name her?'

John said, 'Absolutely we're sure.'

Allegra, who was watching from the bed said, 'Of course, Daddy.'

'You're okay with Kim?'

'I like Kim,' John said.

'Kim is a great name, Daddy.'

'It is,' Hayden said. 'It really is. We were worried about you, Kim.'

'You didn't need to worry about her,' John said. 'That girl is a fighter.'

'Maybe,' Hayden said. 'But it'll be okay. She'll spend a lot of time with her mellow granddad, and after a while some of my peaceful worldview will rub off on her.'

*   *   *

Hayden sat in the passenger's seat, feeling tired in a pleasant way and watching Judith's face as she drove.

'I'm sorry I couldn't answer your question before,' he said.

'Don't be. It was a very personal question.'

'We have a very personal relationship. The answer is, I'm pretty sure I wouldn't have asked for anything. If there's a God, He already knew what I wanted. I would've just said that I wasn't going to fight Him this time. I would've said, "If something goes wrong, I might spend the rest of my life crying about it, but I'm not going to try to dismantle the world." I hope you understand why I couldn't have said that out loud. Not before I knew for sure everything was okay. It would've been almost like giving things permission to go wrong. But I didn't mean it that way, you know?'

'I know.'

'But I couldn't say it. It would've been like accepting a possibility I wasn't nearly ready to accept.'

'It wouldn't have changed anything.'

'I know. That's why I wasn't going to fight. It wouldn't have changed anything. But I couldn't say it then. You can understand that, right?'

Judith reached a hand over and set it on Hayden's left leg. 'Just the fact that you were able to think it is progress.'

True, Hayden thought. He could give himself that much credit. A little bit of hard-earned progress. He put his hand on top of hers.

They rode in silence for a time, a new grandmother and grandfather, Hayden focusing on the feeling of Judith's hand. Not just the feel of it against his hand, but against his leg. It was a mild, muted sensation, but he could feel with that leg. He knew the difference between her hand being there and not being there. He could feel – barely – the comforting weight of it. Another little piece of hard-earned progress.

They drove through the night down the freeway, over the bridge, along the bay, on their way back to the place Hayden now called his home.

Hayden slipped into the Valley Baptist Church and sat in the rearmost pew, a good dozen rows behind the next-closest mourner. Not exactly a packed house. Fifteen people, tops. This seemed sad to Hayden. No matter who you are, he felt, your life should add up to more than that.

He was late, and couldn't seem to spot anyone he recognized, at least from behind. It gave him the queasy feeling that he might have stumbled into the wrong funeral on the wrong day. Then he spotted the back of Peg's head.

The minister was calling Laurel a loving, giving woman, a good soul, a good friend to everyone. Had the minister met Laurel? Did everyone here have the same person in mind?

A moment later Hayden saw Scott head down the aisle in his direction. Scott slipped into the back row and sat close. They exchanged a look and a satisfying nod.

Scott's whisper was quieter even than necessary. 'Didn't think you'd come back, honestly. Didn't think you cared much about her anymore.'

'I don't. I just wanted to make sure Peg is okay.'

'She is,' Scott whispered. 'Not exactly alone in the world. Got a husband and a new baby now. Didn't see her mom a lot. Can't see this'll change her life much.'

Hayden digested this briefly. 'What's the husband like? Good man?'

'Good boy, more like. One of these days he'll get around to being a man, and I reason he'll be a decent one.'

Hayden nodded, then looked above his head, took in the high clerestory, the dark wood, the heavy stained glass windows. Scott seemed to notice.

'How long since you been in church?' he whispered.

'I'm tempted to say not long enough.'

'You haven't changed much, Reese.'

'Yeah, I have.'

A long silence, then Scott said, 'Glad you came back. Hate like hell to admit it, but you're missed around here.'

Hayden wanted to answer, tried, but choked. No answer came.

What might've been ten minutes later – though it felt like an hour – Hayden whispered, 'Peg still got that dog?'

'Good Lord,' Scott whispered back. 'Uglier than he was before. You think it's not possible, but I swear for a fact. She feeds him too much. Now he's ugly plus fat.'

'Is he happy?'

'All fat dogs are happy. Where do you think they get that expression, "happy as a fat dog"?'

'*Is* there such an expression?'

'Don't see why not.'

Peg had a hard look on her face when Hayden approached her after the service. The baby in her arms seemed to be fast asleep, though Hayden couldn't see his face.

'Go ahead,' she said, too loudly for the church setting. 'Light into me. I'm barely twenty, I'm a kid myself. I'll never make nothing of my life now. We got no money, where do we get off thinking we can raise a kid?'

'I was married and had a kid when I was twenty.'

'You were?' Her face changed, opened. 'Was it hard?'

'Very. But I don't regret it.'

'Thanks, Hayden.' She gave him a one-armed hug, waking the baby.

'Now, where's this husband of yours?'

She pointed to a blond-haired young man in a front pew. The baby started fussing, so she slipped out.

Hayden stood alone, leaning on his cane, sorely tempted to go have a talk with the guy. One of the old-style talks. But that wasn't him anymore, was it? 'Oh, what the hell,' he said out loud. 'One more for the road.'

He sat down next to Peg's new husband. The guy looked younger from up close. Skinny, with a trace of mustache that still looked like baby fuzz. Had Hayden looked that young at twenty? He hadn't felt that young.

'I'm Hayden Reese,' he said. 'An old friend of Peg's from way back. Just wanted to come by and tell you that if you even borderline abuse that girl or that baby I'll come back here and reduce you to rubble with my bare hands.'

The boy fixed Hayden with a slightly alarmed, slightly confused look. But then Hayden cracked a smile in spite of himself. The kid looked relieved.

'I don't think I'll be taking you up on that, sir.'

'I was hoping you wouldn't.'

Hayden got up to walk away but the boy called after him. 'Sir? I think it's nice, though, that you cared enough about her to say that.'

Hayden found Scott waiting for him at the door. They stepped out into the light and the heat together.

Scott said, 'Lemme guess. Have yourself a good old-fashioned chat with the boy?'

'Yeah. He's all right.' Hayden squinted and blinked.

'I tried to tell you that, Reese. Lord, you never did listen worth a damn.'

'I know it. How exactly did this thing with Laurel happen, anyway?'

'The usual. Some fool tries to pass on a double line. Only this time the fool was one of our own. Miracle nobody else died. She hit a semi head-on. Shook the guy up bad and his rig was scrap, but he walked away. I reason the worst part of his morning was watching a woman burn to death in her car. I was first on the scene and it didn't exactly make my day. Hate to say it, but it was her own pigheaded fault. You never could talk to that woman.'

'That's what you're always saying about me.'

'Yeah, but *she* went to her grave and never did learn. There's a gathering back at the house. You coming to that?'

'No.'

'Don't blame you.' Scott nodded twice and moved off a step, then stopped and stood a moment, as if weighing how to say good-bye for real this time. Or how not to.

'Scott,' Hayden said. 'Don't take it on yourself, what happened.'

'What makes you say I do?'

'I know you. You think every move everybody makes on that highway is your watch.'

'It is.'

'People die on highways. It's what happens.' Scott only shrugged, and Hayden knew it wasn't that easy. 'Did she have her headlights on, at least?'

'Want one flying guess?'

Poor Scott, Hayden thought. That had to about drive him out of his mind. 'What about Jack? Is he around?'

'Not now, he's not. Stayed a year or so. Drank too much. Then he got a job in the city. Cleaned up his act, I hear. No matter what a guy did, he's gonna move on from it sometime. I mean, what are his choices?'

'I was thinking about him during the service. About that war we had going. All of a sudden it hit me how crazy that is. Fighting a war over Laurel. Why do people do that, Scott? Why go to war to get something that's not worth having?' And another question he couldn't quite verbalize. How could something that felt worth killing or dying for at the time feel so unimportant now?

'You tell me, Hayden. I'll be goddamned if I know.'

'If there's a war inside, it'll find its way out, I guess. You can't just fight with yourself. I have to get out of here, Scott. I hate this place. I can't breathe here. This is hell. I'm sorry. I mean for me. My hell.'

'It's hell for everybody, Hayden. I tried to tell you for years.'

'I don't belong here anymore.'

'You never did belong here.' Scott looked serious. Unusually intent. 'I'm not joking. You never one day fit in with this place. I mean that as a compliment.'

'I take it as one.'

'Now go home to your family. You got no more business here.'

Hayden cruised down the highway in his convertible, the wind ruffling his hair in a pleasant way. On his drive into town, he hadn't liked it. On his way home, everything felt good. He slowed a little passing Jenny's mountain, the spot where he'd laid that good old dog to rest. The marker would have washed away in the flood, but not Jenny. He'd buried her right. Put her down deep, to stay.

'So long, girl,' he said out loud to the only part of this godforsaken hole he would miss.

Then he went home to his family.

THE END

Here's a teaser from

Catherine Ryan Hyde's wonderful novel

Second Hand Heart

VIDA

On My Upcoming Death

I'm probably going to die really soon. Maybe in my sleep tonight. Maybe next week. Maybe three weeks from Thursday. It's kind of hard to tell.

I guess that'll sound like a big deal to you. Whoever you are. Whoever will read this someday. It doesn't sound like such a big deal to me. I'm pretty used to it.

I've been practicing for almost twenty years. Ever since the night I was born.

Not to rock your world too completely, but you're going to die, too. Probably not as soon as I am, but you never know. See, that's the thing. We don't know. None of us. I could get a donor heart and live happily ever after, and you could walk out in front of a bus tomorrow. Hell, today.

Here's the difference between you and me: you think

you're not going to die anytime soon. Even though you could be wrong. I know I probably will.

Sometimes I wonder what it feels like to go to bed every night figuring you'll definitely wake up. Lots of people do, I guess. Every day. But I have no idea what it would feel like to be them.

I only know how it feels to be me.

On My Mother

My mother named me Vida.

I think it's the stupidest name in the world. But I have to try to be patient with my mother. She has issues.

First of all, I'm an only child. And also, even though she's had just as much practice as I have getting used to the idea of losing me, she hasn't made much headway so far. She says it's because she's a mother, and I really have no choice but to believe her. For myself I wouldn't know. I'm not a mother and I never will be, unless I adopt. My heart could never take childbirth.

I'm lucky it got me through today.

In case you don't know any Spanish at all, 'Vida' means 'life'. Get it yet? You know. Like, make sure this kid stays alive. Not that we're Spanish. We're not. But I guess naming your only daughter 'Life' or 'Alive' might be a little weird. Even for her.

My mother has control issues, but I honestly don't think she knows. I haven't told her yet because she has a lot going on, and I'm not sure I want to stack that on top of everything else.

She rules our little world very tightly.

It's funny, too, because . . . Well, it's hard to explain why it's funny. But if you saw her, you'd get it. She's about four foot ten (she says five feet but she's totally lying), and has apple-red cheeks and a big smile, and looks like one of Santa's elves. If Santa had girl elves. She doesn't look like the dominatrix type.

But man, can she hold on.

On My Really Good Friend Esther

Esther used to be in a concentration camp.

Buchenwald.

When I say Buchenwald it comes out sounding different than when Esther says it. Even though she's been in this country for more than sixty years, she still has a very thick German accent. Most people drop the accent after a few years, but Esther hasn't dropped it yet. So she must still need it for something. When she says Buchenwald, the 'ch' sound does this very complicated hissy thing in her throat (which I could not do if I tried, and I've tried), and the 'w' sounds like a 'v'.

When Esther was my age, she was in Buchenwald.

She's very old now. I don't know how old. She won't tell me. But you can figure the years based on when the Allies liberated the camps (I'm very good on the Internet, because I spend so much time indoors, and it's something I can do without anybody getting worried and telling me to take it easy), and then do some simple math and figure she must be at least ninety.

She actually looks older. So I'm thinking maybe she lied a little about how young she was when her whole family got rounded up and put on the train.

I guess it's like my mother saying she's five feet tall when she's only four ten. I guess people do that a lot.

I don't. I tell the truth. I'm not even sure why.

Esther gave me this blank book. The one I'm writing this all down in, right now. The one you must be holding if you're reading this.

She said it's a journal, but it looks like a book. A regular bound book. Just with nothing on any of the pages. I was very excited when she gave it to me, because I figured it was a real book. I like books a lot. I rely on them.

This is true of most people who can't do much of anything without dying.

Esther said if I wanted it to be a real book I'd have to write in it myself. I'd have to write my own. Sounded like a tall order, especially for someone who might be a little short on time. I guess in a weird sort of way that was part of the idea of the thing.

Esther says nobody can tell you when you're going to die.

She says a few days before the Allies came and liberated Buchenwald, one of the camp guards laughed at her and taunted her in German. When she tells me this story – which she does a lot – she repeats what he said in German. I can't do that. But anyway, what he said translates to mean something like, 'You will die here, little Jewess.'

Esther figures that guard is dead now. I figure she's probably right, which is a satisfying thought.

She's our upstairs neighbor and she's my best friend.

She also gave me the worry stone.

On the Worry Stone

The very first day I was in the hospital (and by that I mean this time around – there have been lots of hospitals and lots of times), Esther came to see me and brought me the worry stone.

It's some kind of quartz, and it's very smooth. About the size of a walnut, but flatter. Esther said she brought it all the way from Germany with her. I think that means she must have gotten it after she was liberated. Because I don't think they let you keep any of your stuff when they put you on the train.

I guess it makes sense that when you've spent years in a concentration camp, and you are the only member of your very large extended family to walk out alive, and you're about to go all by yourself to a new country on the other side of the world, you might want something that could possibly absorb your worry.

What I don't get is why she gave it to me. I love it. I just don't get why she gave it up.

She came in that very first morning. As soon as visiting hours started. She was wearing a scarf on her head, and a coat with a big fur collar. And, honestly, it wasn't very cold outside, so far as I knew.

She showed me how she had worried a slightly smoother spot on to the stone by rubbing it with her thumb all the way to America.

She went on a boat and it took weeks.

She told me I could put all my worry into the stone. And maybe it would even wear a groove into solid rock.

I said something like, 'You're kidding. This is only skin.' And I held up my thumb so she could see what was only skin.

'Water is only water,' Esther said. 'But water can wear away stone.'

I took the stone in my hand and held it. I liked the weight of it, and the warmth of it, from being gripped so tightly in Esther's palm.

I said, 'Maybe I won't have time.'

'Or maybe you will,' she said. 'No one can tell you when you are going to die. You die when you are done. Not a moment before. Not a moment after. No matter what anyone says. No matter what anyone wishes for you.'

'Thank you for the worry stone,' I said. 'But I actually don't think I'm very worried.'

'Really?' she said.

'I don't think so.'

'Most people in your situation would be worried.'

'Maybe because they were never in my situation before. I've always been in my situation.'

Esther shook her head and clucked with her tongue.

'Maybe you have worry and you don't know. Just like you have air all around you, but you don't know. If sometimes you had air and sometimes not, then you would know.'

'Maybe,' I said.

'It really doesn't matter what you have,' she said. 'Whatever it is, give it to the worry stone all the same.'

So I've been rubbing it smooth(er) ever since.

On Lying in the Hospital Waiting for a Heart

I'm number one on the list for a heart. That's sort of the good news and the bad news all mixed up into one. Short version, it means I'm more likely to die than anybody else on the list, as best they can figure these things. So it's one of those contests nobody's dying to win. No pun intended. Then again, if there's a heart, it's nice to be number one on the list for it.

It's all very emotionally complicated.

Here's the bad news: there isn't any heart right now for anybody on the list. Not even number one. That could change at any time, I suppose. But this is now. And there isn't a heart.

Ready for the statistics that go with the 'urgent' category? The majority of patients on that list will either die or be transplanted within two weeks.

So this life of mine is coming down to the wire. One way or the other.

Last weekend was a late-spring holiday. One of those ones nobody really cares about. Just a stupid excuse to give everybody Monday off.

My mother was nervous and guilty all weekend long.

She just kept moving. All weekend. She moved into my hospital room. She moved out of it. She walked from my bed to the window. She walked back. She dusted the food tray. (Right, like dust is always a problem in hospital rooms.) Pulled dead petals off the flowers. Went out for a walk in the hall. Came back.

If I'd had more energy I'd have screamed. But I can't even breathe well enough to breathe, not to mention to scream.

Not that I don't get where she's coming from. But when you're nervous and somebody else is nervous, too, you feel like you want them to help you stay calm. Maybe it's not a reasonable request, but you do. Otherwise their nervous kind of stands on the shoulders of your nervous, and then the whole nervous thing is so big and tall that it gets to be too much nervous for anybody to bear. Especially anybody with a bad heart. And then the whole shaky system wants to come crashing down.

So, even though I know it's probably not really fair, it was hard not to blame *her* nervousness. If for no other reason than the sheer volume of it. Figuratively speaking. It didn't literally make any noise. But in another way it drowned out everything else in the room. Hell, everything else in the *world*.

Now. In fairness to my mom, here's what was so hard about this weekend in particular: there are more traffic fatalities on a holiday weekend. Really, if you know the statistics, you know the chances are very good that someone will die.

This is why she was nervous: because maybe nobody would. Or, worse yet, maybe somebody would, but they wouldn't have a donor sticker on their license. Or their family would get squeamish, and decide to bury them all in one piece.

That drives her out of her mind.

Also, this is the part probably nobody knows but me. This is the secret part about why she was feeling guilty: because maybe somebody would. Because part of her was wishing somebody would.

Nobody did.

On Dying

I think I look at it differently than other people do. And I think the way I look at it is right, and the way other people look at it is wrong.

I don't say that about too many things. I'm not vain. I'm not one of those people who always thinks I'm right about everything. I'm just one of those people who always thinks I'm right about this.

Here's why, and I think it's a very good reason: let's say the subject is something else besides death. Say it's a mountain. Or a tree.

Yeah. Let's say it's a tree.

I'm standing under the branches of it. Close enough to reach out and feel the texture of the bark against my palm. The rest of you are two or three miles back, peering through binoculars with foggy lenses.

Now. I ask you. Who knows more about the tree?

Here's what I think about dying: I think it's not so much about being and then not being. I think it's more about *where* you are. Not *whether* you are.

Take me. I'm lying on this hospital bed. Dying. Unless someone dies suddenly in an accident while they're still young and healthy and gives me a heart, and they die in a way that it can be harvested in time, and it gets to me really fast. But let me tell you, there's not much time left for all that stuff to fall into place. Meanwhile, here I am getting weaker and weaker. Like this light that just dims and dims. Until after a while you can't see it at all. Maybe it gives a little flicker. And then nothing. Out.

My mother cries and says, 'That's it, she's gone. No more Vida.'

But somewhere else, in some other place – some very different place – there's this little flicker of light, and somebody is saying, 'Look. What's that? Someone new is here.' And I think they're very happy about that.

And maybe the someone new isn't *exactly* Vida. Definitely not in every earthly sense of the word. And definitely she doesn't have my skinny body. But it's me.

I still *am*. I'm just not what you expected me to be, from experience.

You can live with that. Right?

Not if you're my mother you can't.

On the Heart

It wasn't even a holiday. Just a regular weekday night. And some woman skidded off the road in her car.

I don't know too much about her. Just what my mother told me. That her name was Lorraine Buckner Bailey, and that she went by Lorrie. And that she was thirty-three years old.

And the accident was pretty close by, too. San Jose. Maybe an hour by car, though I doubt that's the way they'll send the heart.

I wanted to know if she had any kids, but I was afraid to ask. My mom gets very emotional around stuff like that. Even though when she was telling me about the heart she was very, very happy. Like, if you didn't know better, you would think it was too much happy to ever knock her out of.

But I know her pretty well. And it was too much happy, really.

It's like when you're a kid and your mom sees you roughhousing with your cousins and screaming with laughter, and she says something like, 'You're laughing now, but in a minute somebody's going to be crying.' Because you're overexcited.

It's like there's a fine line between hyper-happy and falling apart.

Actually, I only know that from watching my cousins play. I could never afford to get overexcited. I wonder if I'll be able to get overexcited when I get the heart. Or whether I'll stay mostly pretty quiet out of habit.

Either way, I don't have it yet, and I definitely can't afford too much excitement right now. And my mother was sort of wearing me down. Actually, my mother was definitely wearing me down. After a while my cardiac surgeon, Dr Vasquez, came in and congratulated me, and said how happy she was for me, and told my mom I needed rest.

So I actually got a little time alone. As you can tell, I'm using the time to write in my journal.

While I'm writing, I'm picturing my mother out in the hallway, jumping up and down as quietly as possible.

Read the complete book.

Second Hand Heart

is out now in paperback!

Second Hand Heart

CATHERINE RYAN HYDE

'Thanks for the heart,' she said.

It was a surprisingly simple statement in the midst of all that life and death and indebtedness.

One girl
Vida is nineteen, very ill, and has spent her short life preparing for death. But a new chance brings its own story, because for Vida to live, someone had to die.

One man
Richard has just lost his beloved wife in a car accident. He hasn't even begun to address his grief, but feels compelled to meet the girl who inherited his wife's heart.

Someone else's heart
In hospital Vida sees Richard and immediately falls in love. Of course he dismisses her as a foolish child. But is she? Can two people be bound by a second hand heart?

She's been given a chance to live.

But does she know how?

Second Hand Heart

CATHERINE RYAN HYDE
BESTSELLING RICHARD & JUDY AUTHOR

'An extraordinary and unforgettable novel' Susan Lewis